A HISTORY OF THE PRESENT ILLNESS

Stories

LOUISE ARONSON

BLOOMSBURY
New York   London   New Delhi   Sydney

Published by Bloomsbury USA, New York

All papers used by Bloomsbury USA are natural, recyclable products made from
wood grown in well-managed forests. The manufacturing processes conform to the
environmental regulations of the country of origin.

LIBRARY OF CONGRESS CATALOGING-IN-PUBLICATION DATA

Aronson, Louise.
A history of the present illness : stories / Louise Aronson. — 1st U.S. ed.
p.   cm.
ISBN: 978-1-60819-830-6 (hardcover)
1. Medical fiction, American.   2. Physician and patient—Fiction
3. San Francisco (Calif.)—Fiction.   I. Title.

PS3601.R67H57 2013
813'.6—dc23
2012018354

First U.S. edition published by Bloomsbury in 2013
This paperback edition published in 2014

Paperback ISBN: 978-1-62040-007-4

1 3 5 7 9 10 8 6 4 2

Typeset by Westchester Book Group
Printed and bound in the U.S.A. by Thomson-Shore Inc., Dexter, Michigan

TO MY PATIENTS

FOR JANE

If you don't care for obscenity,
you don't care for the truth.

—TIM O'BRIEN, *HOW TO TELL A TRUE WAR STORY*

CONTENTS

SNAPSHOTS FROM AN INSTITUTION

1. JIAO

She lies in bed the way a letter lies in its envelope. Her eyes are blank and her mouth is open. The image appears to be black and white.

2. QUINGSHAN

He waits in an armchair by the main entrance dressed in a thick brown suit, a blue plaid cap in his left hand and a battered silver-tipped cane between his legs. The chair—beige vinyl, a two-inch slash in the upper-left corner—is meant to frame him, but he's too tall, too robust; his shoulders exceed the backrest; his legs stretch out on the mosaic floor across an ocher diamond and well into the adjacent roseate square. Each time the scarred double doors of the main entrance open, he smiles. He's waited one hour and forty-five minutes so far. He's missed

1

lunch. His thighs tingle and his stomach growls, but there's no sign of his son.

3. THE PLACE

It's a collection of sandstone buildings in California Mission style, with red-tiled roofs and a hilltop location coveted with equal fervor by real estate developers and urban preservationists. If you bisected the city of San Francisco on both horizontal and vertical axes and went to that location, you would find yourself gazing at the view shown by this wide-angle shot: greenery stretches top to bottom on the left, and a parking lot for two hundred cars does the same on the right. In life, as in this photograph, a vast and gently sloped front lawn popular with local dog walkers fills much of the foreground. Behind the lawn is a traffic circle and behind that a wide staircase and a wheelchair ramp that bring visitors to a terrace where giant pots of native plants surround the main entrance. A newly paved drive lined by twin rows of sentinel palms connects the eleven buildings above with the security gate and busy street below. But the eco-friendly landscaping and handsome square bell tower notwithstanding, only the most inattentive passerby would mistake this place for a college campus or corporate headquarters. The walls and windows are streaked with grime, and too many of the people, coming and going, wear uniforms.

4. QUALITY TIME

This photo was taken a few hours ago, though it might just as easily have been taken yesterday or last week or last month or last year. In it, Jiao and Quingshan sit in the fenced garden adjacent to Building 7. Although it's a warm, sunny morning, Quingshan is perched at the far end of a black metal bench wearing his suit coat and cap and Jiao is beside him in her wheelchair, bundled in blankets and scarves. He visits her seven days a week and stays six hours each day, taking three buses from, and then back to, his studio apartment downtown. Every other Sunday, when his daughter calls by long-distance telephone from her home in another state, he tells her it's no problem. *What else would I do*, he asks, a question for which his daughter has no satisfying answer. And so, each morning at more or less ten o'clock, he arrives, rolls his wife outside, wipes her drool, makes sure she's warm, then watches the bees on the bougainvillea or the liquid food dropping through plastic tubing into a body he once lay awake admiring, timing himself to see how long he could hold back before reaching out with a foot, a fingertip, his tongue. It's much like caring for a baby, he explains to his daughter, except without the sweet smells, without the hope.

5. HISTORY

In the late nineteenth century, when the institution opened, its residents were called inmates. The able-bodied majority worked in the kitchens and laundry (women) or—as shown in this recently colorized archival photograph—on maintenance and road-repair crews (men). They also operated a large working farm and provided mending and tailoring services to other inmates, to the paid staff, and, for a small fee, to people in the surrounding neighborhoods of St. Francis

Wood, Twin Peaks, and the Inner Sunset. Now there are no able-bodied residents. These days, the average age is seventy-six, and even the crazies don't want to live here. Even the homeless, though they do live here, unofficially and undeniably, inside and out. Look back at snapshot 3. Use a magnifying glass. See the colorful mounds beneath the drooping fronds of the sentinel palms and on the margins of the litter-strewn lawn? If this were videography, you'd notice that the mounds move from time to time—a bottle raised to eager lips, an ill-defined shape morphing into something vertical and recognizable, standing and stretching before ambling off. But even with a still image you can appreciate how very many mounds there are, curled under bushes and burrowed in heaps of trash on the extensive grounds the city doesn't have money to maintain.

6. CHARLES

Quingshan and Jiao's oldest son arrives two hours late and doesn't apologize. The camera captures the exact moment when his left hand, with its manicured fingernails and thick gold wedding band, touches down on the sleeve of his father's coat. The only moment it touches down.

He's the piece that doesn't belong, standing in the institution's ancient foyer in his silk suit with his sixty-dollar haircut and limited-edition platinum watch. *Sesame Street!* his made-in-America daughter would shout, delighted, but he doesn't bring her here.

7. CONTEXT

From the street outside, there's a loud pop. The telephoto lens zooms in on a boy facedown on the sidewalk. This image actually is black and white: white cement, black boy.

8. FAMILY MEETING

A group of professionals, all women, three brown and two white, gather in Jiao's room. Quingshan stands by the door, his head pressed against the sun-warmed wall, his discount-store loafers firmly planted on the speckled linoleum. From beneath half-lowered lids, he watches Charles with the doctor and nurses and social worker, watches as his son charms and instructs them. He himself does not speak. There's so much he might say in his language or under different circumstances, but nothing that can be said here.

9. THE DOCTOR

She steals a glance at her watch while explaining to Charles how sometimes families choose to forgo treatments such as resuscitation and hospitalization, and sometimes even X-rays and blood draws and antibiotics, everything but that which increases the patient's comfort. And then, fingering the name badge that hangs from her neck like a long, gaudy necklace, a faded photograph on the flip side of the plastic sleeve, she explains how such decisions are not only perfectly legal but ethical and moral as well, based as they are on respect and compassion for the afflicted loved one. The doctor's slim, stylish watch is secured with a tiny piece of duct tape and her shoes need reheeling, but if she saw this photograph, she wouldn't focus the way most women her age would on the physical indignities of her middle decades: the lips in need of lipstick, the crimped skin forming vertical lines between her brows and furrows around her lips, a body now more attractive clothed than naked. No. This doctor would see only the photograph within the photograph, the years-ago Hawaiian holiday shot of her children from the days when there were three of them, not only her now-teenage baby girl and collegiate boy, but also an oldest child, her firstborn, the lost child who taught her everything she knows about respect and compassion.

10. QUESTIONS

All eyes turn toward Quingshan as the social worker in her smartly tapered skirt, faux-cashmere sweater, and three-inch heels asks in his language—which is also her language, or at any rate, the language of her childhood—*Did you ever talk to your wife about what she would and would not want as she got older?* But before Quingshan can answer, Charles steps into the center of the room and poses his own questions, first in English, then in that other language, flipping easily back and forth and smiling at the staff while keeping his eyes on the older, more foreign version of himself. He asks his father whether he still loves his mother, and whether Quingshan still enjoys spending time with Jiao and wants to do everything possible to help her and keep her alive, or whether he agrees with the staff that his wife would be better off dead. Immediately and simultaneously, the social worker and doctor protest, but the son silences them without even a glance, his hands raised like international stop signs as he completes the translation into his father's language.

Quingshan coughs and smiles at the floor. From beyond the open door comes the click-hum of an electric wheelchair in the hallway. Then Quingshan answers *Yes, Yes, Yes,* and *No.* What else can he say? He doesn't know what Jiao would tell him if she could speak. He imagines, but he does not know.

11. RIGHTS AND PRIVILEGES

With her healthy young son beside her, Jiao looks as if she's already dead. In the distant, impoverished province they come from, she would be. So would Quingshan. Their children might even be dead, at least some of them. But this is America, and in America any person, rich or poor, can be kept alive even when they can't walk or talk, eat or think, even when they can't say, *No, Please, Stop,* and especially when the doctor is told *Do everything* by a man with a good job, good English, and real leather shoes.

12. THE SCORE

On his way out the door, Charles nearly trips over a young man in a wheelchair rolling down the corridor in a hospital gown and backwards baseball cap. White cords dangle from the young man's ears, and a McDonald's milk shake rests in his wheelchair cup holder. It's hard to tell from this one shot—and Charles doesn't notice—but this young man is working, and though the work he's doing is very different from the work of his nineteenth-century predecessors, it's the sort of work he's done since he arrived in America at age eleven, a kind of work that on this particular day looks like this: a kid from outside hoping to make good with the crew slipped him a knife in a thirty-two-ounce milk shake cup, and while the Building 7 social worker was at the Jiao Liang family meeting, the young man, quadriplegic from a gunshot wound, used the knife and his more functional hand to break into her office and steal her laptop computer, an act he considers totally legitimate, since, as he told the kid, *that bitch don't do jack for me, dawg.* Next, with the tidy chrome machine hidden beneath his lap blanket, he wheeled himself down to the Total Care Unit kitchen, where he sold it at one third its retail value to a woman who smelled of garlic and dirty dishwater and barely spoke English but knew her kids needed computers if they were going to avoid ending up like the young man from whom she bought the computer. Now, unaware that he's being photographed, the young man pushes past Charles and heads to the Ambulatory Dementia Unit, where he scores an A-bomb and some baby T off one of the aides. Then he follows the painted green line along the cement walls of the underground tunnel system to the main building, takes the service elevator up to the lobby, and, just beyond a tan vinyl chair with a rip in the upper-left corner, enters a handicapped restroom with a functioning door lock and enough floor space for him to do a back-to-back and have a happy nod undisturbed by staff or security.

13. LOCAL COLOR

At the nurses' station on the Total Care Unit in Building 7, the doctor's left hand rests on a thick binder bearing the name Jiao Liang, and her right hand reaches out toward a dispenser of round red stickers. An assortment of stickers in other colors already decorates the chart's spine: blue (incommunicado), purple (skin breakdown), and yellow (nothing by mouth), the latter two not quite obscuring the stickers they replaced eighteen months earlier: green (fall risk) and orange (danger to staff).

A nurse's thick brown fingers land on the doctor's forearm. The red sticker means *do not resuscitate*, and the doctor cannot put it on this or any other chart without the family's approval.

14. NIGHTFALL

The wide-angle lens again, this shot offering a sunset bird's-eye view of jutting, pallid buildings in the middle of a forested city hilltop, cars like forgotten toys in a giant parking lot, ceramic pots huddled as cockroaches might in the shadows on the terrace of the main entrance, and a huge swath of surrounding land, dark and menacing in the dusk. Invisible at this hour are the institution's raisons d'être, the residents grouped in the eleven buildings by disease and functional status, as if they'd been apprehended at the end of their lives striving for something large and ugly, a defining theme of the sort that would be accompanied by a very modern symphony, its scraping, screeching, and pounding punctuated at regular intervals by a prolonged and disturbing silence.

15. THE GIFT

Long after his usual departure time, Quingshan opens a folding chair and sits down beside Jiao. Her bed has silver bars along both sides, but there's space enough between the slats for him to reach in without taking off his suit coat. For a while he sits quietly, stroking her hair or shoulder, and then suddenly he leans forward and, at a just-audible level, begins to hum. As darkness replaces the grounds and city beyond the window across the room, he moves fluidly from one melody to the next, choosing ballads of love and longing that decades and continents ago he used to tease her for singing, calling them silly and sentimental.

Except when he sings to her, the room is quiet. Except in the late mornings when he wraps her in blankets and takes her outside, Jiao lies in this bed, bars up, wearing nothing more than a blue-and-white gown that ties at the neck and waist and a blanket the aides tuck beneath her chin. When she first moved to the institution, she sometimes also wore a vest that was green and yellow, zipped up in back, and had long straps that the nurses knotted around the silver bars, holding her firmly in place. But she hasn't needed the vest for a very long time.

Jiao and Quingshan did not ask to come to this country. They came for their children and their children's children and their grandchildren's children. They came willingly and without complaint. If he had to do it over, Quingshan would do the same again, and he has only to remember the respect with which the doctor and nurses and social worker listened to Charles to know this much about his wife for sure: so would Jiao.

AN AMERICAN PROBLEM

T HE WATER DREAMS BEGAN the summer before third grade. In the dreams, Bopha ran through hot rain in crowds of muddy, naked legs and blurred grown-up faces or tumbled like garbage in the gutter runoff that coursed down Eddy Street outside her family's apartment after a big storm. Eventually, the cold and wet got so real she woke up. Until the water dreams, she thought she'd forgotten the trip across Cambodia in her mother's stomach and the refugee camp where she'd learned to crawl and talk and play.

The first time it happened, Bopha removed her nightshirt and underpants and curled herself up on the top half of the mattress, hoping the wet would be dry by morning. It wasn't, but she made the bed anyway, and then she forgot all about the stain until her sister pulled back the covers that night. Neary paused and sniffed, then dragged their mother into the room by her arm and pointed.

Bopha's mother covered the wet sheet quickly and without comment while her father sat in the other room in front of the

11

television, picking at his teeth with the very long nail of his left fifth finger.

"*Ot ban*," her mother said, lowering her voice—*it doesn't work*—and Bopha promised not to do it again.

The next morning her bed was dry, but the following night the water dreams returned. They came again two nights later, and three nights after that, until by mid-July they were nightly occurrences and Neary moved onto the mattress across the room to sleep with their two little brothers.

At first, Bopha's mother took the wet sheets to the Laundromat on Turk Street, finding money for the machines in places that made Bopha and Neary laugh: behind the big can of rice under the kitchen sink, in a plastic bag floating inside the toilet's tall back, in the stomach of their baby brother's single toy, a little red monkey with a long, curly tail.

"You must stop," Bopha's mother whispered one morning at the end of the month, dropping the soiled items into the bathtub and turning on the hot water. Before shutting the bathroom door, she glanced over to where Bopha's father lay snoring on the couch, one *krama* cinched around his waist like a skirt and another thrown over his eyes.

In early August, a moist summer fog hung over the city, retreating to the coast for only a few hours at midday. As a result, Bopha's sheets and nightshirt, thrown over the fire escape railing each morning, didn't always dry by bedtime. For three nights in a row, she climbed into a damp bed in the evening and out of a wet one the next day. On the fourth night, she dreamed she fell into a bucket of boiling water and couldn't get out. She woke screaming, kicking the covers away. Her mother came running and turned on the light to reveal an angry red rash from Bopha's waist to the middle of her thighs.

There were tears that night, her mother's, not Bopha's—Bopha never cried—and from her father, lots of yelling. His face turned the dark purple of grape juice, and he used his hands for emphasis, waving them wildly and occasionally aiming his tobacco-stained fingertips at Bopha's face. While he shouted about bad behavior and wasted money and letting the family down, she compared his bare feet, so broad and flat and pale, with her own tiny brown toes and high, rounded arches. She stood with her legs apart because the air felt good on the burn beneath her nightshirt.

Suddenly, Bopha felt a tight, pinching pain in the upper parts of her arms, and the floor pulled away from her feet. Her father lifted her until their faces were nearly level. "Pay attention," he yelled, his mouth leaking the familiar sour smell of old curry and ashtray bottoms and whiskey. Bopha held her breath until she got a funny feeling in her head that made her eyes want to close.

Across the room, her mother repeated a single word like an incantation. At first, Bopha couldn't make out what she was saying, and then she recognized that it was a name: *Vanak*. Her father must have heard it too. Without warning, he let go, and she fell to her knees. For a second, the apartment was perfectly quiet. Then her father grabbed his coat and left, slamming the door behind him. Immediately, the baby wailed, and soon enough, the others joined him. Bopha too felt something hot and hard in her throat, like a small animal trying to get out, but she swallowed again and again, until she made it go away.

Later, she asked about Vanak. Her mother said he was a cousin who'd been arrested in Rhode Island after treating his son's backache with cupping and coining. A teacher had seen the large round bruises and long red lines under the boy's shirt and called the police. Vanak had spent nine months in prison, and when he came out, no one would give him a job. In America, her mother explained, a man could discipline his wife, but he must never leave marks on his children.

The next morning, Bopha's mother put Pheak in a sling on her back, handed Heang to Bopha, and took Neary's hand. Bopha thought they were going to the market, but her mother turned right, not left, outside their building. At the Tenderloin Family Health Clinic, she told the Khmer assistant about Bopha's rash, and an hour later they saw the doctor.

With the assistant translating, Bopha's mother explained the problem and did her best to answer the doctor's questions, even though most of them had nothing to do with water dreams or rashes: Did Bopha like school? How was she spending her summer vacation? Was everything okay at home? Finally, he checked and poked Bopha all over, including her private places, and the nurse escorted her to the bathroom, where she peed into a clear plastic cup.

When she returned to the exam room, Neary and Heang were playing in one corner and Pheak hung from their mother's left breast, one tiny hand suspended in the air behind him. Her mother seemed to be studying something just over the baby's head, but when Bopha walked farther into the room and looked at the same place, all she saw was a wall.

"Well, look who's back," said the doctor. He smiled at Bopha, then wrote something on one of his papers before turning again to her mother.

"So," he explained, "I'm sending some tests, but I expect the results will be normal. Usually, the cause is stress. You need to talk to your daughter and get help for your husband if that's where the trouble is. There are brochures in the waiting room and hotlines open twenty-four hours."

When he finished, the Khmer assistant turned to Bopha's mother and said in Khmer, "An American problem."

The doctor looked at the assistant. "You told her everything I said?" he asked.

"Oh, yes, of course," said the assistant.

The doctor sighed. He wrote a prescription for a cream to treat the rash and a referral to the clinic social worker. "They probably won't bring her," he said to the assistant, as if Bopha wasn't there or as if she, like her mother, couldn't understand English. "And even if they do, she only gets three visits. I doubt it'll be enough."

That night, during a commercial break, her father's face already dark and shiny but the red lightning rods not yet visible in the whites of his eyes, Bopha asked if she could go to the clinic for the appointments the doctor had recommended.

Her father's eyes narrowed. "How much?" he asked.

"Free."

"What do they want?"

"To fix me."

Her father poured himself another drink. He still had on his work clothes, a blue jumpsuit splattered with grease. His fingertips were stained too, and the bottle shook in his hand so some of the brown liquid jumped out of the glass and onto the table.

He wiped at the spill, and little drops flew onto the carpet. "Your mother's too busy to take you."

"It's only three blocks," Bopha said. "I can go by myself."

Her father waved her away.

Bopha took a deep breath. If the water dreams were an American problem, then only an American could make them go away.

She stepped between her father and the television. "The doctor wrote on a paper," she said. "If I don't go, we might get in trouble."

"Come here," said her father.

She took one step, then another.

"Come," he repeated.

When she reached the couch, he pulled her toward him, then sniffed her head and tickled the smooth skin between her t-shirt bottom and skirt top.

"Smart girl," he said.

The following Wednesday, Bopha walked to the clinic, crossing only on green lights, and gave her name at the big desk. She read *Highlights for Children* while she waited, studying the drawings of children playing in sunny backyards on lawns with daisies and dandelions, jungle gyms and swing sets.

"Bo-fa?"

The speaker was a woman with blond braids, long feather earrings, and a smile that took up the lower third of her face.

"Boe-pah," corrected Bopha. "*Bo* like bow and arrow, and *pa* like father."

The woman extended her right hand. "I'm Lenore," she said, still smiling. "And I'm terrible with names, even American ones."

Bopha felt Lenore's warm, bony hand encircle hers. Their arms went up and down, and when Bopha didn't let go in time, Lenore laughed. But Bopha didn't mind because she'd made an important discovery: handshakes meant grown up; they meant you counted. She could tell that the other patients, even the adults, were wondering who she was and why she was getting such special treatment. When their turns came, the nurse just stood beside the desk and called out a name. It was as if Bopha had come to the clinic not as a little girl who acted like a baby at night, but on important business. Whatever she did when she grew up, she decided, it would definitely require lots of handshaking.

Lenore led the way down the hall and into a room crowded with stuffed animals, dolls, cars, blocks, and kid-size furniture. At first Bopha played while Lenore pretended not to be watching and making notes. Then Lenore asked questions that Bopha answered politely but not always honestly. Sometimes, she outright lied: no, she didn't remember her dreams; no, her parents never discussed what happened in Cambodia. Other times, she told half-truths. She talked about how proud she was that her father had a job, but not about how on paycheck days he came home late and made her mother cry. And she mentioned their big television but not the time her oldest cousin had put on a program about the Vietnam War recommended by his teacher and all of a sudden her mother started screaming *murderers* and twisting the skin of her own arms and thighs, creating bruises that took weeks to fade.

The session seemed much shorter than forty-five minutes. Bopha had only just begun tidying the dollhouse when Lenore stood and said, "Time's up, but I'll see you next week, same bat time, same bat place."

"Bat?" Bopha asked. "Like the animal?"

"A joke," Lenore said, a hand on Bopha's back to guide her toward the door. "I'll explain next week."

After the door closed behind her, Bopha stood blinking in the hallway. She felt certain she'd disappointed the social worker but had no idea why.

At their second session, Lenore watched Bopha play for only a short while before suggesting that they sit down on the chairs at the small table with its neat rows of crayons and markers and butcher paper.

"Why don't you draw me a picture of your family," Lenore suggested.

Bopha thought that sounded like fun. She pulled crayons out of the box, choosing a different color for each person as she drew them: yellow for her mother, pink for Neary, bright green for Heang, and Pheak in baby blue. She wasn't sure what color to make her father, but it didn't really matter since the paper was so small, she'd run out of room.

She arranged the crayons in a neat pile at the far end of the desk, the way her teacher had taught her, and waited.

"Are you finished?" Lenore asked.

"My dad's too big. I can't fit him." She should have planned better. Maybe the social worker would make her start over.

Lenore pushed the crayons back into the center of the desk. "I think you can. Why don't you try?"

Bopha studied her paper. Usually she was good at tests, but also usually tests had answers and all you had to do to get an A was study.

The only white space left on her drawing started next to her mother's head and moved across the top of the page. She thought of her father on the couch, where he lay down after work and on weekends, stretched out and snoring even with the TV on and Pheak crying and Bopha and Neary playing keep-away from Heang. Sideways he could sleep just like in real life. She chose the purple crayon and drew. When she finished, her father looked like a giant purple cloud. Bopha liked the picture better before, but now Lenore smiled, and that was more important.

"Very good. Will you tell me who everyone is?"

Bopha pointed at each person and named them.

Lenore's lips disappeared into her mouth, then came back out red and shiny. "Aren't you missing someone?"

Bopha stared at the social worker. She had never met anyone so smart. Picking up the milk-chocolate-colored crayon, she drew the baby in her mother's stomach.

Lenore's head moved from side to side, then up and down. "Okay," she said. "But what about you? Where are you?"

Bopha laughed. "I'm not my family. I'm just me!"

The social worker wrote something down on her pad. "Your parents," she said. "Do you think they're happy?"

Bopha laughed again. She hadn't expected the clinic visit to be just playing and joking.

Lenore's mouth moved into a smile shape, not her great big *Hello, how are you?* smile, but a smaller smile that didn't show in her eyes. "What's funny?"

Bopha swung her legs under the table. Such a simple question had to be a trick, but she couldn't think of any answer except the truth. "Happy's for little kids," she said. "My parents are all grown up."

Lenore leaned forward on her chair. "Anyone can be happy, even adults."

Bopha tried to think of happy grown-ups, but she could think only of fake ones on TV and in books. And maybe Lenore last week; this week she seemed upset.

Down the hall, a baby screamed. On the wall above the table, the clown clock tick-tocked, and when the second hand got to six, it looked like a long hair hanging from the clown's nose.

Bopha giggled.

"Do you know why you're here?" Lenore asked her.

She nodded.

"Tell me?" Lenore said.

Bopha rubbed her top teeth against her bottom lip. She wondered if the enormous stuffed giraffe in the corner of the room was the size of a real giraffe.

"It's because you wet your bed, isn't it?" Lenore asked.

Bopha thought a kid could climb on the giraffe. Her brother, Heang, would like that a lot, though she'd definitely have to give him a boost up.

Lenore put a hand on her arm. "Maybe we could talk about the last time it happened, about what was going on at home that night before you went to sleep?"

Bopha's nose itched, but she didn't scratch it. Maybe she could bring Heang the next time she came and he could ride the giraffe the way people rode horses on TV.

Lenore said, "Or maybe you already have an idea why you wet your bed?"

Bopha peeked at Lenore's face, which now seemed like a giant question mark, then looked down at her lap. She pulled a loose thread off her skirt, careful not to make the material bunch up. Probably she should tell about the water dreams, but they were all different, and anyway, she liked water, especially when she was helping her mother by washing the rice for dinner or taking baths with Neary when they got to use the soap that made big bubbles. Bopha looked at the clock again, but it still wasn't time to go home.

Finally, Lenore asked if she wanted to color some more. Bopha nodded, and the social worker passed her a clean sheet of paper.

The next week, after they shook hands and Lenore led the way down the hall to the therapy room, Bopha opened the door for herself and headed toward the play area.

"No," Lenore said. "Over here."

On the little table, a large shopping bag had replaced the paper and crayons.

"It's a present," Lenore said, her voice rising, as if she weren't sure herself.

The bag was big and white and shiny, with writing on the side. Bopha eyed the long plastic handles. Her mother could use a bag like that for marketing.

"Open it?" Lenore said.

One at a time, Bopha pulled items from the bag and placed them in a neat pile on the table: a bedsheet cut in half, two towels, and two rubber pads.

"So your mattress doesn't get wet," Lenore said. "I'll show you?"

In the middle of the table, Lenore placed a rubber pad, then one of the towels, and, over it all, one of the half bedsheets. Finally, she demonstrated how the lump of cloth could be flattened by tucking the ends of the sheet into the sides of the bed.

"When you wake up wet," Lenore explained, "you can pull all this off, throw it onto the floor, and go back to sleep on the dry regular sheet. Okay?"

Bopha wanted to ask Lenore if one end could be kept loose so she and Neary could sleep together again, but she didn't bother. The towels would never end up on her bed. They were too beautiful, fluffy and yellow and soft, much nicer than the thin, scratchy ones hanging in the bathroom at home. The towels would be for her parents.

She felt the wetness on her cheeks before she realized she was crying.

"What is it?" Lenore asked, but Bopha couldn't speak. The social worker led her to the sofa against the wall, sat down beside her, and held out a box of tissues.

Bopha's body shook and her nose ran. She turned her face into the cushions, but the harder she tried to stop, the worse it got.

Lenore rubbed her back. "Good," she whispered over and over. "Good girl." And then, as Bopha quieted, Lenore began talking fast, her voice low and serious and without question marks. She said that sometimes people felt things that scared them, and when those things couldn't come out the right way, they leaked out in other ways. She said that although Bopha might always have to be her mother's helper and take care of her younger siblings, she didn't have to get straight As or grow up more quickly than other children. She said that if there was trouble between her parents, it wasn't Bopha's fault and it wasn't her job to make it better.

Finally, Bopha quieted. She didn't blame Lenore for not being able to fix her. Maybe the doctor was right and three sessions just weren't enough. Or maybe hers was an especially bad case. Then again, Lenore had helped; Bopha might not get to use the new towels, but she could use the sheets and the pads and maybe even her parents' old towels. If she had all that, she could clean up after herself, and it would be almost as if she didn't have a problem at all. She crossed the room to the table and put the items back into the shopping bag. Then she walked to the door.

Lenore met her there and put a hand on her shoulder. "You know this is our last session?"

Bopha nodded.

"Are you sure there isn't anything you want to tell me before you go?"

Bopha hugged the bag to her chest so no one could steal it on her way home. She smiled at Lenore. "Only thank you very much," she said, and then she walked down the hall and through the clinic's crowded waiting room with her chin on the bag and her eyes on the floor.

GIVING GOOD DEATH

In MANY WAYS, Robert's arrest was liberating. In the county jail, he ate lunch sitting down, exercised regularly, and, with the benefits of 24/7 lighting and permanent lockdown because of what the pedophile one cage over called their VEP or very endangered person status, began tackling some of the great books, large and small, he had always meant to read but never quite seemed to have time for: *Middlemarch* and *The Magic Mountain*, William Carlos Williams's *The Doctor Stories* and *The Collected Works of Anton Chekhov*. After his arrest, Robert had at most one appointment a day, and he was the patient.

Twice a week at ten fifteen, a guard escorted him through the multiple locked doors of a facility that had been hailed in the *San Francisco Chronicle* as "a stunning victory for architectural freedom over bureaucratic stupidity" by a Pulitzer Prize–winning architecture critic who'd obviously never experienced the place from inside its frosted windows. Unlike the architect, Robert's experience of the building had nothing to do with freedom. The guard marched him down the corridors shackled at wrists and ankles, then shoved him into the windowless lime-green room where he was expected to spend a county-designated psychiatric hour—forty minutes—discussing his past. The room had two hardwood chairs that made Robert nostalgic for the comforts of his steel bunk, and a metal table screwed into the floor. The psychiatrist, who introduced herself simply as Dr. Sung, often worked for the DA, though in Robert's case she served as a mutually agreed upon consultant. She was businesslike, younger than he—he guessed late thirties—and wore the weary, harassed expression of a woman with too much to do. From a smudge on the hem of her skirt, he suspected young children, though he never found out for sure. She gave nothing away, which was okay by him. With little to do, he appreciated the challenge.

At their introductory meeting, Dr. Sung said that her job was to provide the judge and jury with an accurate portrait of the defendant and that they'd see a lot of each other because she wanted to understand how Robert came to be the person he was. Robert told her that most people saw what they wanted to see, and precious little in life couldn't be looked at from a variety of equally valid angles.

Though a tape recorder captured his every word, Dr. Sung wrote that sentence down. And so Robert added that one of the reasons he was a doctor and not, say, a lawyer was that suffering was universal while the law varied by state and country, and as a result, sometimes what was right wasn't legal.

Dr. Sung wrote that down too.

Earlier that week, Robert's attorney, Nick Barton, had told him that most prisoners didn't get wireless electronic readers or the time and attention he would get from Dr. Sung, and that he would get Dr. Sung's attention because he was paying for it, and he was paying for it because the usual rapid and ruthless forensic psychology evaluation led to just one conclusion—crazy or not—which in his case wouldn't be useful.

"Why not?" Robert had asked.

"You're not crazy," Nick replied.

"So why the psychiatrist?"

"The DA will try to argue that this sort of thing is always murder—"

"Nick, for Christ's sake, she was dying, and then she died. All I did—"

Nick held up a hand. "I know. Save the next go-round for the headshrinker."

For their first real session, Dr. Sung wore a red suit that didn't quite fit at the shoulders and hips and two-inch heels that might have been weapons in a courtroom or bar but left her vulnerable on the worn, under-waxed floors of the county jail.

Robert was seated when she arrived, but he stood—an awkward, ungraceful effort because of the shackles—when the guard let her in.

"No, no—" she said, trying to wave off his gesture and failing because of the briefcase she carried in one hand and the stack of case files under the other arm.

She didn't look at him until she had deposited her belongings on the floor where he couldn't see them and extracted a blank legal pad and pen. Once settled, she seemed transformed, her body taut and attentive, her brown eyes lit with an intensity she could apparently turn on or off at will.

Interesting, Robert thought. So that's what it looks like.

His ex-wife, Cate, used to accuse him of shifting into doctor mode. He could yell at her one minute and answer a page the next, his voice calm and suffused with concern and compassion. "Why can't you talk to me that way?" she had asked more than once, and for a while he'd try. But she wasn't his patient; she was family, one of the few people with whom he was supposed to be able to be his uncensored self.

"Okay," Dr. Sung said. "Let's start."

He told her he didn't know where to begin.

"Just start. Whatever comes to mind."

For most of the last year of their marriage, Cate went to therapy twice a week and never said a word in her sessions. When Robert asked her why she continued going, she told him she kept hoping it would help.

"What comes to mind is that I don't know where to start."

"Try the beginning."

Beginning of what? he thought. My life?

Dr. Sung put down her pen and sat back. "It's simple," she said. "What do you think of when I say, tell me how you came to be here with these particular charges against you?"

"I think it sounds like you want endings, not beginnings."

Dr. Sung looked at him, her expression neutral.

Robert glanced at his watch. On average, doctors filled silences after just two seconds and interrupted their patients after less than twenty, but psychiatrists were different. Dr. Sung waited without apparent effort or impatience. After a thirty-six-minute standoff, Robert noted the faintest glow of sweat on her nose.

"When you're in training," he said, "you think the worst possible outcome is if the patient dies. But it's not, not nearly."

Dr. Sung slid the pen through her fingers. He could tell she wanted to write that bit down but was afraid to derail his train of thought.

He leaned forward. "Have I considered how I came to be wearing an orange jumpsuit and living in a cell? Of course I have. I have gone over the events dozens of times in my head

26

and several more times with Nick Barton in a room just like this one. I can list facts and events, miscommunications and errors in judgment, but what I haven't been able to do is find an answer to the most important question by far: Why doesn't anyone understand that I've done nothing wrong?"

Dr. Sung scribbled on her pad, then made two slashing motions and stood up. "Sorry," she said, "but we're out of time."

In preparation for their second meeting, Robert read *The Executioner's Song* and *In Cold Blood*, but the session began inauspiciously. Dr. Sung wore a white blouse and tan slacks, colors that made her look pale and tired. No sooner had she uncapped her pen and crossed her legs when they heard a scream and something slammed against the other side of the locked door to the visit room. They both startled, and Dr. Sung's pen flew upward, glancing off her sleeve before clattering to the floor. There was another, even louder thump a second later, followed by a muffled protest, but the door didn't open, and soon enough it was quiet again.

Simultaneously, Robert and Dr. Sung noticed the black stain on her blouse. She swiped at it and swore, her voice not quite a whisper.

It wasn't even ten thirty. She had a full day ahead of her.

Robert picked up her pen and passed it to her, his handcuffs clattering against the table. Since the fabric appeared to be synthetic, he recommended that she wet it, then apply a fine mist of hair spray and a few drops of white vinegar.

"I've read a lot of manuals and how-to books," he offered by way of explanation for his esoteric knowledge. Cate had sometimes questioned his choice of reading material, but after a long day with patients he enjoyed the straightforward prose and unambiguous solutions to problems.

"Thanks," Dr. Sung said. Her tone suggested that he'd done something inappropriate, if not outright annoying.

"I didn't—"

"Let's just get started," she said. "We've lost enough time already."

In the papers, they were calling him the death doctor, which was at times technically accurate but also completely misleading. "Some patients you remember," he told Dr. Sung. "Some patients you can't forget."

She pressed Play on her tape recorder and folded her arms to cover the stain on her sleeve.

The day the DA claimed Robert tried to kill her, Consuela Alvarez had arrived at his office wrapped in her granddaughter's handmade blanket, though the temperature outside was over one hundred degrees. She hadn't walked in five years, hadn't wiped her own bottom in two, but there was nothing wrong with her mind.

Remembering, Robert felt a primal surge; he wanted to escape to some other, better world, with Consuela's tiny, frail body clutched to his chest like an infant.

Dr. Sung shifted, uncrossing then recrossing her legs. "Out loud please," she said quietly.

"Consuela Alvarez first came to see me just after her husband died. This was years ago, in the nineties. Back then, my Spanish wasn't what it is now, but it didn't matter, because she always had someone with her, a daughter or nephew or cousin."

Robert smiled, remembering Consuela as she had been. "She couldn't have been more than four foot ten in heels, and whoever was interpreting told me she supposed she'd grown up poor, though having no experience of anything else, she hadn't realized it at the time. For generations, her family had farmed the sloped coffee fields of northwest El Salvador, and that's what she had done too, when she wasn't having miscarriages or busy with her seven children. But times changed, and once they were grown, her kids didn't want any part of that life. Eventually, they all came north. By the time I met Consuela, she was sixty-two years old and her household included three generations, two teachers, an attorney, five grandchildren, and a one-and-a-half-pound long-haired Chihuahua called Mouse. At that first visit, her only complaints were a left-handed tremor and a tendency to lose her balance."

Dr. Sung took a deep breath. "Okay," she said. "I see where you're going. And I'll want to return to Mrs. Alvarez later. But what we need to talk about first is your earliest professional experience with death. Slow down. Start at the very beginning. You've skipped way ahead."

"I really don't see how—"

"Please," she said. "I know what I'm doing."

Robert stood and took a few steps, but there was nowhere to go, so he sat back down. "Thelma. Thelma Mae Watson, age forty-eight. I was a medical student—"

"Sorry," Dr. Sung said. "Before that. The first person you ever saw dead."

Robert explained that, before medical school, he'd seen a dead frog, several dead goldfish, the usual modicum of roadkill. Really, nothing at all.

"Then start at the beginning of medical school. You've skipped at least one."

He'd forgotten. She was a doctor too.

The beginning, then.

Like every medical student's first patient, Robert's was dead. Four of them shared him, a man so tall his feet dangled off the far end of the metal table, so old he had great gray bristles of hair sprouting from his nose and ears but only a few lonely wisps left on his scalp. Not that theirs was the oldest; the next table over, a team worked on a woman so ancient her skin hung off her body like tissue paper.

It hit him while he was talking. "Almost all of them were old," he said to Dr. Sung. "Our cadavers. Were yours?" He couldn't believe he'd never noticed.

"Keep going," she said.

"I asked you a question."

"My answer isn't relevant."

Robert shook his head. "You're wrong." He leaned forward. "Imagine there's a policy—an unwritten rule—that cadavers need to be people of a certain age. Think of the message that sends."

"Medical school policy doesn't interest me. I want to hear about you."

Robert laughed. Couldn't she see how it all amounted to the same thing?

"During the arm dissection, a bunch of us went over to the next table to check out the woman's bicep. It was thinner than a pencil. No one could believe it. One of the guys at my table commented that she must have been past due."

"Past due?"

"To die. She looked starved, and her joints were contracted." Suddenly he remembered other details, a bald spot on the back of the old woman's head, his own cadaver's long, curved toenails. "Of course, we didn't know what a contracture was back then, but we could see that her hips and knees and elbows wouldn't completely straighten. She'd probably been bed-bound for years." He rubbed his face. He hadn't shaved in a week, and his cheeks and neck itched where the hairs were coming through the skin.

"It was obscene. No one wants that kind of ending."

Dr. Sung nodded, not a *yes* but a *go on*.

Robert leaned back in his chair, eyeing his hired expert, possible enemy, and potential savior. His colleague, first name unknown. "Whaddya think?" he asked. "Should we sign you up to go out like that?"

Dr. Sung didn't bite. "What makes a life worth living?" she asked. "And who has the right to make that decision?"

He refused to answer such a facile question, to make her job so easy. He closed his eyes. In his head, he recited the differential diagnosis for dementia. After a while, their time was up and Dr. Sung pressed the button for the guard to let her out.

Cate's psychiatrist practiced in Pacific Heights, on the sixth floor of a building with views of the San Francisco Bay. Robert had gotten the man's name from a former intern of his who'd gone into psychiatry. The intern had made a lousy neurologist, unable to elicit reflexes, once missing the easy vertebral landmarks on a spinal tap by so many inches he accidentally stuck the patient's liver and nearly killed her, but Robert trusted his judgment of people.

Cate supposed a psychologist would do, but Robert argued that a real doctor would be more likely to understand their situation.

Maybe that was why therapy left her mute. She thought the doctor would take his side.

"I just stare out the window," she told him. "I can see Angel Island, Alcatraz, Tiburon, and the Headlands."

Robert pictured his wife sitting in a soft leather recliner in a tastefully furnished room with throw rugs over the carpeting, floor-to-ceiling bookshelves, and walls hung with discreetly framed abstract art. Cate would offer a polite hello, then avoid looking at the doctor. She would decide on a menu for dinner and make a mental grocery list while twirling a few highlighted strands of hair around her left index finger, creating that one surprising curl in her otherwise straight hair, afraid to speak lest the words dismantled her life in such a way that it could never be put back together.

Robert sometimes wondered whether, if they'd had children, things might have worked out differently. Cate had been willing to consider adoption. He hadn't. He had insisted that they keep trying for one of their own, not because he had anything against adoption, but because he believed Cate would be happier with a little person who was part her, part him, and he thought that if they just kept trying, they'd eventually succeed. By the time it became clear that he'd been overly optimistic, they had settled into a routine that seemed to work well enough.

Robert finished *Crime and Punishment* just in time for his third session with Dr. Sung. She arrived at their usual room in a green dress, belted at the waist, that clashed with the walls and reminded him of one Cate had worn often in the year before she left. Dr. Sung's shoes matched her belt, and her earrings and necklace were the same color as the dress. Cate's dress matched her eyes. Hers had started out as a bridesmaid's dress, and then she'd transformed it. She was clever that way. Dr. Sung's dress bunched at her hips, too tight in some places, too loose in others. Aesthetically, Robert decided, this was not his psychiatrist's finest moment.

They spent the forty minutes in silence. Robert thought of Cate. He couldn't imagine what Dr. Sung was thinking.

Nick Barton had suggested that Robert keep a diary of his life in jail—"just in case"—and Robert was fairly sure he'd been following the letter but not the spirit of the project. That week, he wrote:

Sun—PBJ x 2, warm milk, soggy bread; Forty Niners 21, Giants 28; Stanford 14, USC 35; Invisible Man

Mon—warm milk, The Sound and the Fury

Tues—warm milk, greasy hash browns, bruised apple; Dr. S., black suit, bad shoes, silence; Bleak House

Weds—more Dickens; frozen milk; a call from Nick to say he's hired not one but two forensic pathologists who will independently review the records and find the evidence needed to prove my contentions, "IF IT EXISTS"

Thurs—Dr. S. navy skirt/sweater, silence; Slaughterhouse-Five; warm milk; CSI, Without a Trace

Fri—Dispatches; letter to Cate (not mailed); The Things They Carried; milk actually refrigerated (!!!)

Sat—warm milk, more PBJ; Catch-22

Nine months before she left him, Cate found a new therapist in a public clinic in the Tenderloin, a neighborhood Robert was fairly sure his wife had never been to before even though it was just blocks from some of her favorite department stores. Cate had been in her refugee phase then; previously, there had been rain forest, endangered species, decorator's showcase, and lost art of the American high desert phases as well. She had gone to the Tenderloin Family Health Clinic to set up distribution for a program that gave out children's books with each well-baby check. The therapist (a latter-day hippie type who had a master's degree in social work, not an M.D.) had a no-show and started helping out. They got to talking, and before she left the clinic that evening, Cate had scheduled her first appointment with "Lenore." That night at dinner, what Robert had later come to refer to as the Lenore-isms began, and Cate had told Robert that her new therapist seemed like a real person, something about the woman having an inspiring mix of empathy and humor, traits Cate apparently found lacking in doctors.

By the time of Robert's arrest, Cate lived in Wyoming, where she cooked for a dude ranch that catered to Californians in winter and New Yorkers in summer. He knew this because she'd sent him a postcard a few weeks after the Tuesday he'd arrived home from work to find her gone. She'd threatened to leave the weekend before, but she so often got agitated when he worked late that he hadn't taken her particularly seriously.

The postcard pictured an empty dirt road, distant snow-capped peaks, and lots of bright blue sky. In the foreground stood one of those green-and-white road signs that read:

Owl and Eagle Ranch
Population 18
Elevation 4,527 feet

On the back were three sentences in the elegant cursive Cate had perfected during her years at the French American Bilingual School. Reading it, Robert decided that her parents' decision to send her there had served her well from the standpoint of daughterly handwriting, if not in terms of the development of the basics of interpersonal etiquette such as saying good-bye to your husband of over twenty years face-to-face.

There was no Dear Robert—no salutation at all—though his name did appear above the address.

Beautiful here and gloriously unpredictable—t-shirt weather one day, three layers of fleece plus down jacket the next. People coming next week for my things. They have key and will leave it on mantel when done. C

Dr. Sung arrived late, breathless and apologetic, for their sixth session. Robert kept reading. He'd moved into a Latin American phase and had just transitioned from Borges's *Labyrinths* to Márquez's *One Hundred Years of Solitude*.

When she had settled herself and her usual extravaganza of papers and case files, Dr. Sung said, "Sitting here not talking is just wasting your money and both our time."

"Times," Robert corrected. "Your time plus my time makes it plural, particularly since how we spend our minutes is so very different. Time is one thing I now have to spare."

Dr. Sung looked at him. "Do you?" she asked. "I mean, isn't that what we've been talking about these last few weeks? How there's never enough but also sometimes too much?"

He placed his e-reader on the table and tilted his chair back onto its hind legs.

The weekend she threatened to leave, Cate had complained that they didn't spend enough time together to sustain a marriage. She also said—no doubt quoting Lenore—that she never reached the top spot on Robert's to-do list, and he expected her to compete for his attentions with the sick and disabled.

"Have you ever noticed," Robert asked Dr. Sung, "how most of the time it's much better to be the doctor than the patient, but occasionally there's some little shift, a subtle alteration you didn't see coming, and all of a sudden everything seems flipped on its head and you're not so sure anymore?"

He picked up his e-reader. "I may not have been the world's best husband, but I guarantee you I was a damn good doctor."

Then he pounded on the door for the guard.

The day Consuela Alvarez's grandson had wheeled her into Robert's office and lifted her onto the exam table, a fluke winter heat wave had begun that would bake the city for three days straight. Outside, people wore shorts and t-shirts. In Robert's office downtown, the heater remained on, programmed at some mysterious central location. His staff opened the windows, which helped some but not enough. Robert sweated in his shirtsleeves, but tiny Consuela was burning up. Her grandson wondered about fever and infection, but Robert didn't think that was the problem.

When he told Consuela that he needed to send her to the emergency department, she refused.

"You won't have to stay long," he argued. "It's because of the Parkinson's, because you can't sweat."

Her grandson stroked her head. "Can't you care for her here? Please?"

Asking the grandson to step outside, he and his nurse undressed Consuela. As always, her fingers and jaw shook in short, rapid rolling movements, but they managed to tape ice packs and cool compresses on her forehead, neck, and wrists and cover her with a single thin sheet that he told her grandson to jiggle periodically, creating a fan. While he saw patients in the other room, the nurse gave him regular reports as Consuela's temperature slowly decreased.

Midday, her grandson went out to pick up lunch. In a low

voice garbled by saliva and interrupted by coughing fits that left her red-faced and panting, Consuela told Robert that she needed his help.

Robert said he certainly would help if he possibly could.

Consuela spoke so slowly that several times he had to sing the happy birthday song in his head to keep himself from interrupting. She blinked once every forty seconds, and it took twelve blinks for her to explain what she wanted.

That same day, Paul Massey, kept awake at night by the searing twitches of his right facial nerve, fell asleep at the wheel and drove his car into a stop sign, luckily with only minor injuries, though clearly he needed to be seen that afternoon. Serena Chang was in the ER seizing. Harry Cohen wouldn't discuss how he was managing without the use of the right side of his body. Latrice Jones, only thirty-seven, had an MRI that revealed several new white matter lesions. Tom Julavitz needed a hospital bed, a commode, a night nurse, more medications, a shower chair, a wheelchair, a ramp for the front steps, a night-light, a pill cutter, and a new nervous system. Ten patients had been scheduled for Robert's morning session, twelve for the afternoon. These figures did not include his hospital rounds or the urgent add-on of Paul Massey. There were also five messages on his voice mail, seventy-six e-mails in his in-box, three piles of reports for review, and—as Consuela described her terror at choking repeatedly on her own secretions so she couldn't catch her breath and felt as if she were drowning—a courier waiting for him to sign for the divorce papers that had arrived by certified mail from Cate in Wyoming.

Dr. Sung suspended their sessions. That week, Robert read *Things Fall Apart, Gone with the Wind, Portrait of a Lady, Women in Love*, *The Awakening*, and *Beloved*. The following week, the forensic pathologists hired by Nick Barton concluded that Consuela Alvarez had died of hyperthermia as a result of the unfortunate combination of her many well-documented medical conditions and the extreme heat, and that although the medications she'd taken in the day or two prior to her death might not have been the ones all doctors would have prescribed in that setting, the drug levels were too low to have killed her. The most they could conclude by way of accusation was that maybe Robert's Spanish wasn't as good as he thought and/or he hadn't adequately explained what needed to be done in terms of ongoing cooling to her family. They couldn't explain the initial conclusions of the local coroner, though one did note off the record to Nick that he always read the local paper when consulting in order to give his work a sense of context and he had spotted the coroner on the society page with two members of the Board of Supervisors reported to be against the city's plan for a physician-managed universal health coverage system.

"In light of these reports," Nick said, "not to mention the recent hoopla over the low solve and prosecution rates for murdered black men in the Bayview and Hunters Point, I'd put money down that the DA will drop your case and you'll be a free man by week's end."

"That's it?" Robert asked.

"There will be paperwork, but yeah, basically, that's it."

"My life has been ruined by . . . for what?"

"It's not clear."

"How the hell do you do this work?"

Nick shrugged. "I could ask the same of you."

Two days later, Robert walked out of the county jail into an early-summer afternoon in San Francisco. He couldn't see the fog—it wouldn't come in for another few hours—but he could feel it. A cold wind blew through his shirt as he watched cars race down Bryant Street, honking and swerving in their haste to get to wherever they were going. He carried only his e-reader—he'd just downloaded *Deliverance* and *In Search of Lost Time*, *Housekeeping*, and *Never Let Me Go*—and a stack of letters he'd written to Cate. Having read *Close Range* and *Bad Dirt*, he knew that Wyoming was tough country but also quite beautiful in summer. He thought he might find out for himself.

HEART FAILURE

T̲WO DAYS BEFORE HER father's angiogram appointment, one day before her elder daughter's disappearance, and just hours before a ragged ball of cholesterol and platelets stopped all blood flow through her father's left coronary artery, Marta Perez-Barton prepared for her father and stepmother's arrival for a family dinner. As she chopped and stirred, Marta's three children loitered in the kitchen, supposedly helping but mostly snacking, when Jason, age eleven, the middle child and only boy, asked whether someday they would need to move to a house without stairs so Abuelita Mercedes could still come to visit. Marta realized then that her kids were worried about the wrong grandparent, so she sat them down at the kitchen table and started explaining about heart disease.

Sophie pushed back her chair and stood up. "I've got homework."

"Later," Marta said, using the calm, even tone recommended by their family therapist. And then she waited, as if she had all the time in the world. "Don't let her provoke you," the therapist told them week after week. "If you react, things escalate, and she wins." Marta and Nick sometimes wondered why they paid to be told what was essentially common sense and what she as a practicing physician should already know, but they believed that seeing the psychologist meant they were doing everything possible to help their daughter. And they kept believing, even as Sophie's anger deepened and she stopped accompanying them to therapy.

Sophie slouched back into her seat. "Tic-toc," she said. "Better clue us in before the geezers show."

Marta took a long, slow breath. In the Perez-Barton household, the children were allowed to swear, as long as they did so appropriately and infrequently. Words like *geezer*, by contrast, usually led to discussions on the nature of prejudice and the importance of language.

"Go on, Mommy," Olivia said.

Marta shifted slightly to face her two younger children. "The heart is incredible. It beats one hundred thousand times a day, thirty-six million times a year. And it's able to do this because—"

She stopped talking. Sophie's arms jutted out from her body, and she tilted her torso left and right in wide dramatic sweeps so the dozen black and white plastic bracelets she wore along her forearms fell against one another, clattering arrhythmically. In the sudden quiet, she lifted both hands above her head like an apprehended criminal.

"Okay, Sophie," Marta said. "Go do your homework."

Sophie's lips curled into a tiny, satisfied smile. "And miss a chance to learn about the heart from an expert like you? No way, José."

Olivia's eyes widened. Jason's left leg jiggled under the table. Three more years, Marta told herself. Three more years and Sophie would leave for college. In the meantime, she would be a good mother and follow the therapist's advice.

"Livia," she said to Olivia. "Pass me your crayons and a sheet of paper."

Using pinks and blues and purples, she sketched a cartoon of the blood's path through the heart. Next, she drew a close-up of two coronary arteries, one clean and healthy and the other filled with thick yellow plaque, and then she explained about heart attacks, using a red crayon to clot off the diseased artery.

When she finished, there was a pause, and then Jason said, "I don't understand what this has to do with Abuelo."

Olivia let her bangs fall into her face. "Me either. Sorry, Mommy."

"Yawn," Sophie said, and yawned.

Marta pointed at her drawings. "This is what your arteries look like, and this is what Abuelo's look like. That's why he's going to the hospital for a special test."

Jason said, "But they'll fix him, right? And then he'll be okay?"

"They can help, angel," she said. "But he needs to be careful. And that's what I want you guys to remember tonight. Abuelo looks strong and healthy, but he might be really sick. More sick than Abuela Mercedes. So no games. No running around."

"Mommy," Olivia said. "I still don't understand."

Sophie picked at a pimple on the side of her nose. "Who cares? This is just another one of her 'stuff you kids need to know because I'm a doctor' talks so she can avoid telling you Gramps—oh, sorry, *Ah-boo-eh-low*—is a goner."

"What did you say?"

"Uh-oh, kiddos," Sophie said to her siblings. "Mom's going deaf. Oops! I mean"—and here she perfectly mimicked Marta's professional voice—"*she's developing hearing loss.*"

Marta stood up. "Don't speak to me that way, Sophie."

"Or what, Mom? You'll send me to my room, and I'll miss the Dick and Mercy show, and then you think I'll be all weepy and sorry like you if it's sayonara granddad, time for the big nap six feet under?"

"Get upstairs," Marta shouted. "Now!"

On her way out, just as the doorbell rang, Sophie turned. "Don't worry, *angels*," she said to her brother and sister. "Mom'll make sure Gramps gets therapy or whatever else he needs so she can get on with her life."

Marta's father and stepmother arrived fifteen minutes early for dinner that night as if, like a foreign country, the Perez-Bartons' Glen Park home contained unforeseeable deterrents that might jeopardize their meal.

"We'll get it," said Jason, tugging at Olivia's sweater when the doorbell rang a second time.

"Great," Marta replied. After years of practice, she, Nick, and their two youngest had mastered the art of the rapid switch from private to public selves. Less than a minute after Sophie's outburst, Olivia opened the front door grinning widely so her grandparents might notice her newly missing tooth.

Ricardo Perez wore pressed jeans and a soft sweater the same backlit brown as his eyes. Well into his seventies, he still had the carriage of a military man or the leader of an impoverished but proud people, though he'd been neither, just a community general practitioner, evangelical about the role of the physician in society and the preservation of the city's Mission District murals. After a quick hello, with blatant disregard for his cardiologist's recommendations, he trotted back down the front steps to the driveway. "Was he checking to make sure we were home?" Nick asked while Marta watched her father's comb-over fall into his face as he bent to open the car door for Mercedes.

Overweight and a little breathless, Mercedes grasped her husband's hand in both of hers, still fearful a year after her knee replacement. She wore a halo of tight copper curls— "Someone's been to the beauty parlor," Nick said—and what appeared to be a designer dress, far too fancy for a weekday dinner with the grandkids. Later, she told Marta that the dress was homemade, constructed over six months of Tuesday afternoons at the city college senior fashion class, and she wanted to show it off. Ricardo wouldn't attend the Older Adults Department courses or the Lifelong Learning Institute at San Francisco State. He spent his time up at the University of California Medical Center instead, going to all the free lectures, his stethoscope tucked into his suit-coat pocket as if he'd just come from the office.

Inside the house, Nick helped Mercedes with her coat while Olivia took her grandfather's arm and led him into the dining room. Jason had disappeared after opening the front door. Now he moonwalked in from the den and tucked a small electronic device into his back pocket. He shook his grandfather's hand, then circled Mercedes. "Hmm," he said. "I bet I could rig that so it lights up."

Mercedes looked down in horror at her dress. It was red and covered with hundreds of tiny metallic disks she'd sewn on one at a time herself.

Nick took Jason by the shoulders from behind and tilted him backward until they were eye to eye. "I bet I could rig it so you had to eat dinner in your room."

Jason grinned, shook free of his father, and kissed his grandmother. "I meant that as a compliment. No kidding. You look totally glam."

Mercedes smiled uncertainly.

"*Glamoroso*," Nick explained. "A good thing."

"Abuelo?" Olivia asked. "What are they going to do to you at the hospital?"

Ricardo tucked an errant wisp of Olivia's hair behind her ear. "They are going to take pictures of my heart and maybe clean out its pipes," he said. "You remember last year when you stayed with us and we had to call a man to come fix the kitchen sink? What they will do to me is something like that, like Roto-Rooter."

"Roto-Rooter of the heart?" Olivia laughed.

From upstairs came a stomping. The ceiling shook, then a door slammed.

Nick said, "Why don't we sit down. I'm starved." He pulled Mercedes's chair back from the table and pushed it forward again once she was seated.

"Me, too!" Olivia said, waiting beside her seat.

Jason and Marta went into the kitchen to get the food. Neither Ricardo nor Mercedes asked where Sophie was or why she wasn't joining the family for dinner.

A necessary barbarism. A mutilating assault for an undeniably good cause. In the years prior to Sophie's adolescence, that was how Nick described his oldest daughter's entry into the world to family and friends. For Marta, the birth by cesarean section had been like the Civil War surgeries she'd read about in medical school, chaotic and bloody and brutal.

The epidural wouldn't take. Frustrated, the anesthesiologist treated her as if she were a patient instead of a colleague. "Can you feel this?" he asked over and over, repositioning the catheter and poking her legs and pelvis with a pin. When she answered yes and yes, he tried again, but eventually he gave up, shaking his head in disgust, as if *she* were the problem. So when all the monitors alarmed, signaling fetal distress, and the obstetrician cut a long, horizontal window across her abdomen, Marta felt pain like an explosion that reduced her to a single inflamed sensory bundle. She smelled shit and blood and singed flesh, and she listened with a cringe to volleys of high, piercing sound she only later recognized as her own screams. She watched herself being filleted, and if the pain and the nurses hadn't held her in place, she would have lifted herself up off that table and tried to kill them all.

Perhaps for that reason, bonding with her firstborn hadn't resembled the experiences described in her new-mother books. What, Marta privately wondered, was so terrific about a bald, blemished, inarticulate being who transformed one's life using precisely the same techniques used to indoctrinate people into cults? For weeks that felt like decades, she resented the sudden and drastic change in the way she spent her time, the dietary restrictions and sleep deprivation, her relentless busyness and loss of privacy, the monotonous repetitive tasks, the forfeiture of her former activities and professional identity, and, most of all, other people's assumption of her unconditional surrender to her infant's needs, the universal belief of family members, friends, books, and health professionals that these changes constituted not only life's greatest miracle but her own greatest joy.

And then one evening when Sophie was two and a half months old, she began to cry and wouldn't stop. Nick fed her and changed her diaper and walked her around and sang to her, all to no avail. Finally, he carried their wailing daughter into the bedroom where Marta was trying to nap and placed her on Marta's chest. Sophie quieted mid-scream. Her eyes widened, and a few minutes later, they both fell asleep.

That night, Marta began to appreciate her new role. She returned to work on schedule two weeks later but negotiated a decrease in her clinical responsibilities so she'd have more flexible hours and fewer ancillary demands. Four years and two miscarriages later, they had Jason, and three years after that—to their surprise—came Olivia. As Sophie reached her tweens, Marta watched as her eldest became increasingly strong-willed and serious, less family-focused than Jason, and more needy than her much-younger sister. Conveniently forgetting that Sophie hadn't always been that way, Marta attributed those traits to genetics, birth order, and the unique individuality she and Nick tried to cultivate in each of their children. In other words, long after the signs of serious trouble appeared, she underestimated their significance. She made excuses. Like Nick, she repeated the story of Sophie's beginnings to her friends, as if to say they'd been through hard times before with this kid and look how well things came out. As if the story offered more insight about her daughter than herself.

Over a salad of organic greens, heirloom tomatoes, and home-stewed chipotle black beans, Ricardo—who had turned seventy-six the previous month—lamented his family's lack of longevity. "They all died by their late seventies, more or less," he said, and then listed them. "Lupe at seventy-eight, José at seventy-five, Maria Elena at eighty-one, Tío Miguel just before his seventy-ninth birthday."

"Late seventies isn't so bad," Nick said. "It's beating the average."

Jason asked what the average was.

"It depends," Marta said. But before she could finish an-swering the question, Mercedes—who wouldn't consider even the latest barely visible in-ear hearing aid—interrupted.

"Rico, te olvidas Juan Carlos."

"Oh, no," Ricardo said. "I didn't forget Juan Carlos. Just the opposite." To Nick he said, "Juan Carlos Luis Manuel de Perez, my paternal grandfather. A self-made man like myself. He was not the sort to complain or ask for help. Thought people got where they were by their own strengths or failings and it was not anybody's job to help them out." He looked at Marta. "Juan Carlos was our only centenarian."

Nick nodded, but his attention was on Olivia's plate. They were seated side by side. He reached over with his fork, picked out the orange and yellow tomatoes, then waved them at a grimacing, delighted Olivia before dropping them onto his own salad. Olivia could have done this for herself, of course, but Marta's husband and youngest child were a mutual admi-ration society, each thriving on surprising the other with small, unnecessary kindnesses. If Nick—whose firm special-ized in civil rights law and ethically ambiguous, often high-profile local criminal cases—noticed her father's backhanded slight at his leftist predilections, he didn't let on.

"They used to call him *El Luchador*," Ricardo continued. "The Fighter. And he was. Devil of a man, opinionated on everything from the proper length of ladies' skirts to the his-tory of Mexican-American relations. Even in his nineties, he was always getting into altercations, and not just the kind with words."

Marta refused to argue with her father about the relative influence of genetics and character as determinants of extreme old age. Between her exhaustion and his unshakable confidence, she'd be wasting what little energy she had left after a day of work and family and the latest Sophie drama. With chest pressure when he walked up hills and what the cardiologist called "a better than even chance" of needing bypass surgery, she worried that Ricardo wouldn't reach seventy-seven, much less eighty or ninety or a hundred.

With her patients, Marta considered herself skilled in the art of difficult conversations. It was only when people with options—not those with little money and no access to affordable, healthy foods, but her Glen Park boomer neighbors or her wealthy patients from Nob Hill or Pacific Heights—repeatedly and knowingly made unhealthy decisions that she felt helpless in the way dealing with Sophie made her feel helpless. Those conversations left her speechless—or almost. She went through the motions. She did her job. Often it seemed that her patients couldn't tell the difference. She hoped Sophie couldn't either.

Her father would not only recognize insincerity, he would pounce on it. So rather than respond to whatever question may have been couched in his Juan Carlos story, she asked Olivia what a centenarian was.

Olivia puckered her lips and moved her eyes from side to side. "Ummm."

"Try and figure it out."

The little girl rested her fork on the side of her plate and let out a world-weary sigh. "Cent-ten-a-rian. Cent, like a penny. Ten, that's a number. A-rian. Arian. Ar-ian." Her shoulders sagged. "Oh, boy, I'm in trouble now."

"What's a librarian?" Jason asked his sister.

Marta and Nick smiled at each other across the table.

Olivia squinted at her brother, clearly concerned that this

might be a trick question. Reluctantly, she said, "A library person."

"So if I tell you *centum* is Latin for a hundred," Nick said, "what's a centenarian?"

Olivia sank in her chair until her eyes were just above her plate. Suddenly they widened, and she sat up. "A hundred-year-old person!"

The adults clapped, Jason hooted, and Olivia climbed up on her chair for a bow.

After a dessert of dulce de leche frozen yogurt and out-of-season, imported, and very expensive blueberries bought for the benefit of her father's long-suffering arteries, Marta walked Ricardo and Mercedes down to their car. "What are you doing tomorrow?" she asked.

"Monday," Ricardo said. He pulled a slim black leather datebook from his back pocket. It had gold-rimmed light blue pages and a red ribbon place marker, and he'd had one just like it every year Marta could remember.

Using his index finger as a guide, he read, "At eight, there is epilepsy update. At nine, irritable bowel syndrome, and for lunch, ocular emergencies." He closed his datebook and smiled.

"Tell me you're at least going out for a nice dinner."

Mercedes studied the front of her already buttoned coat.

Ricardo's nostrils flared. "Tomorrow," he said, carefully articulating each syllable, "I will have dinner at home, as always, at seven o'clock *punto*, as I would on any other Monday. And anyone"—he looked from Marta to Mercedes—"anyone who thinks I am in need of a last supper should not bother to come on Tuesday to the hospital."

Mercedes leaned her head against the sleeve of his coat. He pulled her toward him until they were side by side and Marta stood alone opposite them.

"That's not what I meant," she said, though it was precisely what she'd meant. "You may have to stay overnight, and you know how hospital food is."

"And I know also what a fine cook Mercedes is."

Ricardo didn't look at his wife as he said this, but it was clear to Marta from Mercedes's reaction that he'd never uttered those or similar words during any of the twenty-six years of their marriage.

She gave her father a quick kiss and hugged Mercedes. *"Me llamas?"*

"Claro," Mercedes said, and reached up to lay a hand on Marta's cheek. "I will call as soon as he finishes."

The Perezes did not pry into one another's affairs. They did not ask direct, obviously concerned, and conspicuously unasked questions such as, *Why didn't Sophie have dinner with us?* And, *I know you're very busy, but won't you talk to the heart doctor to make sure everything goes okay for your father?* In fact, the Perezes were the sort of family that did not even say *I love you.* Not on birthdays or holidays. Not after pleasant family meals. Not even before angiograms or when confronted by a child desperately trying to get their attention.

Seconds after her grandparents left, Sophie came downstairs and poured herself more cereal than Marta consumed in three days. None of the rest of them ate that particular brand, with its refined sugars, artificial coloring, and television cartoon tie-in. Sophie bought it for herself with money she earned watering neighbors' yards and feeding their cats when they traveled. Because of their busy schedules, the Perez-Bartons had no pets, no indoor plants, and cactus gardens both front and back, facts that appeared at numbers five, twenty, and twenty-one on their elder daughter's thirty-two-item list of complaints, a list Sophie made available to anyone—their friends, colleagues, random strangers—on her Facebook page.

Nick confiscated both bowl and cereal box. "Dinner's over," he said. "And you missed it."

"No problemo. I'm having breakfast."

"No," Nick said, holding the cereal out of reach. "You're not."

And then it started. Red blotches covered Sophie's round face. She picked up a heavy glass serving bowl and dropped it onto the floor. It cracked in two but didn't shatter, so she lifted the largest piece over her head, prepared to throw it across the room. Marta reached for the half bowl and Nick grabbed Sophie by the wrists. A sharp sting seared Marta's palm, then she felt a warmth, and all three of them watched as bright red blood rushed down her arm.

Nick let go of Sophie. "Get out of here!" he bellowed, shoving her with such force that she nearly tripped over her own feet. Marta put her hand under the tap and turned on the cold water. She lifted the flap of severed skin. It was a clean, relatively superficial cut. No glass fragments, no exposed tendons.

"Should I do something?" Nick asked. "What should I do?"

"A dish towel," she answered. "A clean one."

Nick had the good sense to pass a towel well past its prime, and Marta wrapped her hand with it, then held the hand above her head. Regaining control, Nick led her into the den and sat down beside her on the couch, positioning himself so his shoulder was under her elbow and it was no longer any effort for her to elevate her arm.

"What are we going to do?" he asked.

"When the bleeding stops, I'll put on a pressure dressing."

A window had been left open and the fog had come in. Cold air blew through the room. Marta shivered.

"I mean about Sophie."

Oh, she thought. *That.* Marta ran the fingers of her good hand through Nick's hair, blond waves increasingly giving way to gray. Every night, something different set Sophie off. One night it was Olivia, the next it was a look Nick might or might not have given her. The amount of milk in her glass, a t-shirt not yet washed since its last use, her science homework, the trill of her mother's pager—any minor infraction could cause major chaos: screaming, flying objects, punching, scratching, and kicking. One evening a passing pedestrian had called the police.

Marta had lost whole nights—weeks, months—of sleep, running through their parental decisions and actions, trying to uncover the source of Sophie's overwhelming anger. She couldn't figure it out. Not knowing why her child was such a mess was almost as agonizing as the hostility itself.

"Boarding school?" she suggested, only half joking. They'd already tried therapy, first individual and now family, a change of school, and upward and downward adjustments in structure and independence.

Nick frowned. "She's not a chair or a coat. We can't just send her away because she doesn't suit us anymore."

"I know," Marta said, but thought, Where's that law written? People must do it all the time. They couldn't be the first parents unable to cope with a child.

"I pushed her too hard," Nick said. "Way too hard."

"You were upset about me."

"No," he said. "I mean, yes, of course, but that was only part of it. I wanted to push her even harder. I wanted to . . ."

She could guess what he was reluctant to admit. She'd had the same feelings herself, moments when she didn't worry whether Sophie was cutting herself or doing drugs or contemplating suicide, and instead imagined in cold, gratifying detail slapping certain expressions off her daughter's ugly, hate-filled face. Once upon a time, they'd had a wonderful, happy family. She had loved her life. But in the last year, she'd begun coming home filled with trepidation. She dreaded dinners and bedtimes and mornings before school and even weekends, sixty hours without reprieve from a child who had painted the walls of her room black, rarely pulled up the shades, worshipped Kurt Cobain, hated school, and preferred plants and animals to human beings.

Marta took Nick's hand. "Tell me."

He closed his eyes. "I wanted to throw her onto the floor. Beat the crap out of her. Get back at her for all she's put us through." He took a sharp breath. "My own daughter, and I wanted to hurt her so badly I could taste it."

She kissed his palm, then closed her eyes too. The reddish darkness behind her lids seethed with minute speckles of light she couldn't hope to organize into a useful clarity. Against that backdrop, Marta imagined Sophie as a smiling infant, a temperamental toddler, a pretty and charmingly precocious child, and finally, she pictured her daughter waddling into the kitchen, slumping down at the table, and shoveling bite after unwieldy bite of lavender and pink and lime-green cereal into her huge, sneering face, and she felt something inside her tighten, shut down, and turn off.

*

Everyone knows what to do for a heart attack. Everyone, it turned out, except Marta's two useless half brothers, graduates of the nation's leading universities, both of whom still lived at home and neither of whom called 911 when their father's chest pain began later that night. Instead, they squeezed a pallid, sweat-drenched Ricardo and the invisible six-ton elephant on his chest into Carlos's new chrome-and-silver Mini and drove him not to the closest hospital but, at Ricardo's insistence, across town to the University Medical Center.

"What were you thinking?" Marta yelled at Carlos in the waiting area outside the cardiac intensive care unit. And he and Jorge exchanged the look they'd shared as boys when she'd explained to them the importance of learning Spanish or flossing their teeth.

Early the next morning, Marta went home to change her clothes and give her family an update on Ricardo's condition. Nick hadn't gone with her to the hospital, as they were no longer willing to leave Jason and Olivia at home alone with Sophie. After she explained to the kids that their grandfather had had a heart attack and then a surgery he barely survived and might not recover from, Sophie announced that she'd *rather die* than be a doctor.

Marta said, "I can't have that conversation right now."

Sophie smirked. "That's me all over. The inconvenient child."

Jason was on the verge of tears. "Please, can't we just talk about Abuelo?"

"Inconvenient?" Nick turned to Sophie. "What about selfish?"

"I'm going to be a doctor," Olivia said. "I'm going to go work in Africa like Megan's mom."

Sophie glared at her sister. "You can't be a doctor. You can't even kill a bug."

Olivia opened her mouth to protest, then glanced at her sister and closed it again without speaking. Jason turned on his Game Boy and began pounding the keys.

Nick said, "Each of you can be whatever you like. But right now we should be thinking about your grandfather."

Marta nodded.

"Oh, sure," Sophie said. "We can be anything. As long as it's the kind of job that makes people say, 'Wow, you're such a good person.'"

Nick flinched. Marta looked at her daughter and tried to feel something other than exhaustion and a wish that they'd sent Sophie to spend the night at a friend's.

"We just want you to be happy," Nick said. "All three of you."

Sophie cackled. "News flash! Plan not working!"

Marta pictured her father tethered to a bed by tubes and wires and coma. "What would make you happy, Sophie? Tell us. Please."

Sophie threw her head back and slapped the table, as if her mother had just told a great joke. The performance stopped as abruptly as it began, and she glared at Marta. "Like you care."

"Do not," Nick said, "speak to your mother that way. Ever. And you can do whatever you damn please. Just don't hurt other people."

Sophie turned to her siblings. "But," she said, "it's A-OK to degrade and deprive yourself and your family for the sake of strangers."

Jason's fingers froze above his toy.

"Jesus, Sophie!" Nick said. "What the hell does that mean?"

Marta felt dizzy. She had refused Jorge's early-morning offers of vending machine cookies and soft drinks. "We have never degraded you, Sophie," she said. "Never."

"I forget," Olivia said. "What's *degrade*?"

Sophie's eyes narrowed. "Try and figure it out, hot stuff. Start with the Latin root."

"Please," Jason whispered.

Sophie pushed back her chair and stood up. "You two don't even like me," she said, her eyes shooting from Marta to Nick and back again. "If that's not degradation, what is?"

"Like?" Nick protested. "I love you!" The usually unspoken words emerged too loud and with the unmistakable violence of an expletive.

But his words were no match for Marta's silence. The refrigerator buzzed. Outside, a car passed the house, its radio turned up so high that she felt the beat in her bones and gut before she heard the blurred scream of vocals.

Sophie walked over to where her mother was sitting and leaned forward until her pimpled face was just inches from Marta. "And *I'm* supposed to be the problem around here," she said. Then she turned and ran upstairs.

In the cardiac intensive care unit, Marta and Mercedes spent the day sitting side by side in orange plastic chairs beside Ricardo's bed. Machines hummed and beeped. Every six seconds, the respirator made a whoosh and Ricardo's chest rose and slowly fell. Above his head hung bags of medications— the right ones at the right doses, Marta knew, since every time she left the cubicle, if only to use the bathroom down the hall, she checked them on her return. Below him, attached to the bedrail, other bags collected liquids from his bladder and chest tubes. Pumped with fluids during the resuscitation and operation, her father had put on twenty pounds overnight.

"The children are okay?" Mercedes asked for the third time in two hours. Her face, usually round and decorated with powder and rouge, appeared ashen and deflated, as if she'd lost the pounds Ricardo had gained.

"Nick picked them up from school," Marta said again. "They'll be here soon." She looked out the window and watched an aide check the blood pressure of a patient in the next building. "And the boys will be back. They decided we needed real food for dinner."

The aide across the way turned on the light behind her patient's bed so he could read despite the fading daylight. Marta looked at her watch. Nick and the kids should have been at the hospital over an hour ago.

"I have no hunger," Mercedes said. Her eyes filled, and she clamped them closed. They had agreed not to cry in front of Ricardo, not that he would know the difference, as Marta alone knew because she had overheard the residents rounding that afternoon, saying things no one had told the family after the surgery, such as how the team had had trouble restarting Ricardo's heart and the number of minutes his brain had gone without blood and oxygen. It had never occurred to the young doctors that a family member might understand their jargon. At their stage, Marta probably hadn't realized either that doctors were people too.

She wondered what Sophie had done this time. Snippets of the morning's conversation had haunted her in quiet moments throughout the day. Once, remembering Nick's nod toward the stairway after Sophie's exit and her own decision not to follow their daughter upstairs, she'd groaned aloud, sending Mercedes into a panic about Ricardo. She'd have to make amends, she knew, but hopefully not that evening.

"Dr. Perez?" said a voice.

Marta recognized the nurse who'd worked the same unit with the same chipper attitude nearly twenty years earlier when she was a resident. The woman had aged, her hair shorter and more gray. But the same could be said of Marta.

"Your family's here. In the waiting room. I can't let the kids in. Policy. You know how it is." She rolled her eyes before fading back into the hallway.

"I should come?" asked Mercedes.

"No, stay with Dad. I'll be back." More likely she'd send in Nick. Marta needed a break. She imagined that five minutes on the roof screaming at the top of her lungs might help, but how would she explain it to the children?

"Mommy!" Olivia shouted, and threw herself at Marta. "She's gone. She's really, really gone!"

Marta hugged the little girl's body to her own and kissed the top of her head, smelling chalk and shampoo and sweat.

Around her, the busy waiting room seemed glacial, all white walls and haunting silence. Families sat in small clusters separated by one or two empty chairs, and in a far corner, light blinked from a soundless television hung from the ceiling by thick metal cables. Outside the lone window, the sky had turned black.

Gone?

Jason stood beside his father, his eyes huge and his cheeks wet.

Gone.

Marta put an arm out for Jason, who wrapped himself around her and his little sister. She backed up, pulling them with her until she felt the cool of the wall against her legs and shoulders. Finally, she looked at her husband.

"I've called everyone," Nick said. "All her friends. The neighbors. The school. And I tried to file a police report, but it's too soon."

Jason's body heaved against hers. Marta couldn't catch her breath.

"Hospitals?" she asked.

Nick shook his head. He looked pale but composed. "But that's good, right?"

She wished he would come closer, encircle them all. When he didn't, she said, "How can you be so sure? Sophie has keys to neighbors' houses. She could be hiding. Getting back at us—at me. She went to school this morning, Nick. I saw her get in your car."

Marta kept her voice low, but the pitch rose as she spoke. Around the room, a few people looked up, then away.

"Her drawers are empty," Nick said. "Her iPod is gone. Kurt Cobain is gone." He might have been reciting a grocery list.

Suddenly he lurched forward. In the second before she felt his breath on her neck and understood what he had said, his face shattered.

"Marta. She's gone."

Over the next week, as Ricardo failed to regain consciousness, as Mercedes agreed to withdraw life support, as they prepared Jason and Olivia for their grandfather's funeral and heard nothing from or about Sophie, Marta couldn't eat. She couldn't sleep. She turned off her pager, threw bills and catalogs unopened into a pile on the front-hall floor, and erased phone messages as soon as she was certain they had nothing to do with Sophie. She didn't know what was happening at work, and she didn't care.

Twice daily, Nick checked the bus depots and youth shelters. He organized groups of their friends to methodically canvas the Haight, Golden Gate and Buena Vista parks, the Tenderloin, SoMa, and every other part of the city where teenagers were known to sleep in doorways and under bushes. Every three days, they went to the police. "With this type of kid . . . ," said one officer, shrugging his shoulders and not even bothering to finish his sentence, much less write down Sophie's most distinctive characteristics. They stared at him, speechless, coming up with suitable retorts only much later. "Your father would have known what to say," Nick told Marta as they drove home, and his use of the past tense hit her like a blow.

They hired a private detective who repeatedly claimed he found signs of Sophie—in Seattle, then Phoenix, then L.A.—but it was always some other chubby teen with brown hair, pimples, and black clothes. They learned that the country was full of runaway kids prostituting themselves, doing drugs, and somehow getting by on the streets. Before Sophie left, Marta would have converted her new knowledge into donations to charities and letters to the editor about the precious individuality of the nation's faceless, voiceless youth. Now she knew all that social passion was just a role she'd played for her own selfish gratification, a persona she'd invented that had fooled everyone but Sophie.

When Marta finally went back to work, she found she'd lost her taste for the sorts of patients who reminded her of herself in that long stretch of her life she thought of as *before*. Within weeks of her return, she resigned. She could no longer bear the commute across town to the group practice affiliated with the city's best private hospital or the lovely, renovated Victorian with its hushed modern decor and well-heeled patients scheduled every fifteen minutes. Instead, each morning she walked up Glen Canyon Park and through the divide between Twin Peaks and Mount Davidson to the chaotic campus of century-old, crumbling California mission style buildings with red-tiled roofs, where she had enough time to debate the meaning of life and the purpose of medicine with the Americanized children of gravely disabled elderly immigrants and to provide thoughtful, compassionate care for people so down on their luck they put her own life into perspective.

For weeks after Ricardo's death and Sophie's disappearance, friends and colleagues asked how Marta was, openly inviting discussion of her losses. For a few months after that, they graciously excused late school pickups and incomplete patient notes, acknowledging indirectly the dramatic changes in her life. And then they moved on, as she had, at least superficially. At home and at work, she did what needed doing for life to continue for the living and present. She said nothing as Nick took on more and more cases, as Jason, quieter than before, did his chores and Sophie's without ever being asked to pick up the slack, and as Olivia cried at the slightest provocation, since their youngest also continued to laugh as easily as before and so remained their happiest and most carefree child. But Marta felt Sophie's absence as she might feel an amputation. The sensation, relentless and persistent, resembled less the loss of a hand or foot, which would be immediately evident to others and alter her ability to do even the simplest things, and more the loss of an ear or breast, a fundamental and defining feature she could function without but would never stop missing.

BECOMING A DOCTOR

THE THIRD WAVE

I'd been accepted everywhere—all five of the top-ranked medical schools and each of the four second-tier places I'd applied to just in case. Admissions deans or alums called me from four of the top five. All had the same pitch, talking up their school and praising my defense of my roommate's head-scarf in a YouTube video that went viral. Only San Francisco didn't call.

So at orientation, when Dean Rosenthal told our class of one hundred and fifty-two future doctors that although our ambitions might feel as cozy and warm as old fleece sweaters, they were in fact as common as pigeons at Fisherman's Wharf and as cold and slick as late-summer fog through the Golden Gate, I laughed. We all did. Four years later, I know better.

THE SECOND SEX

I come from a family of surgeons—my dad, my grandfather, my older brother—so we all just assumed I'd be one too.

All of us, that is, except for my grandfather, who said the operating room was no place for a girl.

"If that were true," said my father, "none of the rest of us would be here."

My grandparents had met in the OR, where my grandmother had been her future husband's scrub nurse.

"That's different," said my grandfather.

"Right," said my brother. "But only because if you'd been born a few decades later, it would have been Gram giving you orders in the OR instead of vice versa."

"Now, now," said Gram. She stood behind our grandfather with her hands on his shoulders. Then she winked.

From the time I learned to walk and talk, our family had remarked on my astonishing resemblance to my gram, a woman who somehow fulfilled all conventional expectations while also never doing anything quite the way she was supposed to.

OUTRAGEOUS ACTS AND EVERYDAY REBELLIONS

In anatomy lab the first day of medical school, I marveled at the views of the city and ocean seen from the lab's big windows, the shiny metal instruments, and the crisp snap of surgical gloves against my skin. I felt proud in my pressed white lab coat and blue polyester scrubs, though even one of the lab instructors laughed when he saw me. It seemed the scrubs came in just three sizes, the smallest of which didn't take into account that a person might be only five feet tall and barely in the triple digits for weight. Not that I really minded. I tucked the top that otherwise hung to my thigh into the bottoms, triple cuffed the pant legs, and got to work.

The school assigned four students to a table, which meant four students per cadaver. My group consisted of me and three guys—the Wong twins, who had matching class rings from Berkeley, and a preppy wearing penny loafers and a head of long, tight dreads that danced when he spoke.

I wanted to know if he'd interviewed for medical school looking like that, but I couldn't think of a polite way to ask. Instead, I shook Hank's hand and traded answers to the usual questions—hometown, college, anticipated specialty. He had grown up in Seattle, where I went to college, double majored in engineering and biology at Michigan, and planned on surgery too. More surprising was his smell, a mix of cloves and vanilla with an undercurrent of evergreen.

From those first minutes when the four of us introduced ourselves, Hank behaved as if he'd already been selected as our team leader. Pulling the sheet off our cadaver, he correctly diagnosed her as female and said, "Our first patient. Let's call her Cherry."

"Wink, wink," he added, and David and Daniel Wong laughed.

I forced a smile. The dead woman's hands had jagged yellow nails and long, elegant fingers draped in thin, wrinkled skin. I'd never seen hands so pale, so still, and so completely human.

That first morning, according to the anatomy guidebook, we were to fillet Cherry.

"Heads or tails for the first cut," David said, throwing a quarter into the air. The winner would get the privilege of pulling a scalpel from the base of Cherry's neck to her pubis.

Daniel called heads, then shoved his brother and grabbed the coin midair. "Oh, yeah," he said. "This is so mine!"

It was tails. I lost next, and David came up short in the final round. Hank opened the manual to the correct page, drew a line along the torso with a black marker, and handed me his scalpel. "Because I know I'm sometimes an asshole," he said.

My first incision didn't even sever the skin. I made a second pass, then a third before the job was done. The texture was nothing like real skin. The preservative had made it tougher and more rubbery, which turned out to be useful; the harder I pressed, the less my hand shook as I cut.

After that, we divided the work geographically. Up top, Dan and Dave cut along the rim of Cherry's sparse hair. They planned to lift off a window of skull and harvest the brain. A bucket of formaldehyde stood waiting on the counter behind our table. Farther down, Hank and I worked separately, he in Cherry's chest and me in her abdomen. He cut with surgical deliberation; I figured she was already dead, and all that mattered was getting inside.

My hands began to itch in the latex gloves. The smell of formaldehyde, pungent and noxious, seeped into my clothes and hair. I kept glancing at the ridge of thick brown moles under Cherry's right breast, and also at her feet, the gnarled toes heaped upon one another like stacked corpses.

"You okay?" Hank whispered.

I nodded, afraid to speak.

Pulling back flaps of skin, I lifted internal organs to feel each one's heft in my palm. I had so much to learn, and found that my memory worked best through my eyes and hands. I held Cherry's bilobar liver, purple and cobbled when it should have been reddish and smooth; a small, dense kidney, curled up on its side like a sleeping fetus; heaped, pallid coils of intestine—enough, we'd been told, to cover the length of a football field end zone; and, finally, Cherry's uterus, shrunken to a nubbin the size of my thumb.

"Wow," Hank said, moving closer. "Is that what I think it is?"

The guys were all staring.

"Oh, man," Dan said. "Is that possible?" He pointed at what appeared to be a single strand of shredded dental floss dangling from the tiny organ. Maybe Cherry had had only one fallopian tube, the other taken in surgery or atrophied to invisibility. More likely, I'd severed it without even noticing.

Hank's shoulder pressed into mine and he shrugged.

A handful of students, all women, cried during the two-month anatomy course. They left the room, missed entire organ systems. Not me; to those who weren't looking closely, I was as tough as any guy.

PERSONAL POLITICS

Twice a month during that first year, as part of a pilot program to get beginning students out of the classroom and into the real world of medicine, I followed Dr. Bernard Nercessian on rounds on the Rehab and Extended Care Building of the veterans hospital. At one P.M. on alternate Thursdays, he greeted me with an enthusiastic handshake and handed me his spare stethoscope. As we rounded, he introduced me to his patients, lowering his voice to name my medical school, as if the honor was his and my presence beside him proof positive of his own competence and stature.

Dr. Nercessian's patients were mostly returned from Iraq

and Afghanistan, and they followed military etiquette despite being so damaged that dispositions other than discharge were out of the question. They said, "Yes, sir, doctor"; "Copy that, doctor"; "Thank you, doctor, sir." Sometimes they thanked me also, even though almost all I did was watch. But sometimes, too, after Dr. Nercessian was out the door, the patients looked at me and said, "Miss, I need a blanket"; "Miss, change the channel"; "Miss, yo, get the bedpan—hurry." I found blankets, changed channels, and slipped plastic bowls under waiting buttocks of every color, size, and shape before racing to catch up with Dr. Nercessian.

Usually, busy with orders and his notes, he didn't notice my absence. Then one day, I got held up by a guy named Rodney. He was about my age, and his body was so trashed—no right leg or arm; limp, mangled limbs on the left; and half his face missing—that he'd been there for months, and I'd met him on several of my previous Thursdays at the VA. While I struggled to place a bedpan under Rodney, Dr. Nercessian came back into the room, and as soon as I succeeded at what felt to me like my first real clinical challenge, he pulled me into the hallway. "What were you thinking?" he said without letting go of my sleeve.

I had been thinking that the bedpan seemed the very least I could do under the circumstances. I had been thinking that maybe bedpans came in different sizes, but with Rodney praying frantically not to wet himself, I had decided to use the only one I could find in his room.

I was about to explain this to Dr. Nercessian, when he finally let go of my sleeve and said, "Next time, you tell them to call the nurse."

The patient's call light had been on for ten minutes before our arrival and during the entirety of our visit with him.

Dr. Nercessian looked at his watch and shook his head. How was it possible that he couldn't imagine what it might be like to be sick and helpless and desperate to pee?

I followed him down the hallway, smiled when he introduced me to our next patient, and nodded attentively as he pointed out a non-healing amputation stump, a murmur, a nerve palsy, and the tightening scar tissue from a massive chemical burn. I didn't know what I'd do the next time someone asked for a blanket or a bedpan, until two weeks later, when a veteran who'd tried to kill himself and failed—he'd aimed at his temple, not his brain stem—did ask, and I went to get him a blanket. Early the following week, I was informed that Dr. Nercessian had called to resign as a preceptor for the pilot program because, in his estimation, first-year medical students didn't know enough about professional behavior to be allowed near patients.

INTERCOURSE

My girlfriends and I all agreed that it would be a really bad idea to date a member of one's anatomy team, since if you broke up before the course ended, lab would be awkward at best and at worst someone's grade would be affected, and that someone would almost certainly be the girl.

So Hank flirted with me and I flirted with him, but whenever he asked me out, I said no. It got so I knew without looking if he'd entered a room. When he stood near me in lab, I felt as if I had to pull myself in the opposite direction just to remain upright.

Sixteen minutes after the anatomy final, we locked ourselves in the handicapped bathroom on the second floor of the medical sciences building. The odors of hospital soap and piss didn't matter. Nor did the filthy sink and floor. We didn't make it farther into the small room than the two steps needed to clear the door.

Hank's roommate, Ted, also in our class, headed home to Vallejo for the weekend. We spent the next sixty-seven hours in their apartment, never going out, dressing only one at a time and only long enough to pay for the takeout.

IN A DIFFERENT VOICE

It was whispered that one of our immunology professors was a shoo-in for the Nobel Prize in medicine. As the first year progressed, fewer and fewer students showed up for class, but the day of the great professor's talk, the lecture hall was packed.

That evening, my friend Althea and I headed over to Hank and Ted's to study.

On the walk over, Althea said, "I don't even deserve to be in medical school. I didn't understand one word of what that guy said today."

I stopped walking and stared at her, both scared and re-lieved. "I didn't really understand it either."

Althea looked as if she might cry. "I don't mean I couldn't follow the diagrams. I mean, I didn't have the first clue what he was talking about or how his topic fit with the rest of the course."

Althea had won the history prize at Yale and spent two years covering LGBT issues for the *L.A. Times* before med school. Even Hank talked about how brilliant she was. I had majored in biology at UW and come straight to med school from college. My only claims to fame were a two-minute video and having coxswained for the women's crew team that won nationals—both decent achievements to be sure, but not exactly intellectual. If Althea wasn't smart enough for medical school, I was a dead woman walking.

When we arrived at Hank and Ted's apartment, they were talking about the lecture too.

"Can you believe that asshole?" Ted asked. He opened a bag of chips and threw it onto their kitchen table, where we'd be studying.

"Lazy prick," Hank agreed. "Like being hot stuff in the lab entitles him to give an incomprehensible, piece-of-shit lecture."

Althea and I looked at each other and burst out laughing. It had never occurred to either one of us that the problem might lie anywhere but within.

RUBYFRUIT JUNGLE

In our second-year physical exam course, we were sometimes sent to practice our fledgling skills on real patients. When I met Jake C., he was twenty-two years old and panting like a dog. Reverend Frank sat beside him, holding his hand and whispering in his ear. He told me that Jake had had sex only once. The other guy was older, Frank said, told Jake he was negative, showed Jake a lab slip even, then swore on his mother's life and begged to ride bareback. "Live a little," the guy had said. Reverend Frank closed his eyes and shook his head.

A photo of a handsome young man in a suit and tie hung at the head of the bed. On the white pillow below, Jake's nose, lower lip, and cheeks had been replaced by bulbous purple tumors.

I had learned from the chart that Jake had steadfastly refused antiretrovirals. He believed that he'd acquired the virus through sin and stupidity and intended to let God's will determine his fate.

It was Reverend Frank, a teacher at the small local college where Jake had studied until he became too ill, who had called 911. And it was Reverend Frank who, obviously in love with his former student, had pleaded with the doctors to do everything necessary to keep Jake alive.

I touched Jake's shoulder and asked if I could examine him. His oxygen mask fogged and cleared, fogged and cleared. He nodded.

I followed the sequence I had memorized the night before, starting with blood pressure and the other vital signs. When I finished with his chest, I lifted Jake's gown to examine his abdomen. His belly was covered in tiny, glistening pearly growths, and a few inches to the left of his belly button there was something that resembled a moist purple slug.

The nursing notes in his chart said that Jake's family never visited and that Reverend Frank never left Jake's room.

It was impossible to look at Jake's torso and not think plague and curse and infestation and death. But it was equally impossible to imagine how people could stop seeing, touching, and loving their son.

Feeling righteous, I reached forward to examine the scooped-out expanse between Jake's ribs and hips. Reverend Frank stopped my hand in midair.

"Doc," he said with a nod at the box of gloves on the wall above Jake's head. "Haven't you forgotten something?"

THE FEMALE EUNUCH

Our medical school had a two-plus-two format: two years in the classroom followed by two years in the hospital. The demarcation zone consisted of a month in which we crammed facts into our brains for the first of the many board exams designed to certify physician competence. Hank and I had moved in together by then, and in the days leading up to the test, mugs and bowls and plates, papers and highlighters and books migrated onto every surface of our apartment.

"How old do you think this is?" I asked him late one day, holding up a half-eaten sandwich. We'd been quizzing each other on microbiology for almost five hours, working our way through hundreds of viruses and bacteria, protozoa and fungi. I was starving.

Hank moved from his perch on the futon toward where I sat on the floor, placing his feet carefully in the tiny lacunae of visible carpet. He lifted the uppermost slice of bread to reveal wilted lettuce smeared with mayo and mustard.

"Bacteria responsible for food poisoning," he said. "*Salmonella* and *Staphylococcus aureas. Clostridium perfringens. Campylobacter. Bacillus cereus* . . ." He put the sandwich back on the seat of the armchair where I'd found it. "Come with me," he commanded. He pulled me to my feet and led me on tiptoe through the drugs and bugs section of our living room to our bedroom, where the shades remained down and the sheets hadn't been washed in nearly a month.

"But I'm hungry," I protested.

"The ability to focus despite distractions is a key attribute of the competent physician," he said in the exaggerated cadences of our clinical-skills professor. "I think a change in topic will help you regain your focus. Let's review some anatomy." He pulled off his shirt and pointed in turn at his nipple, the paired muscles running down the center of his abdomen, and his belly button. "Areola," he intoned. "Rectus abdominus. Umbilicus." His pants and boxers came off in a single surgical motion. "Your turn."

I took my time unbuttoning my shirt and unhooking my bra, then stood on tiptoe to unzip my jeans and leaned forward. Hank's pulse was visible in the arteries of his neck.

"I have an idea," I whispered, my lips just a millimeter from his ear. "Let's switch to physiology instead."

THE AWAKENING

Neurology was my very first rotation—the start of the second half of our two-by-two curriculum. I was finally in the hospital, finally a third-year medical student. Finally, sort of, or almost, a doctor.

On my first call night, just after midnight, the intern and I went down to the radiology department. We needed to check on an urgent head scan we'd ordered first thing that morning. Though the scan had been done hours earlier, we hadn't had a chance to see it. Busy with a steady stream of admissions, we hadn't gone back to see the patient either. That seemed strange to me, but I figured the intern knew what he was doing, and I kept my mouth shut.

I followed the intern through the mystifying maze of hallways and doors that was radiology at San Francisco General. At regular intervals, open doors revealed darkened rooms with giant machines and glowing view boxes. Making a sharp left, we passed a guy lying on a gurney. Two steps later, the intern stopped walking. I stopped too. And when the intern turned back to the patient, I turned back too.

I thought the guy looked sort of funny.

"Oh fuck," said my intern. "That guy's dead."

Except for Cherry and the other cadavers, I had never seen a dead person before. It turned out that they looked very much like alive people, only completely different.

"Call a code," shouted my intern as he lowered the side rail and began chest compressions.

I scanned the walls, looking for a button or switch.

My intern slammed his arms down onto the dead man's chest. "Phone," he said, and slammed again. "Operator," he said, and down went his arms. "Now!" he yelled.

Since this happened during my first night in the hospital, I really appreciated that my intern took the time to introduce me to such an important diagnosis, even if we didn't also have time to discuss who the man was, or how he'd died, or why he was lying alone and dead in the radiology hallway in the middle of the night, or why we called a code and then did a full resuscitation when the intern had known the patient was dead from the start.

A VINDICATION OF THE RIGHTS OF WOMAN

Walter was a cowboy and Vietnam vet with a failing heart. I took care of him on internal medicine at the veterans hospital, my second rotation. He was from the Wild West somewhere, a place with lots of rivers and streams. He called me honey or sugar, never doctor or doc, wore a bear-tooth necklace with his hospital gown, and taught me to start IVs. "Try again, honey," he said when I missed. "I got plenty more."

I saw Walter several times a day, not only because he was so sick but also because, even though my team had fourteen other patients, being a newbie student, I'd been assigned only Walter. Also, I liked him. From Walter I learned that moose shed their coats late each spring and for months look like mangy dogs, that the best protection against a bear is to sing at the top of your lungs, and that a single elephant turd can weigh eight pounds or more.

"Elephant?" I asked. Even a city girl like me knew that the only elephants in North America lived in zoos.

"Read that one," Walter admitted.

He also admitted that he hadn't killed a bear to get the bear-tooth necklace he wouldn't remove.

"My daughter found it," he said. "Gave it to me for Christmas the year she was six. The next week, her mama packed them both up and took off back to her parents in Phoenix."

"Where is she now?" I asked.

"Dunno, sugar," he said. "She got poisoned against me a long ways back."

Ten days after his admission, on a sunny Wednesday morning when our team was doing morning rounds, Walter announced that he felt better. "Seems like maybe the old ticker isn't used up after all," he told us, sucking air through dusky lips pursed to a crenellated O.

The real doctors on the team nodded and murmured, weighing the pros and cons of sending Walter home. When the senior resident gave his okay, with the usual caveats and warnings, Walter smiled. As the others filed out of the room, I squeezed Walter's hand. It felt cool and limp, like a fresh-caught fish, and I wondered whether his heart, though improved, was doing well enough to keep him going outside the hospital. I told Walter I'd be back later to do his discharge paperwork, and then I hurried off to catch up with my team. Walter winked and said, "Catch you later, sweetheart."

But he didn't.

When I got back to his room, a man bright yellow from jaundice lay sound asleep in Walter's bed. I raced to the nursing station, sure that Walter had died, but he hadn't, he'd gone home. The senior resident had done the paperwork while I was at a student conference.

"Hey," said a nurse, holding out a wadded piece of tissue. "He wouldn't leave unless I promised to give you this."

Inside the tissue was the bear-tooth necklace.

"So creepy," said the nurse.

I held up the worn leather strap. Most of the huge tooth was a yellowish brown, lumpy and ridged, but the tip was pale and worn, with a chip at what should have been the pointed end. I tucked it into the top pocket of my white coat, safety-pinned it in place, and headed down to the emergency department to meet my next patient.

AGAINST OUR WILL

During the first months of our third year, despite the long work hours, Hank and I felt thrilled to be in medicine and happy to be together. I pranced in my rubber clogs. When Hank put on scrubs, he swaggered. No matter how late at night we got home, we lay in bed and presented our accomplishments to each other like gifts in a game of escalating munificence: I did a spinal tap, he caught a baby; he stapled a wound, I did an intubation; he put in a central line, I sutured a laceration.

Since the start of medical school, Hank had debated the pros and cons of each type of surgery: heart or brain, colorectal or transplant, plastic or orthopedic. I hadn't wavered from general surgery, sure that it alone would allow me to indulge my broad interests, play to my strengths, fulfill my family's expectations, and prove my grandfather wrong.

That fall, I began my general surgery at the university hospital with a team considered one of the ten best in the country. Unlike my earlier rotations in neurology and medicine, my surgery team didn't spend half the day talking to patients or one another; we actually did things. In the first two weeks I scrubbed in on more than twenty cases, drained a giant abscess, tied off an appendix, and flew to the Central Valley to harvest a liver. I loved it.

And then in the third week, just minutes after giving what my team told me was a great presentation at the predawn morbidity-and-mortality conference, I was standing outside operating room 14 reviewing the day's cases with my resident when a group of gray-haired surgeons passed behind us. At first, post-call and coming down off the adrenaline of my talk, I thought I'd been stung on the butt by a bee. By the time I realized that my ass had been pinched by one of the august, scalpel-wielding, nationally renowned, and locally revered leaders of my future specialty, it was impossible to know which one had done it.

I told my resident.

"Assholes," he said with a smile.

I told my attending.

He leaned back against the hallway wall and asked me to present our new admissions.

I told Hank, who said, "C'mon, you knew stuff like that would happen."

I didn't call my father or brother, and at the time, I couldn't have explained why not.

THE YELLOW WALLPAPER

Dr. Michelle Hitchens, (former) locked inpatient psychiatry ward attending, taught me a lot about mental illness, and I think the least I can do in her memory is to make sure others realize that depression is a common and crippling disease too often suffered in silence and shame even by those of us in the medical profession. Dr. Hitchens, for example, had all the symptoms listed in my *Diagnostic and Statistical Manual of Mental Disorders* under the diagnosis "major depression," but she seemed either to have no insight into her situation or to be in complete denial.

Every day, we rounded on people who, just like Dr. Hitchens, felt hopeless, slept poorly, ate little, and enjoyed nothing. She worked slowly, cried often, and at the strangest moments would reveal some detail of personal life that was clearly none of my business. One day she mentioned that her husband hadn't worked since about six months after their marriage. Another day she said that he claimed to be writing a play, but really he just went out for coffee and read magazines. She did the grocery shopping, the cooking, and most of the cleaning. On weekends he stayed in bed while she got up to deal with the kids and the dog. He called weekends his days off.

"So," she would say, standing outside a patient's room, gazing at me through eyes bloodshot from fatigue and framed by dark circles, pale cheeks, and sunken temples, "Can we do anything for this sad soul?"

I would dutifully rattle off a hierarchy of potential medications to be tried, recommend that they be used in combination with psychotherapy, and mention that the critical step was not to miss suicidal ideation and intent.

"Good," she would say, running one hand through her obviously unwashed, shapeless hair. "You're just right that those things can help some people."

Then she told me that her oldest son had autism and that he had to wear a helmet and attend a special school. Her younger child was well behaved at home, but they'd been getting notes from his preschool that he was biting and scratching other children.

"What do you do when nothing you try works?" I asked one day.

"Well," said Dr. Hitchens. "Well, then . . ."

My concern for Dr. Hitchens's well-being peaked one morning when we were rounding on the violent, low-functioning schizophrenics and she said she knew it was a bad day when she envied her patients, who were lying in bed with a little cup of green jello on their tray tables. I should have said something to someone that morning about how worried I was. I know that now.

SEX AND THE SINGLE GIRL

When I got home New Year's Eve afternoon, Hank was in bed. He'd been told he could head home early in honor of the holiday.

"Let's celebrate," he said. My Victoria's Secret catalog lay open beside him on the comforter cover.

"I'm exhausted."

"No worries. This won't take long." He threw back the covers so I could see the full extent of his enthusiasm.

Eight minutes later, he was in the shower and I was lying in our bed, suddenly wide awake. Busy and tired as we were that year, we increasingly had sex that was either too fast or too slow and that, by winter, had become for me like one of the experiments I'd had to do in my premed classes, the ones where I followed the rules to an expected outcome, knowing that thousands before me had reached the same pedestrian end by the same rote means, suspecting I was wasting my time.

The eight minutes between Hank's enthusiasm and his shower had included, in addition to the so-called sex, a conversation that went like this:

Hank: "Did you book anywhere for dinner?"

Me: "Nope."

Hank: "Me neither. But I recorded last week's Warriors game. We could order Chinese."

Me: "Okay."

THE BEAUTY MYTH

"Oh yeah," my intern sneered when a dietitian walked by in a short skirt and three-inch heels and all the guys at the nursing station in the surgical intensive care unit turned to watch. "Yeah," she repeated so only I could hear. "I could look pretty hot too, if I worked eight hours a day instead of twenty-eight."

This was at the university hospital on my obstetrics and gynecology rotation. The next day, I caught my first baby, a seven-pound boy. His father held him up, and everything in the delivery room just froze. It was like a medicalized and modernized religious tableau: the father—bearded and decades older than his wife—glowing, the child wailing above his head, the two of them bathed in fluorescent light.

That month, I worked with my best team yet. The attending had won every teaching award the school had to offer and had allowed a medical student to deliver each of her three children. My senior resident, headed into gyn-oncology, was equally skilled in the most challenging surgical techniques and in giving bad news so the grieving could actually hear and make use of what she said. The intern had conducted groundbreaking research on domestic violence in the South Asian community while she was in medical school and had since published three research articles, the last of which had been picked up by the national media.

That they treated me as one of them blew my mind. By the end of the month I decided on obstetrics and gynecology as my specialty. It was perfect: both surgical and medical, inpatient and outpatient, young patients and old. Similar to what the rest of my family did, yet entirely my own.

Hank had finally decided as well. "Really?" said the future neurosurgeon when I told him my choice. "Everyone knows OB-gynies are lame. They're like medieval with the scalpel. And anyway, what do you get to do that really matters?"

THE FEMININE MYSTIQUE

One night toward the end of our third year, Hank came home and called me a slob. I looked at his pants on the floor, at the piles of his journal articles obscuring our futon. For a while I'd picked up after him, but I no longer had the time or energy.

"Sorry," I said. "But I was under the impression I was your girlfriend, not your maid."

I'd just worked a sixteen-hour day and was expected at the hospital by five the next morning. I took a big mouthful of strawberry yogurt. A perfect pink circle fell onto my textbook. "Dinner," I said. "Yum, yum."

Hank opened, then shut the empty fridge. I kept reading. I was on peds with Raj Patel, our class genius. If I wanted honors—and I did—I was going to have to bring my A-game every day. Besides, the more I knew, the more they'd let me do, and I wanted to do it all.

Hank said, "We live like shit."

I looked up. "You haven't shopped or cooked either, and you're on an easier rotation."

"Then let's go out for dinner."

I turned the page in my textbook, though I hadn't finished the page I'd been reading. "I can't. Sorry."

He knelt beside my chair, a position that would have raised my pulse and expectations just a few months earlier. "C'mon. My treat."

"I've got yogurt." I wanted him to earn my attention, to beg for it.

"That's not dinner."

"It is for me." I pretended to keep reading, noting with satisfaction that the hair at the far end of his part was thinning.

"Well, that makes one of us, doesn't it?"

He went into the living room. I heard the sound of rustling paper and a while later the roar of our ancient vacuum. I returned to studying Ewing's sarcoma. When Hank came back into the kitchen with my coat a half hour later, I shut the textbook and we went out for Chinese.

THE BELL JAR

Three weeks after Hank broke up with me, Althea came over. I hadn't left my apartment except to go to work, and I'd been ignoring phone calls. In honor of my first full weekend off in months, I had decided to do nothing but watch sentimental family dramas on television, crying as frequently and noisily as I pleased.

"Up," commanded Althea.

When I didn't budge, she pulled me to my feet and led me into the bedroom. Then she tried to pull my sweatshirt up and off. I pushed her away. "What the hell?"

"Don't be stupid," she said. "You are so not my type. But you do need to shower, and you need to do it now. I'll be in the kitchen."

Apparently she'd brought groceries. I hadn't noticed. As I showered, then dressed—"Clothes," Althea shouted from the kitchen, "not pajamas"—she cleaned and cooked, transferring pots of food into labeled Tupperware, filling both freezer and refrigerator before moving to the bedroom, where she changed the bedsheets and straightened the closet, spreading my clothes beyond the half to which they'd previously been confined.

I watched from the futon. She had muted the sound on the TV while I showered, and I couldn't even be bothered to press the one little button that would have restored the current sound track of my life.

Finally, she flopped down beside me. "What's the difference between a family doc and a pizza?" she asked.

I didn't have a clue.

Althea smiled. "A pizza can feed a family of four."

"Family?" I said, feeling interested in something other than my own misery for the first time in weeks. "You're going to do family medicine?"

"Ba-da boom!" She grinned, throwing her arms wide. "So I'm ordering pizza, and since you'll make twice what I do at least, you're paying."

While we waited for our vegetarian special, she organized

my medical journals and textbooks, using little pieces of paper color-coded by organ system and enumerated by order of importance.

"For the record," she said, looking up from the *New England Journal*, "you've done nothing but complain about him for months."

"So?"

"So, breakups suck. But (a) you might eventually be happier without him if you let yourself, and (b) you've worked too hard to blow it now."

REVOLUTION FROM WITHIN

I did my emergency medicine rotation at San Francisco General over the winter holidays of my fourth year. Assigned to the night shift, and with all my friends working days, I developed a ritual of sleeping until midafternoon, then going for a walk to remind myself of things like fresh air and conversations that didn't include words like *pus, gunshot, pain, hemorrhage,* or *heroin.*

Outside Macy's in Union Square on Christmas Eve, a homeless man in a SAVE THE WHALES hat held out his cracked palm. After deciding he was *not* the patient whose boil I had drained the previous night in the emergency department, I told him I gave at the office.

"Where you work?" he asked. He sat on a filthy army-issue sleeping bag. At his feet lounged a gray-and-white pit bull wearing a red velvet collar studded with small silver bells.

I told him.

"I been there," he said with a smile that lifted the right side of his face but not the left. "Okay, baby, you get a pass. Merry Christmas."

In the square across the street, a tree rose three stories above the crowd. Baubles hung from each limb, and a huge gold bow had somehow been fixed to the narrow top. People swarmed around it, holding hands, carrying packages, and pushing strollers. To me they all looked like patients or potential patients, people who didn't realize that their lives could change, or end, in an instant.

I crossed back to the Save the Whales man, handed him all the cash from my wallet, and went home.

That night, the doctors and nurses in the emergency department all wore Santa Claus hats and red T-shirts under their green scrubs. The atmosphere was festive. Someone had loaded the CD player with Christmas music and pressed both the Random and Repeat buttons, so Christmas carols played all night long. Between patients, we drank hot apple cider and ate tree-shaped sugar cookies decorated with sprinkles. Except for the suicides, the shift was fairly quiet.

BACKLASH

I was on the gynecologic oncology service in February, when most of my friends, having submitted their residency match lists, were lying on beaches or doing "research" months in places like Kenya or Paris or Guatemala. Althea was in the Punjab at the Jawahar Children's Hospital. Hank, I'd heard, was at Harvard doing an extra sub-internship. Me? I was hoping to stay in San Francisco for residency, and as my father reminded me several times a month, this was no time to let my guard down.

I spent my cancer month going to work in the dark and coming home in the dark. In between, I devoted an absurd number of hours to changing dressings, hunting down fevers, and replacing the essential minerals that seemed to drain from the cancer patients' bloated bodies like water through gravel. As if that wasn't bad enough, I'd somehow decided that if I could deal with the sickest patients, I could handle anything, and so had set the personal goal of racing to the scene every time a code blue blared from the loudspeaker announcing some desperately ill person's effort to die. No matter the hospital floor or medical service, seconds after the announcement fifteen or more residents, students, and nurses would pack into the patient's room and vie for the chance to run the code, put in the breathing tube, or somehow otherwise appear useful. Usually I watched and handed people things. Then one morning I was the second person to arrive at the bedside.

The first person to arrive, who later turned out to be a cardiology fellow named Sheppard, said, "You're a student?"

I nodded.

"Then go to it," he said.

I started the chest compressions and felt the patient's ribs shatter with my very first thrust. The cancer must have been all through her bones.

Thirty-six minutes later, after Sheppard had made the official call that the woman was surely and irrevocably dead, he looked over at me and said, "Hey, stick around."

"Why?" I asked. There were low potassium levels in need of my attention.

He grinned and whispered, "Because you're gonna line her up."

I stared.

"You know," he added. "Put catheters in her."

I looked at the patient's sunken, frozen face and all the tubes already hanging from her arms and neck. "But she's dead."

Sheppard nodded. "Right. So she won't mind."

I put in four lines that afternoon, one after the next, until I had the process down cold. I felt elated, especially when Sheppard said he'd never seen anyone get so good at it so quickly.

That night, Sheppard and I went out to dinner to celebrate my new skill set. He held doors and chairs for me and insisted on paying the bill, but not on sleeping over. We dated for the next two weeks, until the night he took me to see a romantic comedy and afterward happened to mention that he'd never marry another doctor.

"You can't do work like we do and be a good mom," he said. "There's just no way. And I totally want to have a family."

OUR BODIES, OURSELVES

For my final rotation as a medical student, I did anesthesia at the private hospital across town. This was late spring of my fourth year, when I'd already received my first choice in the match and knew I'd be staying in San Francisco. With no move to plan and orchestrate, I could focus on getting ready for internship. Anesthesia provided the perfect practice grounds, as it was all about doing procedures and giving medications.

My first day on call, I got pulled off an elective gallbladder to help with a Jane Doe who'd been found crawling down the sidewalk on the block of Market Street where historic landmarks and prominent department stores gave way to discount retailers, gentlemen's clubs, and bars. She had a business card for one of the private hospital's doctors in her sweater, so the cops had brought her in to us. In the ER, they'd figured out that she'd taken a beating and also that Jane Doe was actually

Joan Kendall, a former CPA who'd become homeless after having three or four glasses of wine at a party and driving her family into an oncoming semi in an accident that made local headlines for its six instant fatalities (her husband, their four kids, and the trucker) and one intoxicated but unscathed driver.

The day I met Joan, the surgeons suspected that she had a slow internal bleed, and they wanted to open her up to find out for sure. I explained to Joan that she needed a second IV for surgery and that I was going to numb up the spot before inserting the needle. When I reached for her arm, she pulled it away and tucked it between her legs. When I tried again, after at least a minute spent reassuring and cajoling her, she howled. And when I moved to her feet, still looking for a decent vein, she kicked me in the chest.

I told my attending that I thought it was time to move to Plan B.

"No, please, no!" she wailed as I tied her arms to the bedrails with soft restraints. "No. No. Noooooooo!!" she screamed, louder still, as I pinned her head and torso and my attending held a mask of nitrous oxide over her filthy, scarred, and screaming face.

As soon as she was out, I put in the lines and we took her to the OR. I ran the whole case, the attending occasionally pointing at a dial or a drug but mostly telling me the story of his solo trip up Mount Whitney that weekend.

"You're ready, you know," he said after we'd dropped Joan in the post-anesthesia care unit. "For internship, I mean. You don't need this rotation. You should drop it and go on an adventure. Do something wild and crazy while you can."

I thanked him but didn't take his advice. Putting people to sleep so they could be painlessly cut open and made healthier was wild and crazy enough for me.

LOUISE ARONSON

WRITING A WOMAN'S LIFE

The Saturday before my medical school graduation was one of those perfect late-spring days in San Francisco when there's no hint of fog and the locals who usually complain about the cold complain about the heat instead. Althea and I decided to brave the lines at the dive restaurant on the pier at China Basin in exchange for the pleasure of sitting outside by the water and the seagulls, drinking beer and eating oversize burgers. She too would be staying in San Francisco, doing the Family and Community Medicine Residency at SF General. We joked about how great it would be the day I delivered a baby and handed it off to her for its first full physical.

We were well into our second beers and discussing all the weddings taking place in the two weeks between graduation and internship, when out of the blue Althea said, "Did you ever feel, you know, like you hated them?"

"Who?" I asked.

"Patients," she answered into her glass. "The ones you were taking care of." She leaned forward. "You know. All that whining and manipulation and wasted time. The way they made you look stupid and useless in front of your team when you were killing yourself just to keep going and learn and not hurt anyone."

Just then our dessert arrived. "*Signorine,*" said the obviously Latino waiter, with a small bow and an exaggerated sweep of the arm not laden with other customers' dirty dinner plates.

"Cappuccino? Espresso? More beer?" he asked without waiting for our answer.

"Patients are sick," I said. "Probably they can't help it."

We'd been given a generous slice of tiramisu with three

92

and a half ladyfingers along the edge and a decorative spray of shaved chocolate across the plate.

"A work of art," Althea said, pushing the plate toward me. "You eat. I don't deserve it."

I eyed the cream bulging voluptuously between the thin layers of sponge, then moved the plate back to the center of the table. "Not all patients," I said. "And not all the time."

"No," Althea agreed. "Not even most of them. So why do I keep thinking of the hard ones?"

A seagull landed on the railing beside our table, opening and closing his beak as if he wanted to join the conversation.

"You know what Dean Rosenthal would say."

Together we intoned, "Focus on your strengths, and you are weak; focus on your weaknesses, and you get stronger."

I looked out at the bay. Three middle-aged women glided past the pier in bright orange kayaks. Farther out, a windsurfer struggled to remain upright in the scant breeze. The water wasn't quite the blue green of the tropics, but it sparkled in the sunlight.

And I had at least four more years in San Francisco ahead of me.

Althea must have been having similar thoughts. "Mostly it's amazing, though, isn't it?" she said. "Medicine, I mean. Interesting, challenging, important—everything you'd want in a career. And we get to do it here."

I nodded. "And it probably gets better once you're really a doctor."

"You mean the week after next?"

We laughed and picked up our forks. The tiramisu was as good as it looked.

AFTER

In the rehabilitation and Extended Care Building of
the San Francisco Veterans Affairs Medical Center, where
some people came and went but most came and stayed, Rodney Brown, a.k.a. A-Rod, nudged the Bible off the edge of his
bed. It hit the floor with a slam, and across the room, K.C.'s
eyes opened, scanned, then rolled up, and he said, "Shit, man,
not again. What the fuck time is it anyway?"

Rodney ignored K.C. and turned on his call light by slapping his left arm against the pressure-sensitive pad beside
him on the bed. And then he waited, something he was getting good at, not that he had much choice, though at least he
was better off than Danny Stockton, who had taken one in
the head, or Pablo Villela, who lived two floors up on the
ward where you didn't have to do anything for yourself, not
even eat, not even breathe.

He listened for footsteps. Sometimes he could tell which
girl was coming by the way her shoes touched down on the
linoleum: Esther did a tap-shush, Celeste made a squeak-sigh-
squeak, and big Grace—full of self-importance—sounded as

solid and steady as a man. With Rita, his favorite, there was only the nearly inaudible brush of one nylon thigh against the other.

Unfortunately, Rodney's nose also worked well—too well—and now it was telling him that someone somewhere not far enough away was crapping himself. He hoped it was K.C. and not himself, since the hall was completely quiet, meaning it was still the night shift, the staff sacked out in an empty bed or in the med room or wherever the hell else they hid when you needed them most.

Hallway light bled through gaps above and beneath the door, then diffused across the room. It was just bright enough that Rodney could see K.C.'s open eyes trained on that place where—for a few months—there'd been a *before* photo: K.C. standing on the two legs God gave him outside the projects up on Cashmere and La Salle, his arms around the woman who'd visited daily until the afternoon she hadn't pulled up the tan vinyl chair, but stood to one side of K.C.'s bed and announced that she loved him, but she was too young for all this, that she needed a life, a real life like the one she'd always dreamed of, that she wished him well and he'd always be in her prayers, and, finally, that she really, really hoped they could be friends forever, no matter what.

Footsteps sounded in the corridor. Rodney listened, then smiled. It was Grace for sure, and he was about to advise K.C. to turn his head and catch some of the eye candy as big Gracey bowed and reached for the Bible on the floor, when pain exploded in his right foot like the sudden, excruciating burn of a lighter held to his toes.

"Oh fuck!" he yelled, though the pain faded as quickly as it had appeared, replaced by a smolder with a throbbing behind it.

K.C. asked if he was okay, but Rodney didn't answer. He was concentrating, relaxing into a hurt so familiar it was almost as if he could smell the strange German pizza a nurse named Eva used to sneak him at the hospital in Landstuhl in those last, best days before they transported him back stateside. "You are lucky," she had whispered, placing tiny rounds of sausage and melted cheese on his tongue and jerking her chin at the other beds. Her breath, warm and sharp from cigarettes and coffee, had traveled into his ear and down his torso, landing between his hips, where it blossomed into a problem he could no longer solve.

Rodney shook that memory away by conjuring the image of his mother when she finally arrived at his foreign bedside. She had changed planes four times to get from San Francisco to him—her first air travel in nearly a half century of life, a trip for which she'd been given the cheapest ticket instead of the most direct route, a trip she'd made without hesitation even though he'd signed up against her wishes, even though he'd fucked up again, ending just as she'd feared he would.

He had watched her scan the ward, skipping the white boys but slowing down at the brown ones, as if the desert sun might have lightened his color. If he could have shouted out while her eyes lingered on the black bodies covered in bandages, he would have. Finally, she saw him. Her lips parted and her eyes closed. Then she crossed the room, and it seemed for a second that she might climb over the plastic side rail and into the bed beside him. Instead, she leaned way over and kissed his forehead, then moved to stroke his arm. But before her fingers made contact, she'd done a visual sweep of his body, then stopped short, her hand trembling above his chest like those crazy birds after the bombing of Fallujah, unsure where—or whether—to touch down.

Rodney blinked and dragged his left wrist across his eyes; the pain was better now, no more than an ember. He looked down the bed at the bump that was his feet, a short, sloped ridge that might have been anyone's feet or even part of the bed itself, and there was no movement down there, but that didn't matter, because this time he knew he felt something.

"Grace!" he shouted, wondering where she'd gone.

He slapped the call light again, slapped it and slapped it. "Yo," he said to K.C. "Help me, man," but K.C. only grunted and pulled his pillow over his head.

Twenty minutes later—long enough for Rodney to be certain it was all coming back: the toe, the foot, the leg, everything—he heard the solid, steady steps again.

"Hey," he called. "Gracey, please," and the door opened.

The person in the doorway wasn't Grace or any of the other girls, but a guy Rodney had never seen before, a guy who would have been a total waste of his time earlier, since he would never, ever watch some Joe bend no matter how hard up he was. In fact, he decided, he wouldn't even mention the fallen Bible to the guy, he'd just call again later, hoping for Esther with her small, soft fingers, or Rita with her high-riding ass. But the guy could help him with something more important than a quickie thrill, more important—at least for this one moment—than even the good book itself, and so he said, "My right foot, man! I feel it!"

The aide nodded and pulled back the covers, and together they stared at the long white space on the sheet next to Rodney's mangled and scarred left leg. Rodney closed his eyes and waved the aide away.

Every morning, he somehow forgot. Every morning he woke up and recognized the hospital bed and the colorless walls he shared with K.C., and he remembered he was damaged, but he forgot precisely how or why, and for a while—seconds at least, but sometimes much, much longer—he imagined that it wasn't really so bad, and that he might have a normal life with a job and a family and the ability to wipe his own ass. He imagined that what was left of him was worth saving.

TWENTY-FIVE THINGS I KNOW
ABOUT MY HUSBAND'S MOTHER

1. She was born in the Ahmedabad district of Bombay province, India, in 1947, two weeks after partition, thirteen days after independence, the second of six children of a petty bureaucrat and a housewife with repressed artistic ambitions that seeped out in silent tears and storms of uncontrolled hilarity.

2. By age ten, her hair reached below her buttocks. She never cut it.

3. She did well in school and hoped to go to college. Her father said no.

4. At seventeen, she had her first bout of depression. Or so we assume. All we really know is that she stayed in bed for a year, and neither the local healers nor the specialists her father took her to see in Bombay offered a plausible diagnosis or effective treatment.

5. During that year, she read all of Jane Austen, the Brontë sisters, George Eliot, Thomas Hardy, and D. H. Lawrence. Twice.

6. To everyone's surprise, she married well, the youngest

son from a good family, a doctor with a growing practice in Springfield, Illinois, an aloofness reminiscent of Mr. Darcy, and a skin condition that sometimes stained his shirt and trousers. The year was 1967. They were the only Gujarati in central Illinois.

7. Her husband worked long hours and expected her to manage everything else. He didn't love her, and she knew it.

8. She had one son, then five miscarriages. After the first four, she took root on their living room couch. Her husband prescribed antidepressants, which she flushed down the toilet. "Life's disappointments," she explained to her boy, "one cannot be treating with pills." Of that time, her son recalls a heavyset woman hired by his father to keep house; pale, bland foods; and relatively happy afternoons spent combing the tangles from his mother's hair as she began to recover.

9. After the fifth miscarriage, she moved into the guest room and enrolled in classes at the university. Three years later, she graduated with honors and a double major in English literature and business administration.

10. That summer, her husband announced that he was relocating to Kentucky with his nurse, who, though neither especially young nor particularly pretty, was five months pregnant with his child and belonged to a pink-skinned but surprisingly open-minded extended family outside Louisville.

11. After her husband's departure, she spent a week in the hammock on the screened back porch, in what turned out to be her last such sojourn. Her son shopped and cooked and cleaned until one afternoon he returned from the store to find his mother trying on business suits. Before that day, he'd never seen her in anything but a sari.

12. For the next twelve years, she worked at the university from which she'd graduated, first as the administrative assistant to the chairman of the English Department, then as the dean's special assistant, and, finally, as the registrar of the College of Arts and Sciences.

13. When her son was a sophomore in college, her ex-husband collapsed in the smoking lounge at the Dallas–Fort Worth International Airport. Attempts at resuscitation were unsuccessful. At the time of his death, he had four children. His estate went to the three youngest.

14. Her husband was the only man she ever slept with. "Love," she told her son, "especially romantic love, is an invention meant to distract the lower classes by compelling them to strive for the unimportant and unsustainable."

15. When her son inquired how she could feel as she did about love, on the one hand, and study romantic literature on the other, she said, her accent thickening as it always did when she was annoyed, "You are too much focusing on logic and science."

16. When, several years later, her son told her he'd been accepted to the University of California, San Francisco School of Medicine, she said, "I suppose you must learn for yourself that form is not always content's container." He had no idea what she was talking about.

17. She was one semester short of her Ph.D. in nineteenth-century British literature when she was diagnosed with widely metastatic cancer. Her son flew home from San Francisco, where he was midway through his fourth and final year of medical school. Scans and biopsies revealed an aggressive, primitive tumor of unclear origin, for which there were no good treatment options. "Go back to school," she commanded her son. "There is nothing to be done here."

18. Upon hearing her fate, she took up walking. Before and after work and all day on weekends, she crisscrossed the small city and the university campus, sometimes venturing so far as the surrounding farms and fields, always in pain. When she became too weak to walk, her son took a leave of absence and moved home to care for her.

19. People he'd never heard of sent flowers, books, and a remarkable array of foods. The breads and curries of his childhood arrived from small towns in Illinois, Wisconsin, and Indiana, while neighbors and coworkers dropped off such exotic dishes as fried chicken with bacon stuffing, mashed sweet potatoes with marshmallows, and jello molds with canned pineapple. The less his mother ate, the hungrier he became, until one morning he could barely button his jeans.

20. She died sixteen days later.

21. Her son sat with the body, reviewing his every memory of his mother, and in the end he concluded that he had never seen her happy, only less sad.

22. In her top dresser drawer he found plane tickets to India in her name and his for the ten-day break between his medical school graduation and internship and also a stack of aerograms to which were stapled photographs of young women, the ones on top gazing right at the camera, the bottom ones with downcast eyes and demure expressions.

23. If she hadn't died that April, her son might not have married me, a fellow Indian who has never been to India, a modern girl who is both a doctor like his father and a romantic like his mother and so sometimes kisses her patients and admits that she loves them.

24. Her only child became a radiologist. He spends his time scrutinizing and analyzing those parts of people that re-

main invisible to the rest of us. To this day, he claims strictly intellectual origins for his professional interests.

25. She never met her grandchildren, though the youngest, a girl, looks just like her. Whenever that child sleeps in, her son holds his breath, and when she laughs, he closes his eyes as a once-blind man might upon waking to the excruciating beauty of an ordinary sunlit morning.

SOUP OR SEX?

MAURICE KASMAREK WAS MY second admission on the first day of my first real job as a doctor. I'd been hired as a hospitalist by the same large San Francisco health maintenance organization where I'd finished my training just two weeks earlier, and I marveled that the world suddenly and somewhat arbitrarily considered me fit for unsupervised practice. My inaugural patient that day, a twenty-two-year-old with cystic fibrosis, came in every three months carrying preprinted orders from her pulmonologist detailing every aspect of her care. I was fairly sure I'd admitted her at least once before during residency, but though she knew all the nurses by their names and significant others and children and even pets, she didn't remember me at all. When I walked into her room, she said, "Do you really even need to examine me?" I said I really did, and she said, "All right then, let's get this over with. But you're gonna have to read my chart to get the history."

Maurice showed up an hour later and, after being wheeled across the street from oncology, refused to let the transport guys push him down the hallway to his room. "If I've got to go into this place," he argued, "at least let me get there under my own steam." It took him twenty minutes to cover twenty yards.

I tracked his progress from the nursing station. "Look out, honey," said the nurse beside me, who, despite his omnipresent five o'clock shadow, was rumored to be one of the locally famous transvestites, the Sisters of Perpetual Indulgence. "This one's a heartbreaker."

Once Maurice caught his breath and settled in, I went into his room to do the history and physical.

"Mr. Kasmarek—" I began.

"Oh, hell," he interrupted. "The name's Maurice. We're both grown-ups. Why don't you call me that?"

"Okay," I said, though usually I'm a bit of a traditionalist when it comes to patient-doctor etiquette.

He raised the part of his forehead that should have had eyebrows. "So what's your name?"

"Chitra," I replied. "But you can call me Dr. Agarwal."

I waited a split second, and then I smiled.

"Ha!" he said. "You had me going. Yes you did. Bravo, Dr. Chitra, bravo!"

And so, in the first two minutes of our acquaintance, we became Maurice and Dr. Chitra, a compromise arrived at without any negotiation and a solution that pleased us both.

Nearly an hour later, in addition to the medical essentials, I learned that Maurice was twice divorced, had no children, and prior to the cancer had been a supervisor for Pacific Gas and Electric. When we finally finished the history and physical, I explained Maurice's medical condition to him in case they hadn't in oncology or in case the physician telling him, uncomfortable him- or herself, had mumbled or obfuscated, and also because it was entirely possible that Maurice himself, not wanting to hear the bad news, had chosen denial or belief in divine intervention over the dismal facts. It seemed that he knew and understood his situation, but when I showed him the Preferred Intensity of Treatment form, hoping he'd choose comfort only, so I could page the palliative care team and get going on my next admission, he said he wanted everything done: chemo and radiation as needed, intensive care, even cardiopulmonary resuscitation.

"But it won't work," I told him, referring to his odds of surviving CPR. "I know they're always saving people on television, but in real life, in your circumstances, I wish I could say it would help, but it won't."

He grinned. "Sure it will."

When he smiled, he looked eighty, not sixty: sagging gray skin, narrow ropes of withered muscle securing head to torso and elbow to shoulder, and indentations at his temples from all the weight he'd lost. Since he'd managed databases and distribution schedules, I tried to seduce him with numbers. "There's good data on this," I explained. "If you have cancer and it has spread—"

"Metastatic," he said.

"Right. Anyway, if your heart stops—if you're *dead*—even if we could restart your heart—which we almost certainly *couldn't*—there's a less than one percent chance you'd make it out of intensive care and *no chance* you'd leave the hospital alive."

"Dr. Chitra," he said. "Give it all you've got."

I tried explaining again, but Maurice wouldn't change his mind. "Let me tell you a story," he said, and pointed at the chair beside his bed for me to sit down. I looked at my watch; I had at least two other patients waiting by then, but I took a deep breath and sat.

"There's a woman," Maurice began. "No spring chicken, but not far into middle age either, forties maybe, something like that. Anyway, one day she lets herself into the front hall of the house she grew up in and calls upstairs to her father, 'Dad, it's time. You almost ready?' She's a good daughter, you see. Since her mother passed, she does her best to take care of her father even though her cooking isn't what it could be and she's able to tolerate a whole lot more dust than her mother ever did, which the father's having a hell of a time getting used to."

He checked to make sure I was listening.

"She gets no answer and calls again, this time raising her voice. Nothing. So she goes upstairs, taps her father on the shoulder, and, when he turns around, says, 'Dad, for the fourth time, we need to leave,' and the father says, 'Daughter, for the fourth time, I'll be there in a minute.'"

I didn't laugh.

"Don't you get it?" he asked. "It's the daughter who's deaf, not the father. But everyone just assumes it's the old guy that's got the problem. Dr. C., you disappoint me."

"You're not that old," I protested.

"You still don't get it."

But I had understood the story; I just didn't see how it pertained to Maurice. Unlike the father in his story, he was sick, very sick.

Maurice's eyes seemed overlarge in his shrunken face. Radiating sadness and hope, he looked like one of those children on television where a voice-over says that for just five cents a day, you—comfortable, healthy, and wealthy American sitting on your couch—can save a life.

"I'll call your oncologist," I offered. "There must be something else we can try."

Maurice slapped his bed with one hand and smiled. "They told me you were smart!"

That time, I laughed. "And the clinic nurse told me you'd asked."

Defying all my predictions, Maurice survived a first and then a second cycle of chemotherapy, though every time I tried to discharge him, he developed some complication that required him to stay in the hospital. One morning more than three weeks into his stay, he asked to see me. I found him not in the vinyl armchair from which he usually held court, but in his bed. Framed by the pillow, the whites of his eyes appeared yellow.

"How are you?" I asked.

"Never better," he said so softly that I had to step closer to hear him. It was as if he didn't have the energy to force out the air required for speech.

"No nausea. Even the plumbing is A-OK. I'm gearing up for the next round."

"Maurice."

He managed an unconvincing smile. "You must mean the back pain."

For a week he'd had worsening pain that he hadn't mentioned. I told him I'd give him a shot and send him downstairs for X-rays.

"Ha!" he said. "This is all a ploy to drum up business for your husband."

Somehow, on a previous trip to radiology, Maurice had noticed that the radiologist and I shared the same last name, put two and two together, and then charmed my usually circumspect husband into disclosing much of our family history, including our rocky early courtship as Atul's mother was dying of cancer in central Illinois.

"We're on salary," I said.

"I hope you don't think that's an excuse for losing your sense of humor."

"Cancer isn't funny. And you need an X-ray."

"Don't be silly," he said. "I've been sitting around this place for weeks. Of course my back hurts."

Either he really didn't understand what the back pain might mean—which seemed unlikely—or he was playing tough guy again.

"Let me tell you a story," I said.

Maurice shrugged. I pulled up the vinyl chair and sat down.

"A man goes to see his doctor because his knee hurts. The doctor asks the usual questions—when did the pain start, what makes it better and worse, and so on—then moves the knee up and down and back and forth. Finally he stands up and says, 'The knee's fine. It's just everyday wear and tear. Try resting and icing it.' The man looks at him. 'Doc,' he says, 'my knees go everywhere together, and the other one doesn't hurt a bit.'"

"Easy for him to say. Lucky chump's still living his life."

"Okay, but my point—"

"I get your point." He looked out the window. "Knees—and backs—don't hurt for no reason. So probably the cancer's spread more. If that's the news, do I still get my next chemo?"

"If you're sure you want it. And maybe some radiation too."

"Well then. Tell the hubby I'll be right over, and tell the boys downstairs I'm ready to be zapped when they're ready to do the zapping."

*

In accordance with Maurice's wishes and because the oncologist said some response still wasn't completely out of the realm of possibility, he began the next round of chemotherapy that afternoon, despite the disease up and down his spine and in his liver and almost certainly in his lungs as well. My days off started the next morning, so I didn't see Maurice again until the end of the week.

"There's a woman," he whispered. I was barely through the door. I hadn't even said hello.

"New. In a place like this." He paused and took a deep breath. His hospital gown had come untied, and they'd forgotten to put in his teeth.

I walked quickly to the bedside and turned on the overhead lights. His eyes looked glassy and unfocused, the kind you sometimes see in dolls, which, however lifelike, never actually look like real human beings. He needed intensive care. I reached over his head and depressed the nurse call button.

"The woman waits," he continued. "By the elevator. Person comes along. She lifts her skirt." He stopped speaking and panted.

I pulled the oxygen tubing out from behind his pillow and tried to slip it over his head. He batted me away.

"Woman lifts her skirt," he said. "Shows off her legs. Says, 'Supersex!'"

I turned on the oxygen, put one hand on his arm so he couldn't stop me, hooked the prongs into his nostrils, and coiled the tubing around his ears.

A nurse came into the room and looked from Maurice to me. "ICU?" she asked. I nodded.

"One day," Maurice said. With each inspiration, the skin at the sides of his face sank beneath his cheekbones.

I put my hand on his arm again. "It's okay. You can tell me the rest later."

"I'll tell them we're on our way," said the nurse.

"One day," Maurice repeated, "a man comes by. In a wheelchair. And this woman. Offers . . . 'Supersex!'" He grimaced.

The nurse spoke into her cell phone, then gave me a thumbs-up.

Maurice's voice was barely audible. "Man says, 'Soup, please.'"

I had just unlocked my side of his bed. We had everything secured for the quick dash down the hall to intensive care. And now, finally, Maurice was ready to stop chasing sex and choose soup.

I stopped the chemo and radiation, called the palliative care team, and started the morphine. Before I left work that day, I returned to his room. Maurice seemed comfortable, but also not at all himself. Already his legs and fingertips looked purple and mottled. I readjusted the oxygen tubing on his face. His breath smelled rancid, but when I leaned over to kiss his forehead, his skin was warm and soft against my lips.

As I walked to my car, the feel of him lingered. I realized that I loved Maurice—if *love* is the right word for the irrational and wholly asexual passions I have since felt many times for the men and women in my care—and because of that love, I had done things for him that made no sense medically, and I had done those things to please him, and also and most important, if I could turn back the clock, I would do exactly the same things for Maurice for exactly the same reasons.

FIRES AND FLAT LINES

I.

The boy kept hold of the match until he could feel the flames on his fingertips.

His mother's name was Vivian; her identical twin was Sarah.

After the fire, I dreamed of exuberant rose-colored cells with ectatic blue-streaked nuclei and stippled tufts of lavender cytoplasm—of cancer, in other words, but not any cancer, not the disfiguring or painful or lethal kind, but a tumor of my own devising, one I might conquer at both bench and bedside, liberating me from the facts and fables of strangers' lives.

Vivian never worried about the future, hers or anyone else's.

Early on, Sarah flew from Michigan to San Francisco.

I came late into the story and knew Vivian only if you consider palpating the warm pink lining of a woman's mouth and rectum, cutting yellow-gray strands off what was once her left breast, injecting poisons into her bloodstream, and harvesting her sister's dusky marrow, but not actually introducing yourself as her new oncologist and having a conversation—if you consider that knowing.

Every time they left to go home, the boy thought—no, he was sure—his mother would die.

His mother was young, but he was just a child.

Theirs was the sort of situation that neatly divided people into one of two types: those who bucked up and carried on, and those who sought comfort in culinary perversions and carnal oxymorons.

"Read your book," said the father to the boy.

A is for apple . . .

There was a calm to Vivian, as if, even unconscious, she recognized that her condition was only part of a larger hurt, a whole ocean of ache, cool and dark and menacing, stretching out in every direction.

This is a story I've pieced together from gestures and glances, assumptions and fragmentary knowledge, a story that may not be true.

II.

Imagine that every day you made decisions of consequence, decisions that changed the shape of other people's bodies and the content of their lives.

One day, the boy overheard his father and aunt: "Don't be crazy," Sarah said. "Nobody's ruining anyone else's life."

"Give me a chance," I said to the family. "Cancer is what I do."

A was for apple but also for adenocarcinoma and arrogance and atrocity.

"Try this," the boy's father said to Sarah. "It's delicious."

I pushed the probe into Sarah and extracted what Vivian needed.

Much later, when he heard the term *palliative care*, the boy thought it sounded just right; he had wanted the doctors to take good care of his mother, to be her pals.

"Read your book," said the father to the boy.

B was for bald, *C* was for cure, *D* was for death . . .

In those days, I remembered test results but not names, doses but not stories, achromatic jokes and medical mishaps, each family's folklore buried beneath my own.

E was for Excelsior, the neighborhood he loved and, as his father explained to Sarah, the only place they could afford to live.

His father said it wasn't sexual.

His father said, "For you, because big boys ride two-wheelers."

L was for lies.

The boy wondered where the ants went as they streamed along the sidewalk below his black, spinning tires.

I explained that Vivian's expression, though disturbing, was only a reaction to the tape holding down her eyelids and the tubes running into her mouth and nose and neck.

The boy liked the ants, liked flipping them over and watching the flailing of their little legs.

"I know it looks bad," I said, "but there's plenty more left to try."

At the bar on Geneva Avenue, his father said it was only sex.

The boy dropped the match, and the ants burned from the outside in, like crumpled paper, starting with their little legs.

P was for pneumonia and pressure sore, for pathos and pro-longation.

The death doctors, the famous ones, said you could bring closure to any death.

"Your aunt and I . . . ," his father began.

Until my wife moved in, I had radios in my kitchen and bathroom, a clock radio by my bed, radios in my office and car, all tuned to news, not music, unless the music was something fast and funky, no more sentimental than a sportscast or a weather report.

III.

For years, all the boy remembered of the end was a nap when it wasn't nap time and his father's pale, pinched face through automatic swinging doors.

What doctors don't talk about is how grief swells and festers, how endings are never really the end.

The nurse said, "The child never cried, not even once."

R was for rage and retribution.

"I love you," my wife said recently, "but you'd have me fight to the end, and I might not want to try something experimental. I might not want to be alive any way I could."

"She's a strong one," I told the family two days before Vivian died. "No reason to give up now."

The boy liked that the bike's tires burned first, liked that they burned with very little flame and lots of dark gray smoke.

S was for sadness, for secrets, for shame.

I read about the fire in the paper and right away recognized the boy.

"Eat," his aunt Sarah had said. "I'm your mother now."

"Two people inside," a witness told the newspaper reporter. "A man and a woman."

Above the house, over the flames and through the smoke, the boy watched as the sharp edges of Twin Peaks and San Bruno Mountain blurred.

Until the green line beside Vivian's bed went flat, I continued the perfectly timed bursts of electricity, the great thrusts of humidified air, and the steady drip of clear and potent liquids.

The boy watched the fire, and then he spread his legs and put his wrists together behind his back.

V was for vindication.

As my wife and I drive out of McLaren Park and past the charred house, I launch into the story, and when I finish, my wife says, "For you, this city is a graveyard," and at first I'm tempted to agree, but then I remember that a graveyard is a place without memory or imagination, without guilt or regret, a place of closure and rest.

THE PSYCHIATRIST'S WIFE

S HE DRINKS LIME SWITCHERS by the pool while her husband swims through a ship sunk by Blackbeard in the days of the Atlantic buccaneers. *Alcohol abuse*, her husband, the psychiatrist, would say if he could see her now. But he would be wrong. She knows, because she's a doctor too. More of a doctor than he is, in fact, since she repairs damaged bodies and removes diseased organs while he sits in his chair talking, labeling, judging, then talking some more.

When someone she knows approaches—another wife, occasionally a husband—she closes her eyes. Even in the shadow of an oversize sun umbrella, her pallor glows, startling and unfashionable. Brown hair hangs below her scrawny shoulders in careless wisps, but closer to her scalp it too lacks color. An inch above her ears, gray meets brown at a sharply demarcated line, like the place on a hillside marking the path of a recent, all-consuming fire.

She looks at her watch and smiles. To constitute abuse, the dysfunctional relationship to the substance must be present for at least one month. She sips her drink. They'll be here only another three days, twenty-two hours, and thirty-seven minutes. Then she'll stop.

The psychiatrist has come to the island for a medical conference on post–traumatic stress disorder, and his wife—as she has come to think of herself now—is accompanying him. He has been preparing for months, finding reprieve from his latest claim-to-fame role as director of the working group revising the *Diagnostic and Statistical Manual of Mental Disorders* in his research comparing the brain scans of Gulf War veterans with those of healthy civilians, rape victims, middle-aged Cambodians, ancient Jews, and young Somalis. Here in paradise—the brochure promised unrelenting sunshine and resplendent blue waters, but also escape and the ability to anticipate a guest's every need—her husband disappears for three hours each morning and two hours each afternoon, emerging from the grand ballroom overstimulated and horny with triumph. She waits in their room as if stranded, responds against her will, lying like a corpse on skin-soft sheets, washing slowly when it's over. He invited her on the scuba cruise, but she won't go into the ocean any more than she will walk back into an operating room. *Generalized anxiety*, he argued. *The unrealistic or excessive worry about two or more life circumstances for at least six months.*

They had flown from San Francisco to Miami, then traveled by cruise ship at her insistence. He lost an extra week of work. She didn't, because when they made the booking four months earlier, she had already quit.

For twenty-two years she had worked in a community hospital.

Saint Specialist, they called it, half joking, because most patients had a different doctor for each of their organ systems.

Her husband's University of California Medical Center colleagues, she knew, sometimes called it the Death Star.

On call for the surgical intensive care unit, she was paged every twenty minutes. She got called about high fevers and low blood pressures, about oozing wounds and racing minds, and too often—once a month, sometimes more often—about a death.

One of those nights, around two A.M., her husband said, "Effective supervisors set limits."

They were in their new bed at the time, with its Italian hardwood frame and pricey French linens. She turned on the light, and he covered his face with a pillow.

"This isn't someone's neurosis," she said. "It's multisystem organ failure."

"You've misunderstood."

"Of course. I'm not the famous expert."

He lifted one corner of the pillow. "I was simply suggesting—"

"People get sick," she told him. "They try to die."

He let the pillow fall back over his face. "And even then, most fail."

That anecdote, she knew, gave a misleading impression of her husband. Still, it happened.

At least she came on the trip. "Plane or boat," their only child, a teenage son, had said to his father, "no way am I going on your so-called vacation."

* * *

An ebony man in white shorts and white gloves brings the psychiatrist's wife another lime switcher on a tray that may be real silver. As he approaches, she smells his sweat and cologne and turns to look.

A green-gray blur, a hummingbird, hangs above the bougainvillea. A child squeals in the pool. The child is not her child. Her child is older now and refuses family vacations. Her child cheats on tests he could ace without studying, simultaneously achieving social acceptance and academic mediocrity. Her child wears a ring on the fourth finger of his left hand to honor a vow of celibacy and burns books he considers untruthful or impure but thinks nothing of piercing his nipples, nose, scrotum, and umbilicus with cheap silver hoops and beaded baubles.

The ebony man hands the psychiatrist's wife her drink. The ice-filled glass contains a subtly jaundiced, not quite transparent liquid that burns going down. It gives her gooseflesh. It warms her, then makes her shiver.

For years—five and a half decades, her whole life—she thought like and love were parts of the same emotional spectrum. Now she knows they exist on separate tracks, ones that periodically intersect but don't necessarily run parallel.

The ebony man wipes condensation from the base of his tray. He has a scar on the side of his neck that emerges, thick and pink brown, larval and accusing, from beneath his shirt collar. The psychiatrist's wife wants to ask where he got it and why he doesn't have it removed, but this is the real world, not work, and the answers to those questions are none of her business.

"Not to worry," her husband had said. "A man quits, and the word that goes out is nervous breakdown. But a woman? She's applauded for her devotion to family and openness to innovative and alternative career paths."

*

Symptoms she'd developed in recent years:

1. She waited until all the operating rooms were fully booked before giving her assistant the list of her upcoming cases.
2. Knowing families wanted to talk to her, she took the stairway, not the elevator, so she wouldn't run into them.
3. She let her practice group's physician assistant help with all but the most complicated procedures so he would scrub with her instead of the other surgeons and she'd rarely be alone in managing her patients.
4. She started telling patients about similarities between her life and theirs, as if what was going on between them was a friendship.

Years earlier, already a surgeon but not yet a mother, she'd gone to art openings, guerrilla theater, readings of playful postmodern novels, the sorts of events where technique and interpretation mattered as much as outcome. "The thing about him," a critic once said of a writer who had lived a long, full life but wrote again and again about a certain personal trauma, "is that he doesn't shrink from the travail of understanding, even when no true understanding can be found. With each effort, he tries to come at the same material in a crazy new way, as if by doing so, he'll eventually make sense of the inevitably tragic ending."

But another night, there had been a tribute to an artist who'd spent her career exploring her life and fantasies using soft woods and pliable metals, found objects and slivers of colored glass; she had created and re-created, until she could no longer distinguish the autobiographical facts of her real life from the fiction of her sculptures, until she believed she'd tasted failures she'd deftly eluded and she'd heard the rapturous wails and touched the tiny tufts of darkly bristled finger hair of men she'd never actually slept with.

She'd crossed countries off the list: "Iraq, Afghanistan, Lebanon, Sudan, Israel, Congo, Nepal, Iran—"

"Dude!" her son interrupted. "Is there anywhere I *can* go this summer?"

"If you would just please make an effort," the psychiatrist said at the end of their first full day in paradise.

They were in the bar then: indoor-outdoor, thatch roofed, wall-free, calypso music coming through invisible speakers. They were watching the sun drop through a mango-berry sky onto a slick, flat edge of ocean that made the world seem at once finite and limitless.

His colleagues scanned the crowd as they transitioned from the afternoon's passive learning to poolside evening cocktails or, somewhat less steadily, from the tall wicker barstools up the two steps to the open-air ocean-view dining room. The glances of more than a few lingered on the psychiatrist and his wife while they pretended to look for an errant child or a waiter.

"Perhaps if you tried to articulate," he said, speaking in the same wounded tone he used to say *You're drinking again* or *He's my son too.*

She snorted. The way he spoke. The affectation, the absurdity. He'd spent one year at Oxford. One year, thirty years ago. And he hadn't even been a Rhodes scholar—it was just an ordinary year abroad.

That made her smile.

"What's funny?" he asked.

She looked at him. She knew she was behaving badly. "Nothing," she said. "Not one little thing."

* * *

After her second switcher, the psychiatrist's wife signals for the ebony man. When he reaches for her glass, she holds it up, then doesn't let go.

"How many of these do you think one person can drink?" she asks.

He squints, as if she's suddenly out of focus, but he neither releases the glass nor pulls it from between her fingers. And so, their hands nearly touching, she tells him that she's drinking because her father recently died, writhing and grimacing in intractable pain. Gunshot wounds, she says. And: the wrong place at the wrong time. The ebony man lowers his eyes and shakes his head. He mumbles something she can't understand, then slides the glass from her grasp and vanishes with it, only to reappear seconds later with a new one.

After her third switcher, she tells him that she got it wrong, that in fact her father died by drowning, pink-tinged fluid filling his lungs, thrashing and gasping in a way she can't forget, the walls of his damaged heart flaccid and unable to pump.

The ebony man puts a hand on her shoulder so quickly, so briefly—like a fly on a too-hot light, the flick of a lizard across a wall—that she isn't sure it happened. And so she tells him that she got it wrong again and that what really happened was this: her father died well, calm and comfortable, and that she, his daughter, was present both in the traditional physical sense and in the more modern and spiritual version of the word.

But none of that is true. Though she attended each one of

those deaths and too many more, her father is not merely alive, but well, a nimble, athletic eighty-two, still managing his small-appliance-repair shop in the Outer Sunset, still turning heads, and it's the psychiatrist's wife who is uncomfortable, writhing, and drowning in some modern and spiritual way.

She and the psychiatrist dated in medical school. He was handsome and smart and, unlike her other boyfriends, listened to what she said, thought about it, and, sometimes days or weeks later, commented in an understatedly supportive way. But that wasn't what she wanted back then. She wanted someone who took charge, someone driven and decisive. They split up during residency, married other people—she an entrepreneur, he a psychologist—divorced, and then, united by surprise at the smallness of their lives and achievements, married each other just in time to convert one of her last viable ova into a son. That was when he took the job at the university hospital. "For him," he said, lifting their wailing infant up over his head, "so he'll be proud of us and ambitious for himself."

In those early years of their marriage, busy with diapers and playdates, she hardly noticed as her husband began amassing awards and publications, responsibilities and prestige. What she did notice was the disappearance of his abdominal muscles below a generous layer of excess flesh; the phone call from the day care center when their son waited, forgotten, long after the drop-dead hour on her husband's day for pickup; his impatience with her new, young, and not terribly accomplished but unfailingly supportive friends from the Noe Valley No Nanny parents group.

"Oh, please," her son said when they discussed where he'd stay during his parents' Caribbean absence. And then, pulling his jeans well below his slim hips and running one hand over his buzz cut, he added, "Like my plan for the three weeks you're gone, yo, is to throw a bitchin' party and let the other kids trash the place while I hook up with some totally fly chick, knock boots, and let the baby gravy swim. You feel me?"

People made assumptions. They assigned values. She knew people who said *Holocaust* as if, in recent human history, there had been only one. Newscasters and journalists said "the tragedy of September 11, 2001" and meant New York City, as if those who that day succumbed to malaria or malnutrition, to ruptured abdominal aneurysms or perforated intestines deserved less sympathy because of the quiet and unoriginal way they chose to die. In the cruise ship ballroom, she winced as her husband said his study of a promising new drug showed negligible mortality, as if one death in four hundred was the same as none.

Signs:

1. Dreams in which her pager flashed a phone number and then the three digits 9 and 1 and 1, and she raced from elevator to elevator, then down one empty corridor and along another, into and out of every hospital and clinic she'd ever worked in, unable to find the right operating room.
2. The way a hand on her forearm here in the Caribbean for whatever benign reason provoked for her both an unwarranted startle and memories of a different hand, warm but insistent, and with it her colleague's voice saying *stop*, saying *that's enough*, saying *you can't win 'em all* . . .

3. The ebb of her sanity and the flow of her self-absorption;
   the certain knowledge that she was theoretically right
   but pragmatically going about everything in just the
   wrong way.

"For me," her husband proclaimed one late afternoon as she
cut up fruits and vegetables and laid out expensive cheeses
and pâtés for his biannual departmental open house, "medicine is to life as mold is to Stilton. For you, it's more like the
rind of overripe brie."

"Excuse me?" says the psychiatrist's wife.

The ebony man's nostrils flare. "Madame is American,"
he asks a second time, though his tone is not that of a
question.

"Yes," she says, and he nods, as if that explains everything
he knows about her.

* * *

A perfect sky. A landscape of red rooftops and white sand
beaches, of blues and greens and azures. Even the plants
standing tall, slick and robust, dripping with sweat.

The heat and alcohol pin the psychiatrist's wife to her chair.
Low to the earth, she droops. She doesn't need an infinity
pool to float, to drown.

"Do something," her husband had said, donning his swim
trunks. "Do anything."

And, standing at the door with his snorkel and fins:
"This morning, a propos of coping skills in combat veterans,
Dick Tan quoted Confucius, who said, 'Learning is like

paddling a boat upstream; stop paddling and you go back-wards.'"

In the beginning she had noticed nothing but the saves. Right away after such triumphs, families brought presents—candy and flowers and fortune cookies, curries and tamales, kimchi and lumpia, cheap, tarnished jewelry, hand-knitted scarves, paintings and Bibles and poetry. And for a while, once they were whole and healthy again, patients sent cards or stopped by her office just to visit. Years later, some still called, sent her e-mail, invited her to family reunions—lavish affairs where she was hugged, kissed, cried over, and fed to the point of physiologic jeopardy, where she received the welcome of a sibling lost in a long-ago, faraway civil war, a folk hero, the risen dead.

She'd needed to be a doctor for so many reasons—for security and self-esteem and social approbation, or, as the psychiatrist put it, for id and ego and superego—and so she was. She'd been a great resident, efficient and technically skilled, had eas-ily secured a job at the hospital of her choice after she finished her training, and for more than two decades had excelled at her work, earning more referrals than she could keep up with, a good salary, and, way back when, the hospital's award for outstanding devotion and compassion.

The night their son came to the dinner table with a metal rod punched through his nasal septum, her husband said, "Iden-tity isn't an abstraction. It's more like a ceramic pot, carefully molded over time, then decorated, and finally glazed and baked to maintain a certain look and feel. Break it, and no matter how well you remember the original look and feel, you have to start again from scratch."

She hadn't gone to medical school hoping, like the Cowardly Lion in Oz, to become someone she wasn't. But she'd be the first to admit she'd imagined that knowing how to save a life would make it easy to do so. Or straightforward. Or, at the very least, more possible than not.

"It is," her husband argued. "Crunch the numbers."

In medicine, numbers conferred prestige and legitimacy. Sometimes she thought of Albert Einstein, who said, *Not everything that matters can be measured, and not everything that gets measured matters.*

She didn't mean that she couldn't save a life by removing a tumor from a lung or a bullet from a liver, but that doing so didn't stop people from smoking cigarettes, or from shooting each other, or from doing any one of thousands of other dangerous and deadly things she couldn't control or fix or even imagine, until they appeared on her operating table—like the man whose third-degree burns were the result of a house fire intentionally set by his young son after weeks of practicing on bugs and bicycles and just six days after the boy's mother's death from cancer.

Her mother-in-law was very ill. The psychiatrist was very busy. The psychiatrist's wife took family medical leave and stayed with her mother-in-law night and day for a week, then just days, then night and day again, then days again, then hours. Hospital, rehab, hospital, rehab. Finally, after nearly two months, her mother-in-law got better. Knowing the worst was over, she felt as if she had money in the bank, food in the larder, a stockpile of marital credit. She felt entitled to her own life again. Desperate for it, in fact, like a refugee willing to trample others to catch a bag of rice thrown from a relief truck.

"It's not about trying to feel something," their son said casually, as if reporting what he'd eaten for lunch. "I feel plenty. I feel too much. It's about saying, *Look at me!* and also FUCK YOU, FUCK YOU, FUCK YOU, FUCK YOU, FUCK YOU, FUCK YOU FUCK YOU, FUCK YOU, FUCK YOU FUCK YOU, FUCK YOU, FUCK YOU . . ."

So much of life was contextual, but she wanted to believe there were absolutes as well, that some choices, viewpoints, and activities could be considered more moral than others, better by some universal standard of human decency and societal need, however unrecognized, however hopeless, and that the flip side held other choices, viewpoints, and activities that could be written off as unwise or simply wrong.

Theirs wasn't one of those families afraid to call a thing by its name. The psychiatrist had no patience for false solace, half-truths, or religion. Their son never heard the expressions "passed away," "with the Lord," or "moved to the great beyond" except from his friends and in books and movies. When their cat died, they said, "Sorry, honey, but Hippocrates is dead."

Relief hit like an endorphin rush. A switch thrown by a single unplanned thought: she could quit. She tried to be rational, but it was over. She was done. She could think of nothing but getting out. She smiled at patients and nurses, ignored pages, and canceled cases. She wrote orders for follow-up in hours, days, a week—anytime when the problem wouldn't be hers. Load lifted, the heels of her shoes touched down without sound on the speckled linoleum. As she made her way to the elevators, explosions of light and color lit the periphery of her visual fields where once there had been only clichéd art in mass-market frames, red crash carts, black-faced monitors, and sliding glass doors to dimly lit rooms of mechanized furniture and malfunctioning humans. "I quit," she incanted, her lips clenched, her tongue trembling to resist the devastating allure of emotional incontinence.

The ebony man asks the psychiatrist's wife if she wants another switcher.

"Oh, yes," she says. "Please."

He puts her empty glass on his tray.

"Madame's vacation," he says, "is for how long?"

"I don't know."

For a fraction of a second, his smile wavers—there's the slightest narrowing of his eyes, a flicker along his jaw.

"Madame works?" he asks.

She looks at the pool, the palm trees, the tanned feet and pink, pedicured toenails of a passing stranger, and she shakes her head, wishing she had a scar like his, for all the world to see.

* * *

It's lonely at the top, or so the saying went, and the psychiatrist's wife used to wonder if it had to be that way, whether nice guys really always finished last while those better able to maintain the demarcation between Self and Other would—like scum—more surely rise to the top of the sweet organic mélange that sustained them.

Her husband told her it wasn't so. But that was decades earlier, when they were peers in both stature and passion, when her mind still resembled a well-organized catalog of scientific information rather than an endlessly unfurling commemorative scroll, when she too believed that a person's profession could and should define her life.

Morbid preoccupation, the psychiatrist said, not unkindly, in the days before she stopped telling him her dreams.

Histrionic personality disorder, he whispered on one of his rare visits with his hospitalized mother.

Adolescence, he recently said of their son. *No longer a child but not yet an adult.*

"*Please*," he says not infrequently, even now. His hands touching, reaching.

She had a colleague who said that sometimes, when nothing else he'd tried worked, he figured the last thing he could do was to give good death. He told families that he was sorry he couldn't move things along, but if anything happened, any little thing, he'd treat it with morphine only. No more machines, no electricity, no antibiotics. Some families fired him; others clasped his hands in theirs as if he were an angel.

"I just want to make a difference in the world," her son said. "Why can't you understand that?"

In medical school they'd been taught the words of the great physician Francis Weld Peabody, who said, "The secret to caring for the patient is to care for the patient." Too late, she knew that Dr. Peabody was wrong. Too late, she understood that the secret was caring for the patient—for anyone—just a little. Enough, but not too much.

The ebony man asks if the psychiatrist's wife has come for the conference. She shakes her head. "No," she says. Then, "Yes.

My husband is there now." The ebony man smiles. "So your husband is a doctor?"

She nods.

"That is good," he says. "That is very, very good."

"Why?" she had asked her son when the piercings began.

For the longest time, until after the fourth switcher, until the ebony man with his scar and his questions, she hadn't understood her son's answer, the *Look at me* followed by the stream of *FUCK YOU*s.

When her husband returns from his scuba cruise, the psychiatrist's wife sits waiting on a bed stripped of everything but a single white sheet. Her hair is stylishly short and newly bleached, a blond so pale it trifles with light and time. She's wearing an ocean-blue spaghetti-strap dress that tapers at her waist and thighs and stops above her knees. Her makeup is perfect and her suitcase is packed.

BLURRED BOUNDARY DISORDER

D EAR DRS. SAPERSTEIN and DiBenedetto:
It has come to my attention[1] that you are, respectively, the director and associate director of the working group charged with revising the *Diagnostic and Statistical Manual of Mental Disorders* for its much-anticipated (and long-awaited) fifth edition.

Below please find (again)[2] my[3] suggestion for an addition

---

[1]After sixteen phone calls and hours of research; this isn't exactly a transparent process, is it??

[2]Yes, this is the third time I've sent this proposed diagnosis because I have yet to receive even a standard-issue form letter by way of reply, and although I realize you're both at that post–traumatic stress disorder conference in the Caribbean, I checked online and know for a fact that your hotel has Internet access. The recent unjust and all-too-publicly exaggerated charges against me notwithstanding, I keep asking myself how an entire committee can simply ignore a well-articulated, life- and judgment-disrupting diagnosis? A diagnosis, I might add, that bears both accurately and acutely on the suffering of an undervalued and often unfairly penalized segment of the population, namely those almost invariably female and of-

to the second section of the "Personality Disorders" chapter, which I heretofore will refer to as Cluster[4] B.

301.8[5] BLURRED BOUNDARY DISORDER

The essential feature of this disorder is a pervasive pattern of personal boundary instability exhibited by a caregiving pro-

---

ten also otherwise marginalized people who are and always have been disproportionately overrepresented in poorly remunerated and oftentimes dangerous jobs that require enormous emotional and temporal investments at equally enormous and not infrequently devastating personal costs. (Costs, I might add, that may explain why this majority segment of the population is represented on your committee only by Drs. Georgia Brown and Ethel Liu—there's a word for their role, the noun of which used to get a person onto ferries and buses.)

[3]Noemi Kadish-Luna, B.S., M.D., M.A., M.P.A./H.S.A.(c)

[4]I'm not sure *cluster* is the best word choice here, given that when the average American hears that word, she or he will likely have a mall- and/or holiday-based association to that increasingly ubiquitous and tooth-decay-inducing bite-size morsel, the pecan cluster, which, if you think about it, is what? Well, a cluster of *nuts*, of course, which I know is not the message you want to be sending, to say nothing of the other sort of cluster that might appear in people's (especially women's) minds when confronted with the image of a group of mostly middle-aged, mostly white, mostly male doctors sitting around a meeting room in some fancy hotel casually critiquing and summarily pathologizing people, many of whom are not middle-aged, not white, and not male, and most of whom are (for unclear reasons) not present while, between sips of Seattle's Best and bites of poached salmon with endive salad, the aforementioned middle-aged, mostly white males discuss nothing less than the very personhood of the un- and underrepresented absent majority. (Hint: it's a two-word phrase and the second word is *fuck*.)

[5]Final digit dependent on number of new diagnoses accepted (see other potential Cluster B additions in footnotes 15 and 16 below). And in case

fessional, affecting mood, self-image, and not just intimate relationships (e.g., lovers, friends, and—where applicable[6]—spouse and children) but also professional ones.[7]

---

you're wondering how one person comes up with so many apt solutions to the DSM's glaring (if publicly unacknowledged) deficiencies, the answer is simple: I don't just drop into the real world from my ivory tower for one or two half-day sessions a week; I actually live there.

[6] I wish!!

[7] I often find it helps to put a face to a diagnosis, so let me just mention here that for several years I practiced primary care psychiatry at the South of Market Community Health Center here in San Francisco, working fourteen-hour days while meth heads (active clients and a former employee, according to the police reports) broke into our on-site pharmacy, depleting our already inadequate supply of cold medicines and painkillers, and other criminals (guys who were probably also our clients) took apart my car, a maroon secondhand '86 Honda Civic with VOTE VEGAN / GIRLS RULE / DIVERSITY / NOT EVERY SPERM NEEDS A NAME / DOGS FIRST! stickers artfully arrayed on the back bumper. The Civic was all I could afford on what they were paying me at SMCHC and certainly wasn't much to look at even prior to its broad-daylight dismantlement, and yet its loss precipitated the single instance in which I wondered whether, rather than pursuing a life in the world of mental illness, I instead should have followed the leads of my friends who went into specialties like dermatology, pathology, radiology, and cosmetic surgery and who, since finishing training, have wed, slept late on weekends, traveled, and had children. Actually, to be perfectly accurate, while all the men have enjoyed these myriad fruits of their well-chosen professions, only some of the women have, and they were either those perfect ones who could do everything well, or the slimy types who gave up their careers without a single backward glance upon the first sign of their successful impregnation, as if doctoring had been for them nothing more than a loop in the holding pattern of their trajectory toward marriage and motherhood. (I can't resist digressing a bit here to comment on the irony that it was the members of what I think of as the M.D.-Mrs. contingent who criticized me most strenuously when that whole business between me and a certain postdoctoral pharmacy student—not under my direct supervision, not even

In BBD sufferers, a marked and persistent belief that personal value depends on professional reputation is often present.[8] This may be evidenced by tendencies to give in to patients/ clients (and even colleagues) if not doing so results in disappointment or anger and doing so leads to praise and affection for the professional.[9]

Ethical lines often appear unclear,[10] a desire to please is prominent, and performance-related affective instability is common.[11]

---

from the medical center with which I have an affiliation—made the papers, even though easily two thirds of the published account was an obvious and blatant distortion of the facts conjured by the press to justify their lurid, bold-type headlines and sell this first-rate city's second-rate rag.)

[8] I must admit here to not only the expected psychic *Sturm und Drang* but also to actual physical pain (occipital, primarily) when I learned I hadn't been invited to participate in the diagnostic revision process, particularly since (recent events notwithstanding) no current committee member has credentials remotely equal to my own.

[9] *You're so pretty*, Mike Reed, M.A., Pharm.D., said to me his first day at the SMCHC, as if looking at me were akin to gazing upon the idyllic (and perhaps imaginary) Hanging Gardens of Babylon or some other largely inaccessible and supremely exotic global treasure and he felt fortunate beyond his (admittedly limited) powers of verbal expression to have the opportunity to gaze upon my corporeal self while clarifying one of my orders or less than optimally legible prescriptions. And the next week, just after my supervisor suggested (using his favorite deceptively quiet but devastatingly harsh voice) that I try a little harder to stay on schedule, Mike added, *You're so sexy*. And then, *I've never met anyone like you*. And also, *You know you're the smartest doctor I've ever met, don't you?*

[10] *C'mon*, Mike said later that same day (and on several subsequent occasions in the weeks prior to our discovery, his firing, my suspension, etc.), *I really, really want you and there's no one in the med room.*

[11] I lost my temper just once, after receiving the suicide threat fax (see below), when I thought Mike was dead and that his death was caused, at

BBD is characterized by subtle and varied presentations including: inability to turn off pager and/or cell phone even while vacationing;[12] receipt of copious presents from patients absent any traditional gift-giving occasion (i.e., holidays—Christmas, Chinese New Year, Mardi Gras—

---

least in part, by clerical error. On the other hand, it's true that sometimes, when I got off work, knowing I'd had a productive day, I'd find myself standing at the intersection outside the SMCHC looking past the usual assortment of lost tourists; shivering, half-naked leather daddies; bedraggled, intoxicated homeless veterans; loft-living, gym-bound yuppies; and dilapidated working girls and boys, and I'd feel unsure which of the traffic lights was meant for me and also whether the latest designer antidepressants and colorful PET scan patterns mattered in a world where life was more pleasant for most patients off their meds than on, where schizophrenic diabetics with fungating foot sores didn't qualify for emergency housing and teenagers in lipstick and high heels traded sucks for falafel and fucks for shelter of the most temporary and dubious sort.

[12]No doubt you heard (or have heard about) the pager that went off repeatedly during the profound and moving Convocation of Fellows at the American Psychiatric Association meeting last year here in San Francisco, and I'll admit now (for the first time) that the pager was indeed mine, but I offer my confession with the dual caveats that (1) I had brought it only because when Freddy "I know they're wiretapping me even though I'm homeless and phoneless" Ramboteau gets it in his head to try for another dive off the Golden Gate Bridge, I'm the only one who can talk him off the outer railing and into the locked unit at San Francisco General and (2) I'd forgotten that I'd removed my suit coat (with the pager clipped to the right front pocket) and left it stacked against the wall with my three-ring binder and accumulating pile of free pharmaceutical company conference loot (which I take not for myself—I belong to the anti-freebie group No Free Lunch—but for our patients and their children who love the canvas carrying cases, the mega-grip Day-Glo medium-point pens, the logo-imprinted cerebrum/pill/heart-shaped bouncing rubber balls, and the colorful oversize striped shoelaces).

and/or following the successful diagnosis/treatment of a po-
tentially serious medical condition);[13] and inability to let go
when treatment termination is in the client/patient/family's
best interest.[14]

---

[13]Mr. Quintanilla gave me a conch shell from the Philippines. *Inside that one,* he said, *you can hear my country and maybe you remember me.* He missed all his subsequent appointments. I checked the hospitals and obituaries for months but never found him. Basim Rashad brought me a rug as broad as my largest room and the bright red of the morphine he dropped on his only son's tongue in the weeks after we stopped the antiretrovirals and Ahmed lost his ability to swallow. Bud Stanton's wife, Myra, said if I could get him into Napa State, the inpatient psych hospital north of San Francisco, she'd take me to lunch. Anywhere in town, Myra said, price is no object. Each time I did a home visit, Fele Tafatolu's sister gave me a palm-size present wrapped in burlap and tied with string. Fele thought water was poison, their shower stall a cell. The whole apartment reeked of urine and stool and open wounds. Inside the burlap was soap. Lavender and rose, chamomile and lilac and gardenia. For months before it was stripped and gutted, my Civic smelled like heaven.

[14]Three weeks after Tina Ball died, I got the most incredible note from her daughter Daisy. Tina's death certificate said cancer, but that was the least of it. She'd been schizophrenic, a horrible mother until Alzheimer's gave her a second girlhood. Daisy said that last year and especially the months of her mother's dying were the best of her life, and she couldn't thank me enough for noticing the yellow tint in her mother's skin and referring them to hospice. But Daisy's note also said that since her mother's psychiatric disease had burned itself out and clinic visits were a physical and logistic challenge, I should not have insisted on continuing weekly appointments right up to Tina's admittedly painless blessing of an end, an accusation that shocked and surprised me and one that I wanted to (but did not) reply to by way of self-defense that I sincerely thought Daisy (if not Tina) benefited from the visits, that in my mind I had shifted to a sort of family systems approach that I believed would serve them both at that crucial juncture of their lives and that I could justify to our medical direc-

Associated features: Frequently this disorder is accompanied by Overachievement Disorder,[15] the Good-Girl Syndrome,[16] and a variety of subsyndromal anxiety, depressive, sexual, eating, and substance abuse disorders.[17]

---

tor only by billing for schizophrenia, since the clinic received some reimbursement for that diagnosis (albeit a small fraction of what is given for "medical" diagnoses), but no codes exist for finding oneself orphaned in adulthood, for grieving, or dying, or death.

[15] See proposal for new DSM diagnosis "Overachievement Disorder," arriving under separate cover.

[16] Ditto preceding footnote for "Good-Girl Syndrome." (Surely this one has been recognized, at least by astute clinicians in urban and academic centers, since the dawn of feminism nearly a half century ago???)

[17] Contrary to public reports (the source of which, I'm sure, was the clinic admin who never forgave me for losing my temper; see below), I had not been drinking on the day Mike and I were apprehended doing the two-step nasty in the med room, and while it's true that I grew fond of a certain cost-friendly Australian varietal after his dismissal and my pre-suspension probation, I never drank before sundown and feel confident that I never imbibed enough at night that anyone would be able to tell the next day. That said, I believe I understand the source of people's mistaken conclusions and hereby propose the following as an eminently reasonable alternative explication: I worked in a neighborhood where most people smelled of alcohol, weeks and months and years of it polluting their breath and seeping from their pores, and I commonly hugged such people (my patients) because it often seemed to me that I was the only person in their lives who did so and that it was just possible that my hugs were at times more helpful to them than all my talk and hard-won Medicaid-approved prescriptions. Of course, such details aren't even relevant if, as the Review Board claimed, the issue was abuse of power (which it wasn't), as if what transpired between Mike and myself was pedophilia or reverse rape(!) or something actually illegal and definitively pathological, when in reality, Mike came on to me, not the other way around, and I wrote his letter of recommendation weeks before we

Impairment: Affected individuals often, if not always, run late in both social and occupational arenas.[18]

---

hooked up. Moreover, if Mike had the wherewithal to earn a doctorate, he was certainly also capable of (1) deciding the interrogatives (who, where, etc.) of his private/sex life and (2) obtaining a letter of recommendation without sleeping with the clinic psychiatrist. While I concede both my affliction with BBD and my poor judgment vis-à-vis Mike (yes, I saw the scars on his arms and belly), I must most adamantly object to the diagnoses given to me by the Review Board's smug, obscenely well remunerated and therefore *de facto* biased and corrupt consulting psychiatrist (a man who has never worked in community health, who in fact has no continuity psychiatry practice of any kind, and who earned for each hour he spent on my case 8.7 times what I earned in an hour at the SMCHC).

[18]Anyone will tell you that I was busy—panicked, if you must know—finishing my master's thesis in transformative studies, "Cross-cultural Approaches to Individuation in Psychiatric Patients with Triple Diagnosis and a History of Geographic Fluidity," and after my official reprimand, I had been barred by the Review Board from contact with Mike, so I hadn't seen him for weeks or maybe even months by the time the whole fax thing happened (which of course they blame me for too), but let me assure you that Mike knew perfectly well that I always ran late, and stayed late, and didn't get to my mailbox until evening, because I prioritized patients first, not paperwork, not even my own bodily needs like using the restroom or eating lunch or even my little interludes with him (he hated that . . .). And what of the admin who put the fax that said "Call me by 3 or I'll kill myself" into my mailbox instead of into my hand?!? If that wasn't just typical of the SMCHC and all such places where you work with no support or the sort of support that's actually worse than no support, not that the referrals you make on behalf of your helpless and hapless patients go anywhere anyway, since the city and state and federal government keep cutting services, making it impossible for even the most professionally rigorous clinician to follow practice guidelines, and then those same august bodies turn around and give the clinic and its doctors a

Complications: May include but are not limited to attempts to buy love and abolish disappointment with excessive gifting.[19] Premature death (i.e., suicide) is rare because of primal fears of letting others down.[20] More common is a change to an alternate career of equal or greater social utility but with intrinsic boundaries.[21]

---

bad rating because those selfsame guidelines weren't followed, which can and, as you may know, in the case of the SMCHC did (two months after my return to work) lead to closure of a facility desperately needed by the neediest among us.

[19]The newspaper listed "a car" among the objects I gave Mike during his two months at the SMCHC. The "car" to which they refer was the Civic, which, as I've already explained, had been gutted and so had no apparent value and didn't run. Mike wanted it anyway; I have no idea why.

[20]For a while, when the story broke, I set my alarm for four-thirty each morning and drove the thirty-two miles to my parents' house in the Los Altos Hills to wait for the paper boy, then removed the Bay Area section from their *San Francisco Chronicle*, that section being the one detailing the so-called abuses at the SMCHC, including an unnamed (but otherwise obviously identifiable) psychiatrist's on-site liaisons with a visiting "student."

[21]I decided to apply to the Master of Public Administration Program with emphasis on health services administration at USF after my temporary suspension and before my self-prescribed Prozac kicked in, on a day when I stopped by the SMCHC just to say hi and came upon Zbigniew (a.k.a. "Big Z"), whom one of the internists wanted to commit because Big Z had claimed in his peculiarly accented English (he's from Minnesota, not Poland) that he'd not only seen but talked to Jesus that very morning and that Jesus had told him he'd find cigarettes behind the register and not in aisle 5. I had to explain to my well-meaning but medically myopic colleague that it wasn't Jesus but *Jésus* who had spoken to Big Z—*Jésus*, whom I also sometimes asked for help, who pronounced his first name *Hay-zeus* and worked as an assistant manager at the pharmacy down the street—and

Sex ratio: The disorder is much more common in females than in males.[22]

Prevalence: Recent data suggests increasing prevalence and widespread underdiagnosis.

Predisposing factors and familial pattern: There is some evidence that firstborn children are particularly susceptible,[23] as are those professionals with a predilection for low-status, low-reimbursement, patient-centered specialties such as social work and community psychiatry.[24]

---

that Big Z therefore was not hallucinating and so would not require a costly inpatient stay. Right then I realized that if a person designed a universally applicable language- and culture-sensitive medical personnel training program for docs like my internist colleague, that person would be making an important, ultimately cost-saving, and consequently bipartisanly popular contribution to the future of our tragically dysfunctional American health-care system and that a very smart first step toward such a contribution would be enrollment in an M.P.A./H.S.A. program.
[22]!!

[23]I have two much-younger brothers (my mother had a string of miscarriages until diagnosed with and treated for her "incompetent" cervix).

[24]I must strenuously protest the comments in the press by certain well-known lights of the psychiatric establishment (including you, Dr. Saperstein) suggesting the high incidence of hero complexes in people willing or even eager to work under socioeconomically challenging conditions. While I did not use the best judgment in allowing Mike to seduce me, it seems to me even now, in retrospect, that I behaved as I did, not because I had found someone to fulfill an insatiable need for worship, but because occasionally a person needs a brief interlude of semiprivate vasculo-muscular and neurochemical bliss, an opportunity, if you will, for the evanescent release of the otherwise rigorously repressed but still wildly vital animal within in order to punctuate the daily horrors of her job and the uniformly dismal realities of her patients' lives. It wasn't, after all, as if I planned my encounters with Mike. They just came over me in that way cravings might justifiably overtake

Differential diagnosis: In Overcompensation Disorder, residual type, there is a history of a clear medical[25] mistake followed by a sudden change in practice style that may resemble Blurred Boundary Disorder in some aspects, but the key distinguishing feature of OD (not to be confused with OCD) is a tendency to order frequent and unnecessary services, tests, and specialist consultations. Not uncommonly, professionals with Borderline Personality Disorder also meet the criteria for Blurred Boundary Disorder, but the instability

---

even the most disciplined among us after hearing from a person (who, no matter how derelict and odoriferous, is a fellow human being) about how a group of perfect strangers, well dressed and out for a night on the town, kicked him and urinated on him and set fire to his bedroll, his only possession, and how, as a result, he might have frozen to death were it not for the actions of a buddy of his, another person who, by all standards of conventional society, is a nobody. Fortunately, this nobody had earned only enough change from passersby that afternoon (while napping, hat in lap, outside the McDonald's on Van Ness Avenue) to score a single pint and so was in the optimally functional zone between withdrawal and falling down drunk, and consequently not only spotted his beat-up, half-frozen friend but was cogitating sufficiently well to fetch the local cops, who got the friend to the emergency department at San Francisco General just in time. Imagine, if you will, hearing that story and then walking down a gray-carpeted, fluorescently lit hallway and seeing Mike's lean, rectangular torso or his tightly sculpted runner's thighs and wanting them for yourself, if only for a few minutes (which, I'll be honest, was about all I ever got because, his later denials, protestations, confabulations, and retractions before the Review Board notwithstanding, Mike certainly seemed the eager little beaver in the heat of that and other similar moments, grunting and panting like those funny small dogs with the smashed-in faces), and then perhaps you can understand how, in the twilight zone of the SMCHC, I decided that maybe a quick fuck wasn't such a bad idea.

[25]Perhaps this should read "medical *and/or personal*"?

of identity, interpersonal relationships, and affect, the self-damaging impulsiveness, inappropriate anger, and recurrent suicidal threats or self-mutilation so common to those with Borderline Personality Disorder[26] will not be manifest in those with pure BBD.

Yours sincerely,

Noemi Kadish-Luna, B.S., M.D., M.A., M.P.A./H.S.A.(c)[27]

---

[26]I know what you're thinking: How did she, a well-trained professional—a *psychiatrist*, for God's sake—not see that Mike was Borderline? The answer is simple: the usual way; I was charmed.

[27]In conclusion, I cannot resist pointing out what you as my fellow psychiatric professionals no doubt already know, namely that although personality disorders carry an ethically indefensible if sometimes well-earned historic burden of negative associations even in our own small psychiatric community, there are those among us who would benefit from receiving the sort of diagnosis that might be employed to explain our thoughts and behaviors not only to ourselves but to others, a diagnosis we might metaphorically hoist before us when we disappoint our families or lose a job or are subject to humiliating pseudo-public professional scrutiny, using it as protection in much the same way a soldier girds himself for combat with a bulletproof vest and helmet and grenade. Because, let's face it, the tragic truth is that even now, in the twenty-first century, too many people fail to understand and appreciate the huge and significant difference between differentness (i.e., me) and true insanity (i.e., Freddy Ramboteau, Tina Ball, Big Z), how the former can make a person needy and might even periodically impair her decision-making capacity but may also be responsible for precisely those traits that make her a unique, even special human being, a person striving to make daily contributions, large and small, to the faltering social experiment we call life on behalf of those too ill to do so for themselves. In fact, it might behoove the committee to pause long enough to consider whether, in fact, the selfsame constellation of traits

might account for not only the BBD "disordered" person's character weaknesses and psychological vulnerabilities but also for those "gifted" and "good girl" aptitudes and interests that enable her both to excel in academic pursuits such as earning graduate degrees and developing new diagnostic categories and to feel a profound and sincere sympathy for those among her fellow humans who are too often ignored, written off, insulted, and abused by the sorts of people (including, I'm sorry to have to mention, certain media-hound-type members of the "Cluster B" revision subcommittee) who can look at the downtrodden and desperate and feel no sympathy or empathy, no bathos or pathos, and whose behavior leads some of us so-called crazies to wonder who among us really deserves the label of deeply and irredeemably psychologically deficient. Which brings me back to my relationship with Mike. I admit he was a manipulative, self-serving cutter, quick on the manly trigger and prone to dramatic exits both actual (he left a rainbow-colored trail of pills on the gray carpet the day the SMCHC fired him) and threatened (in addition to the fax, he twice left suicide notes on the handlebar of the bicycle I've used for transportation since the Civic's demise, though last I heard he was alive and well and collecting disability while awaiting a trial date for his wrongful dismissal lawsuit). But unlike most of the other people in my life, Mike also seemed able to see the parts of me that are so often misunderstood, and he not only loved those parts but valued and treasured them, and as a result, for a time, so did I.

VITAL SIGNS STABLE

A CHUNK OF WET CLAY on a linoleum floor, a pair of black suede pumps with leather mignons and two-inch heels, a scream. At ninety-eight—her bones like a frivolous dinner set from early in the last century, the china still functional but thinned to near translucence, its pieces prone to shattering as might an heirloom dropped on the ground from even the modest height of four feet, ten inches—Edith Picarelli had been shrinking for decades.

"I heard it," said the nursing home's art-room assistant. "This sound, like chimes?"

"Too many pieces for counting," commented the radiologist in New Delhi by teleconference.

"Damned heels," said the English administrator when informed. "Her right hip, I'm afraid," she explained to Frank Picarelli's answering machine when she called Edith's son with the news.

It was a cool summer Saturday morning in San Francisco. From his cell phone at the window table of a popular brunch café, the on-call physician told the nurse to send Edith to the hospital. After he hung up, he put a spoonful of scrambled eggs in his toddler daughter's mouth and said to his wife, "Sweet. That was easy."

An hour later, a teenager smoking in the designated area outside the University Hospital ambulance bay said, "Yo, what's that noise?"

The ambulance attendants lowered the gurney to the asphalt and push-pulled it up over the curb and through the sliding glass doors of the Emergency Department. "Hang in there, dear," one of the attendants advised, patting Edith's shoulder as her screams intensified and they parked her in the hallway near the triage desk.

The nurse pretended to cover her ears with her hands. "Gee thanks, guys," she said while sizing up Edith's arm to decide whether she'd need a small-adult or a child-size blood pressure cuff.

"On our way," the paramedic with Edith Picarelli's paperwork in his back pocket said into his radio as he and his partner disappeared back through the sliding doors. They'd just had a call about a near-fatal accident on Nineteenth Avenue and had to hurry.

Quentin Chew, the new intern in the emergency department, didn't know what to make of the almost feral cries or the fact that no one else seemed troubled by them.

"Stand back, stand back! Coming through!" shouted an orderly who couldn't see over the supply cart he pushed down the hall.

Quentin flattened himself against the wall to avoid being hit by the cart. He'd heard similar awful screeching only once before, while watching a documentary on the great migration of herbivores across the Serengeti. The film consisted mostly of sweeping vistas and the occasional mother and baby shot, so he'd grabbed Ralph's arm when, without warning, the action cut to a group of trophy hunters shooting into the herd. They missed their target, an impala with massive spiral horns, and hit a wildebeest instead. As the herd dispersed, the angry and frustrated hunters took turns shooting the injured wildebeest, aiming anywhere but the head or the heart. The animal, down on its side, its hide soaked with blood, made surprising high-pitched cries that Quentin, watching years later and continents away, had felt on his skin and in his gut. The same feeling he had now.

He reached for the next chart in the "to be seen" box.

The chart contained no information except "Picarelli, Edith, room 5" and the patient's vital signs.

"Why's she here?" Quentin asked the triage nurse, hoping for the sort of problem that required suturing or some other procedure.

"You should lose that and most of those," the nurse said, pointing first at Quentin's chewing gum and then at the pockets of his pressed white coat, which bulged with equipment readily available in each Emergency Department patient-care room.

"About the patient?" Quentin asked.

The nurse smiled. "Ancient, not accompanied by family. You figure it out."

In room 5, Edith Picarelli lay perfectly still, her eyes closed. But for the tiny trail of saliva on her lower lip and her crescendo-decrescendo wails, Quentin would have diagnosed the old woman as dead.

He started his exam at Edith's head and finished at her toes, careful not to miss any part in between. This seemed a surefire strategy for avoiding error while maintaining the clinical independence expected of him now that he had his M.D.

An hour and a half after picking up the chart, he presented Edith's case to the supervising physician. Two hours after that, following an impressive array of nonspecifically abnormal tests and several injections of psychiatric medications that quieted but didn't eliminate the wails, a nurse suggested that Quentin call the nursing home to ask why they'd sent Edith in.

"Oh shit," he said when told of the broken hip. "Oh shit, shit, shit." He ordered morphine and X-rays. And then, vaguely light-headed, he paged ortho.

"Not with a ten-foot pole," said the consulting orthopedist.

Quentin called the general medicine team.

"No freaking way," said the admitting medical resident. "This can and should be managed at the sniff."

"Sniff?" asked Quentin.

"Her nursing home. Skilled nursing facility. S-N-F. Sniff. How the hell do you get to be an intern and not know that?"

"But—" Quentin began. And then for nearly twenty seconds he listened to a dial tone.

"Very well then," said the home's English administrator when Quentin informed her of the plan. A realist, the administrator didn't argue. Edith Picarelli wasn't the first of their patients to fail to capture the interest of the fancy university hospital doctors, and she wouldn't be the last.

So Quentin sent Edith back.

"If she was comfortable when she left, what difference does it make?" Ralph asked when Quentin paged him. Midway through his first continuity clinic at the New Israel Care Home as a primary care intern, Ralph seemed distracted and impatient, so Quentin didn't tell him about the wildebeest or how many hours had passed between Edith's arrival and her diagnosis.

"Sorry," Ralph added. "But she got good care, right? Time to move on." Then he softened his voice and added, "Q, I've got like fifty old ladies just like her here in my clinic, and anyway, if you let things like this get to you, you'll never survive residency."

Late that afternoon, Quentin jogged along the Crissy Field promenade without paying much attention to the dogs frolicking on the beach or the windsurfers leaning low on their boards off Fort Point. Since Ralph was on call and not coming home, he reheated leftover spaghetti for his dinner and curled up on their bed with a textbook to study the surgical management of hip fractures. He would have liked to read about the nonsurgical management of hip fractures as well or, more important, about how to approach patients who can't talk, or what to do when you've made an inexcusable mistake, but his book didn't have chapters on those topics.

* * *

At the nursing home, Edith Picarelli shared a semiprivate with a woman young enough, at seventy-four, to be her daughter. In one half of their room—Edith's half—sculptures rested on every flat surface, poked out from beneath the bed, and stood like barricade soldiers against the walls. There were tropical plants with bladelike leaves and ostentatious flowers, miniature replicas of each of the Picarelli family's now-deceased forebears and four-legged companions, and an abundance of child-size chamber music instruments, many in the orange brown of clay that had been fired but not glazed. In the other half of the room, across the statuary demarcation line and surrounded by white, unadorned walls and blond institutional furniture, her young-old roommate slept in an oversize wheelchair before a blaring television.

Earlier that afternoon, shortly after Edith's return from the hospital, Frank Picarelli had noticed the blinking light on his answering machine. Now Edith's family gathered around her bed.

A nurse came in. "Hello!" she said, smiling first at Frank and then at the children. "But so many people. You did not need to come all at one time!"

Edith's grandson, Frank Junior, who went by FJ, rubbed his beard with two fingertips. "I called the hospital. They said she might die?"

"Oh yes, of course," said the nurse. "But it is very slow at this age."

All eyes turned toward the bed. Already the necessary painkillers had made Edith smaller, paler, flatter. She'd forgotten even the basics, such as who they were and how to stay awake.

Still scratching his beard, FJ itemized the changes. "Seems quick to me," he said.

"You will see," said the nurse. She looked at her watch. "I come back after."

"After what?" asked Lily, Edith's ten-year-old great-granddaughter.

FJ put one hand on the top of his daughter's head and another across her mouth. "Terrific," he said to the nurse. "We'll see you then."

"What'd I do?" asked Lily once she'd wriggled free.

When nobody replied, Lily walked over to her nana. Close, but not too close. Not scary close. And Nana was scary today, even more so than usual, but in a different kind of way. Usually Nana might say, *Come here*, and grab Lily's ponytail and pull off the elastic band and start brushing Lily's hair in a way that hurt at first (that was the scary part), then felt kind of good. Next, without discussing what Lily wanted (that was the other scary part), she'd put in some bobby pins with bows and flowers on them, and when she'd finished, Lily would see in the mirror that she looked better, maybe even pretty, but she wouldn't get to stay that way long because as soon as they left Nana's room, her mom would sigh and look at her dad and pull out the bobby pins and remind Lily that Nana had used those exact same pins and bows on the little white fluffy dogs she always had until she moved into the home.

"You didn't do anything, honey," Melissa said now, and as if she'd read her daughter's mind, she ran her fingers through Lily's bangs and tightened the elastic band on her ponytail.

On Edith's roommate's television, a man's voice said, *We're getting word now of hundreds, maybe thousands, of refugees driven to the border and forced at gunpoint . . .*

"Oh joyous, happy world," said FJ.

Lily's younger brother, Frankie, lifted a small cello from the clay string quartet on Edith's dresser. For the first time in his six and a half years as a member of the Picarelli family, no one said, *Don't touch*. He threw it up into the air, caught it, and looked around. Then he grinned and slipped it into his pocket.

An aide coming into the room talking rapidly into a pink cell phone saw the Picarellis, shoved the phone into her smock pocket, and pulled a curtain that split the room in two. "For more private," she said, bowing slightly and backing out the door.

. . . and in local news, a drive-by shooting left two teenagers . . .

Edith sighed.

"I couldn't agree with you more, Gran," said FJ.

Frank signaled to his wife to turn off the television, but Edith had gone back to sleep, so Jean pretended she didn't notice Frank's outsize gesticulations. "Once," she said, glancing at her mother-in-law, "years ago, after the first hip fracture, when I took care of Edith for two months, she gave me a sculpture. A Yorkie that looked just like our Maxie, who'd died the year before. This was back when she still painted them, and she knew the little dog with his shiny black nose was my favorite. She gave it to me the afternoon she moved out of FJ's old bedroom and back to her apartment, but the next morning she called to say she needed it back."

Frank laughed. "She can never part with them."

"It was the only sculpture of hers I ever liked," said Jean.

"Gran sure does like to have her things around her," Melissa said, trying as always to keep the peace. She opened Edith's closet door to reveal three double racks of high-heeled slingbacks, pumps, and sandals. "Look at this one." She blew dust off a steeply sloped wedge. "Such a fabulous red—and those feathers over the toe!"

. . . I just turned away for a second. One minute she was there playing with her doll and then . . . Oh my God, this can't . . .

FJ jumped up, threw open the curtain, and turned off the TV. Edith's roommate opened her eyes. She stared first at the blank screen and then at FJ.

Frankie moved so that his mother stood between him and the roommate.

"Sorry," FJ said. "I thought you were asleep."

The roommate looked at the adult Picarellis one at a time. Then she unlocked her wheelchair and rolled out of the room.

A while later, an aide appeared and saw the red shoe on the bedside table where Melissa had left it. "Many times, we try to take them," she said, "but her feet too crooked, like this—"

She tilted her arm so her elbow pointed at the ceiling and her fingers at the baseboard of the opposite wall. "She walk not good in normal shoes."

The family stared at the aide, Frankie captivated by the excursions of the woman's exceedingly bushy eyebrows, FJ because even though he didn't want Melissa's feet to end up like his gran's, just thinking about her legs and ass in high heels turned him on, and Frank senior mystified because his hearing wasn't what it used to be and he'd understood only a few words of what the aide said.

Eventually, as promised, the nurse returned. She and the aide leaned over the bed. "Edith! Wake up! You want something please?"

"Scotch on the rocks," said FJ.

The nurse looked at him, squinted, then turned back to her patient. She repeated the question, louder.

Eyes opened, stared, blinked, and blinked again.

"Hello, Mother!"

"Hi, Gran!"

"Nana, Nana, Nana!"

"We're all here, Edith," said Jean.

The response from the bed: a grunt, an almost smile.

"We sit her up," said the nurse. She nodded at the aide. The covers came down. Together, they lifted, one on each side, their fists curled around a sheet that had been folded twice and laid perpendicular to the bed.

The body wobbled. One hand shot out—a flash of pale, cobbled knuckles, a gold band with a small diamond solitaire, long pink fingernails.

"Aya!" yelped the aide, and the transfer sheet jerked to her side before it was lowered hastily back onto the bed. A second later, they all watched as three parallel red lines bloomed on the brown background of the aide's slim, hairless forearm.

The nurse took a long, audible breath. "Lucky," she said. "No blood." And then she and the aide exchanged a glance in which they agreed on a call to the evening supervisor and an early end to the aide's shift, with full pay but no incident report.

That settled, they returned their attention to Edith. Left-side down was exchanged for faceup, the head was elevated, the pillows were puffed, and the heels were floated. Finally, from one of the large front pockets of her smiley-face-patterned scrub top, the nurse produced first a syringe of pain medication, then a squat purple box into which she inserted a thick white straw. She extended her arm, rested the bottom of the box on the ruffled collar of Edith's pale yellow nightgown, and carefully positioned the straw.

The mouth opened, a fault line between cracked lips. Edith drank.

"Atta girl," whispered Frank.

"You drink more now," the nurse said, gently patting Edith's arm with one hand as she squeezed the box with the other.

There was a gurgling sound and the hint of a cough, but soon enough Edith drank more.

On a paper taped to the wall above the head of the bed under the word "In," the nurse noted the time, the product name, and the amount consumed.

"She doing good," the nurse announced to the family with a big, encouraging smile.

"Now can we go home?" asked Frankie.

*

Sunday morning, the family met for breakfast before heading to the nursing home. When they got to Edith's semiprivate room, her bed was empty.

"Holy . . . ," said FJ as Melissa grabbed their children and pushed them back into the hallway. On their way out, they had to squeeze between the doorjamb and Frank, who stood frozen in the entryway, staring at the naked mattress.

He was sixty-seven years old and wholly unprepared to become an orphan.

Maybe his mother hadn't been the best parent—certainly she hadn't been as attentive to him as he and Jean had been to FJ—but he felt sure she'd done her best. On the second-to-last day of the war, when his father died—not from the injuries he'd sustained in France, which had included the loss of half of his left leg, most of his hearing, and all of his sense of humor, but from a car accident—his mother had become a pregnant thirty-one-year-old widow. Ancient by the standards of the day when she married for the first time, there seemed no chance she'd get lucky a second time, so she'd gone to work. As he grew up, her job had changed from telephone operator to sales clerk to ticket agent to office girl. The office job, her last and best, was where she met James Michael McMurray, the closest thing Frank had had to a father. Mac taught him how to throw a curveball, how to check the tires and change the oil in his mother's car, and why he might want to consider shaving a second time on Friday and Saturday evenings. For the better part of a decade after Mac moved in, Frank hadn't caught on that the reason his stepfather spent so much time away from home had less to do with job-related travel than with his wife and six children across town. After Mac's death, his mother retired and shifted her focus from people to pets. The sculpting had come later but with equal passion.

Frank heard the rapid, staccato click of heels on linoleum and turned to see Melissa hurrying toward him, flushed and excited.

"I found her," she panted. "She's out here. She's fine."

He closed his eyes and exhaled. Then, for only the fourth time in the thirteen years since Melissa Wong had joined the family, Frank Picarelli smiled at his daughter-in-law. She took his hand and led him down the hall to a bed-shaped chair by the nurses' station.

Jean watched Frank latch on to Melissa and had a vision of him—of herself—debilitated and dependent in one of these places. They were nearly old enough already. If it weren't for Edith's characteristically stubborn hold on life, they'd already be next on the chopping block.

The family stayed all day, though there wasn't much to do but watch TV, flip through magazines, or play card games.

Pillows and blankets hung off the recliner's edges like the drooped leaves of a dying plant. Edith's hair, tinted and usually perfectly set, resembled the surface of a once-beloved throw, bobbled in some places and desperately worn in others. Unlike the previous evening, she no longer moaned or sighed or swatted away the aides who returned at regular intervals to poke a thermometer under her tongue, wrap a blood pressure cuff around her arm, and clip an oxygen sensor to the tip of the one finger from which the hospital had removed the polished fake nail.

"I'm so glad she's more comfortable now," said Melissa. Edith, unlike Frank, had welcomed Melissa into the family, giving advice on the care and feeding of Picarelli men and sending small checks for the kids whenever she could afford to and whether or not it was Lily's or Frankie's birthday or Christmas.

In the late afternoon, a nurse told them that the doctor would be in early the next day and suggested that they head home for dinner and a good night's sleep.

Edith Picarelli hardly noticed when, one after the other, her family kissed her good night.

Just before noon on Monday, most Picarellis having now missed a half day of work or day camp, the doctor ambled into the semiprivate. His stylish goatee and round, rimless glasses glistened in the fluorescent light, competing for the family's attention with a Grant Wood *American Gothic* necktie.

He leaned over and loudly announced himself to Edith's right ear.

"She hasn't been doing much talking," offered Frank.

FJ snorted. "Much? She hasn't spoken since the day before yesterday."

The doctor examined her, then went into the bathroom to wash his hands.

FJ picked up a sculpture, one of the recent ones, judging from the asymmetric shape and unglazed, clay-orange color. He'd already missed two meetings and a deadline at work.

"How is she, doctor?" Frank asked when the doctor re-appeared.

"She's great, Dad," said FJ. "She's really having a bang-up week."

The doctor draped his stethoscope over one shoulder like an ornament.

"I think what Frank's trying to ask," said Jean, "what we'd all like to know, is how long—"

"She's always been a very active person," interrupted Frank. "It will be a problem if she can't get around on her own."

"Dad," said FJ. He looked over at his children and lowered his voice. "Mom. Jesus Christ. Look at her. She's dying."

The doctor held up a hand. "Now, hold on. This is a fracture, not a stroke. She's dehydrated. We give her some fluids, and she may perk right up."

"Right," said FJ. "Like a plant someone forgot to water."

The doctor smiled. "Exactly." He and Frank shook hands.

FJ looked at his parents. "Mom, Dad, please. Listen to me. Maybe—for Gran's sake . . ."

Though it hadn't beeped, the doctor swept the edge of his jacket to one side and touched the pager hooked onto his belt. "Pain medication, some salt water. We're not talking about heroic measures here." He nodded at Frank. "And now, if you'll excuse me . . ."

With the doctor out the door, Frank looked at his son. "Over my dead body."

And just like that, the crisis ended. The next morning, Edith sat upright in the reclining chair, eyes open. The day after, she began drinking again, and on the third day, after dispensing the other residents' bedtime medicines, the nurse they'd met the first evening removed her IV.

Lily and Frankie went back to day camp, FJ and Melissa returned to work, and Jean drove to check on the Napa house, a two-hour trip in stop-and-go traffic past a nearly uninterrupted series of strip malls and cookie-cutter houses, most of which hadn't existed fifteen years earlier when she and Frank had bought the property so they could eventually retire to the country.

Frank, often but not always accompanied by Jean, continued to visit Edith daily, reading the newspaper while she dozed and, when she woke up, wheeling her along the corridors and through the tastefully planted garden before leaving her in the fluorescent-lit atrium by the nurses' station.

As days collected into weeks, Edith seemed neither better nor worse. The recliner became her home—she ate, slept, and bathed in it. "Chocolate," she said sometimes when the box the nurse gave her was green and the liquid food inside it vanilla flavored. "No," she said when the aides asked if she wanted to go to the art room or to a concert in the main auditorium. "No," she said when they informed her that her grandson was on the phone and wanted to talk to her. Otherwise, she didn't speak.

Two months later. Still in the recliner. Still drinking.

Three months. Four. Seven.

Her hair grew long and straight, until only the tips still had color, as if she'd been turned upside down and dipped into a near-empty well of platinum paint.

"That's not Gran," Frankie whispered loudly to Lily one Sunday afternoon on what his parents decided would be his last trip to the facility. "That lady doesn't even look like Gran."

Eventually Edith Picarelli stopped talking altogether. She ate little, though apparently enough, and made few spontaneous movements. The aides bathed her once a week, tied her wispy white hair into a bun each morning, changed her diapers five times a day, and turned her every two hours—left side, back, right side, and so on.

On the one-year anniversary of the fracture, when FJ

called the doctor's office, the nurse told him that according to the doctor's notes, his grandmother's skin was in great shape, her heart strong, and her vital signs entirely normal.

"What does that mean?" FJ asked.

"Well," said the nurse, "I'd say it means she'll be around for a while longer."

*　　*　　*

By the Labor Day weekend of his fourth and final year of emergency-medicine training, Quentin Chew knew that he could handle whatever came through the hospital doors: overdoses with obscure, nefarious poisons; bones and organs crushed by two tons of accelerating steel; screaming babies with projectile vomiting; and violent psychos in drug-induced frenzies. What he couldn't handle were days like this one, shifts so slow even the medical students had time to eat, take a piss, and text their friends about the latest of their youthful Saturdays lost to the hospital.

To kill time, Quentin checked labs on a couple of patients in holding patterns pending the daily discharges and deaths that would free up beds upstairs. Next, he invented reasons to talk to the unit clerk, a kid still in college who thought he might want to be a doctor someday and whose huge blue eyes followed Quentin around the department. Quentin enjoyed the flirtation but hoped the boy understood they were just playing around. As soon as the state completed its inspections, he and Ralph were set to become the parents of one- and two-year-old half sisters whose repeatedly incarcerated mother had relinquished custody.

"Hey, Quentin," called one of the nurses. "You might want to get in here."

The patient was ancient, a nursing home dump in the eleventh hour. The single sheet of paper accompanying her listed a questionable diagnosis of pneumonia and the name and phone number of a son.

"I called already," said the nurse, a woman so smart and experienced that Quentin always felt like the frosting to her cake in patient care. "Left a message on the machine. It sounded like a landline to me. Let's hope they're just out to lunch and not out of town for the weekend."

"A landline." Quentin laughed. "Who the hell still has a landline?"

The nurse looked at him over her bifocals as she secured the IV. "You need to get out more, Dr. C., mix it up with the over-forty crowd. Besides, this lady's a hundred and one years old. Her baby boy could be pushing seventy or eighty himself."

"Tell me she's DNR."

"She's DNR."

He couldn't hear a blood pressure. He inflated the cuff again and this time felt for the pulse with his fingers.

"You're saying that to make me happy."

"I don't like you nearly enough to do that. I called the nursing home. She's okay for antibiotics, no for everything else."

Quentin ordered antibiotics and increased her fluids. "She must have been okay for hospitalization, too. Just our luck."

The nurse shook her head.

"You're shitting me. Then why's she here?"

"Staffing issue at the SNF. Apparently they have a rule not to do palliative care unless they can do it right."

Quentin watched the patient's heart on the monitor. She was already having runs without beats. He turned off the machine.

"On a theoretical level, I'm all for that. But who gave them

167

the impression that we could do it right here? I'm calling the team now. They need to get their asses down here."

Quentin did the handoff quickly, reading the patient's name and unit number to the resident, then giving her a one-liner on the patient's precarious situation. He didn't recognize the name Edith Picarelli, and since she was dying, there was no reason for him to read the chart in which he would have found his note from the first time he met her, when she'd come in three years earlier wailing like an injured wildebeest.

As they did every year over Labor Day weekend, the Picarelli family had gathered at Frank and Jean's house in Napa. Every now and then over those three days, while flipping burgers on the barbecue, taking a walk along one of the grapevine- and tree-lined lanes, or watching a baseball game on the tiny television with its rabbit ears antenna and six viable channels, one or another of the adults—usually Frank—would mention that they missed Edith, and shortly after that, someone else—usually FJ—would wonder aloud whether they should have done things differently from the very beginning. But each time the subject came up, at least one other person—usually Jean or Melissa—pointed out that they hadn't done much of anything at all, and nothing other than what had been recommended by the doctors and nurses, so they shouldn't blame themselves for what had and hadn't happened to Edith since her fall and fracture. Invariably then, someone—most often Frank but sometimes also Jean, since they were at that age when conversation often turned toward symptoms and illness—told a story recently told to him or her by a friend or acquaintance with a supposedly similar experience that sometimes really was similar and ended in the same way but other times became either a litany of suffering followed by death or an almost evangelical tale of months of intensive care and constant worried vigilance that were not called torture, because they were followed by a miraculous recovery, the ancient relative stronger and healthier than they had been before the heart attack or infection or surgery. And it wasn't clear to FJ and Melissa, who were already anticipating having to deal with the decline of Frank and Jean, whether the ultimate outcome of these stories depended on the older person him- or herself, or on the doctor or nursing care, or even on the underlying problem and its treatment, or whether it all came down to less tangible factors such as luck and timing and personality and imagination. But the entire family agreed that in any case, at this point, there was nothing they could do about their outcome, which was, of course, also and especially Edith's outcome, and which, while thankfully devoid of torture, had become—at least according to Jean's niece Pam, who was visiting, having flown north from Mexico to finalize her divorce—a different sort of tragedy: a life that wasn't much of a life in a home that wasn't much of a home, a place of so many bodies in so many beds, a place where some people went to live and others went to die—or not die, as the case might be.

"At least she's comfortable," said Melissa.

"Amen to that," added Frank.

At dinner, Frankie—hoping to make up for having kicked his soccer ball into his grandmother's favorite rosebush earlier in the day—raised his glass. "To Nana," he said, and the rest of the family followed suit, lifting their glasses high and taking big sips of wine, Scotch, juice, or milk, each of the adults hoping to remain healthy forever or, failing that, to die quickly, without warning or prelude.

DAYS OF AWE

For weeks he'd been planning. By the morning of Rosh Hashanah, the pieces had fallen into place: his election to the Residents' Council, an open room in the Jaffa building, and a signed contract for his trio, We Three Hebes, to play at the Hardly Strictly Bluegrass festival in Golden Gate Park. Now only two obstacles remained between Harold Chaikin and a happy ending—the small challenge of telling his wife and the larger one of securing his room change.

He felt badly about Ruth, but he refused to feel guilty. They had lived at the New Israel Care Home for seven months already, and she hadn't once made an effort to adjust. Instead, she let it be known—to him, to the staff, even to other residents—that debilities notwithstanding, only fools willingly gave up the real world for an institution. She would leave in a heartbeat, he knew, would prefer to live almost anywhere else, but they hadn't had children, and most of their friends were in similar straits or worse, so he'd reasoned they'd be better off here than alone at home with only each other and paid help for company. But since their arrival, while he explored the New Israel's possibilities, Ruth wallowed in their losses. As he worked to adapt, always encouraging her to do the same, she chose, again and again, to give up on life.

The sun was barely over the horizon when he made his announcement.

"Moving?" Ruth repeated, pushing up from her bed. "Where are we going?"

"Not we," he said. "Me."

Her hair, unbrushed for days, hung limp at the sides of her face.

"Nearby," he said. "Another building, one closer to the music room and gym. That way I won't keep disturbing you with my practicing and comings and goings."

She put on her glasses. "Wait a minute. You bring me to this prison, then leave? Is that what you're telling me?"

He'd promised himself he'd be patient and kind. "Not so loud. You want everyone to hear our business?"

She laughed. "These people? Who the hell cares? Oh, it's great to be you, isn't it? Able to see and walk and do what you want. You self-serving bastard . . ."

He pressed the call light. On and on she went, as if that kind of talk would make him want to stay. She never took responsibility for her part in their mess. Plenty of others at the home had every one of her admittedly many medical problems, which were real and horrible to be sure, but which the doctor himself had said might slow her down but wouldn't kill her. And slow he could have lived with, slow he would have been happy to help with. But Ruth had chosen to stop. All day she stayed in bed, whining and watching TV. She refused to accompany him to concerts or services or on any of the field trips the home arranged to the symphony or the

Marin Headlands or, just last week, to the new exhibit at the Academy of Sciences in Golden Gate Park. Instead—again—she was making a scene.

The door to their room opened, and an aide stood in the entryway. It was the short, almost deformed-looking one who often took care of Ruth. She had one of those crazy names like Lovey or Peachy or Happy.

"What happen?" asked the aide.

He explained.

Ruth snorted and turned to face the wall.

"If you see it differently," he said, "then sit back up and say so."

Silence.

The aide pointed at the door. "You go now please."

He left gladly. After all, he had things to do.

In the hallway, he nodded at the janitor and smiled at Deborah Wasserman, who was leaning forward on her walker to study the bulletin board that listed the day's events.

"Beautiful sweater," he said as he passed her. "Great with your eyes."

Deborah looked down at her sweater and smiled.

Everywhere he went at the New Israel, women outnumbered men three, sometimes four, to one. As a result, the home was socially the opposite of real life—his real life, at least. From the moment he arrived, he'd been sought out by women who, fifty, thirty, even ten years before, wouldn't have given him the time of day. To his astonishment, in his ninth decade he'd become the cream of the crop. And all because he could still walk and think, because he still had hair and a talent for social graces.

At the end of the hall, he glanced behind him. Deborah turned quickly back toward the bulletin board. Gotcha, he thought, and whistling "Blue Moon of Kentucky," he turned the corner toward the nurses' station.

Zeni stood behind the broad blue counter wearing a uniform top imprinted with alternating Band-Aids and teddy bears. Blue was Tel Aviv 5's official color. The walls were blue, the fifth-floor residents' medical charts bore big blue stickers, and on the elevator, there was a blue square next to the number 5 button, a visual reminder for those who had trouble remembering which floor they called home.

"You tell her?" Zeni asked. Unlike the rest of the mostly Filipino staff, who were so polite that he could never tell where he stood with them, Zeni had no trouble speaking her mind.

"I said I would."

"No shouting from Ruth?" she said, pulling a red SIGN HERE arrow off the edge of the counter.

"You missed it." He glanced down the hallway. People were starting to emerge from their rooms and make their slow way to breakfast. "Did you get her an appointment? For this morning?"

Zeni nodded. She was efficient, that much he had to admit.

"And where *you* will live?"

So far he'd told no one but Gisela the answer to that question in case she, as the newly elected head of the Residents' Council, might be in a position to help him. And sure enough, Gisela had come up with a plan that she'd unveiled on the way to the Academy of Sciences, the two of them sitting in the back row of the transport van and whispering to each other as if they were still in high school.

He jiggled the change in his pocket. "Only one place to live—Jaffa."

Zeni covered her mouth with one hand, shaking her head and laughing as though he couldn't possibly be serious.

The breakfast bell rang like some faraway chime. Not that she cared to eat. Drained of color, the food at the New Israel looked awful and tasted worse. She'd lost so much weight already that her skin hung on her body as if she were wearing one of Harold's man-size sweaters. And anyway, it wasn't even eight in the morning, much too early for anything but coffee.

Lovey had said she'd be back, but of course she hadn't returned. This was the staff's busiest time of day, when they had to get everyone up and ready, breakfasted and medicated. So there was nothing to do but stare at the walls of her soon-to-be-single room, a rectangle with two beds, two sinks, and two dressers.

As they did about everything else, she and Harold had disagreed about how to decorate. In the end, they'd divided the room like children, an imaginary line down the center. His side had furniture brought from home, a huge CD player, and, on the walls, his bluegrass posters and instruments, with the Martin guitar and his five-string banjo in the places of honor visible from the doorway. On either side of the instruments, Bill Monroe, Hazel Dickens, Earl Scruggs, and J. D. Crowe plucked and crooned on framed oversize posters he had kept in a document tube until two months after moving to the New Israel.

She hadn't decorated her side. Nice things only reminded her of all she'd lost in moving here—her home in Presidio Heights, the garden she'd planted and tended for fifty years. Her right to sleep and wake and eat when she wanted.

And now she was losing Harold too. She had no idea how or why she'd go on.

She pressed the button that moved her bed to an upright position. Maybe she should have gone to more social programs or worn the damn wig as he'd asked. "Have a little self-respect, will you?" he'd said too loudly and too often in the days and weeks after they'd first moved in. But at the New Israel she gave her clothes each Tuesday to a girl for the wash. If they came back damaged or ruined—as they did, more often than not—what could she do about it? So she'd taught herself not to care. As for the wig, why couldn't Harold, with his better-than-new-after-cataract-surgery eyes, see what would happen if she wore it? From twenty feet away she might look well put together and not unattractive, but up close would be another story, the young hair a shock against her rumpled old face. In late middle age, she'd begun noticing such women in Laurel Village and, a few years later, among her friends from the Mount Zion Auxiliary or his from the Concordia Club. She didn't care to join their ranks.

Harold had changed since their move. Each morning, he visited people newly arrived at the home, just returned from the hospital, or otherwise in a state of transition. When not in the music room or at an activity, he fretted about the well-being of women and men he barely knew—everyone's well-being, it seemed, but hers.

Not that his concern about the opinions of others was new. For decades, when they'd gone to the symphony or the theater, Harold had never known what he thought of a performance until the following day. Only after reading the reviews in the morning paper and consulting with a few friends—those who might themselves have spoken to someone who'd rung up a society page regular, one of the Goldsteins or Lillienthals or Blums—only then did he have an opinion. Her own take on such matters rarely coincided with his, but in the early years of their marriage he'd appreciated her homegrown uniqueness. When they'd begun dating, she with nothing more than a high school diploma, she'd believed that he, with his fancy East Coast education, would guide her to all that was remarkable in the world. Once married, she'd quickly learned that his years at Princeton and Harvard meant little to him beyond their utility as accessories, like the handkerchief placed just so in the breast pocket of his dress suit. She'd had to find culture for herself and had done so through books and women's groups, her cooking and her garden, a wonderland of herbs and edible plants for which she'd been presented a key to the city.

She looked across the room at the photograph proudly displayed on his dresser: Harold's arm around her waist as Mayor Moscone handed her the oversize key. Two weeks later, Moscone was dead, killed by a jealous supervisor, and Harold had removed the photograph from above the sofa in their den and taken it downtown to his office, where he had used it to impress the beautiful people with whom he had had a lifelong unrequited courtship.

Unrequited, at least, until now. When they forced her to eat in the dining room, she heard the gossip—there was nothing wrong with her ears. Ironically, at the New Israel, where Harold at last had decided to be his unedited self, right down to his previously secret love of bluegrass, he'd attained the social status he always wanted. For this reason if no other, she was glad they'd moved in.

As soon as Jerusalem opened, he crossed the courtyard toward the imposing Greek revival, three stories of granite, with narrow rectangular windows and a portico framed by thick fluted columns. The administration building's classic elegance reminded him of the stock exchange, where he'd spent most of his working life—it was the sort of place a man could go with a complaint or a suggestion and expect to be heard.

He straightened his hair and stepped into the reception suite.

"Running late," warned the secretary, tossing her head in the direction of the CEO's closed office door.

"I'll wait," he said. He would miss his tai chi class, but so be it.

Forty-five minutes later, Andrew Ross greeted him with a warm handshake and a cursory apology.

Furious, he followed the CEO through his office door, then stopped short.

A mural covered the room's back wall, a giant cityscape of Jerusalem painted floor to ceiling, creating the illusion that the CEO's oversize desk sat atop the hill beside the Knesset, sharing its fabulous views. He'd never seen anything like it. Everywhere were perfect likenesses of actual structures: the Shrine of the Book, the Israel Museum, and the Judean Mountains. Years earlier, he and Ruth had visited them all.

Andrew Ross grinned, then motioned at the visitor's seat, a wooden armchair emblazoned with the home's logo and situated near the part of the mural portraying slightly run-down and very ordinary houses. "Have a seat. I haven't got much time."

Without mentioning Ruth, he explained his situation. He used the word *urgent* in a way that might have been construed as misleading and said, truthfully, that most of his friends lived in Jaffa. Since he spent his days exercising, going to activities, playing music, and attending the Residents' Council meetings with those friends, it only made sense for him also to live in the same building and eat in the same dining room as they did. He admitted that he couldn't imagine living anywhere else.

Andrew Ross positioned a pair of glasses halfway down his nose and typed into his computer. "There's a wait list."

He'd been prepared for that. "Three fourteen is open. Has been for months. Maintenance says there's a problem with one wall." Fred in maintenance had also told Gisela that the home, following the capital campaign for the new end-stage-dementia building, lacked the funds to repair it.

Andrew Ross removed his glasses. "Go on."

"I'll pay to fix it up, but then it's mine. You get free repairs and another room rent. I skip the wait list."

The CEO took a cloth from his pants pocket and cleaned his glasses, first the front and then the back. "It was my idea, you know," he said without looking up. "One of the first things I did when I took this job was to make Jaffa home for the healthiest and most independent residents. A few years back, it used to be psych, and of course, no one wanted to be there. Or to have dad there, or grandma. But now Jaffa's got prestige. Now everyone wants in."

"Pure marketing genius," Harold agreed, hoping the conversation wasn't going where he suspected it was.

"It's not just that room that's beat-up, you know," said Andrew Ross, leaning back and using his high-end ergonomic chair to full advantage. "From the outside, Jaffa might look handsome, but inside it's a mess. Faded paint, chips in the plaster, exposed pipes. The 'New' in New Israel doesn't apply to Jaffa."

There could be no question that Tel Aviv was superficially newer and nicer than Jaffa. But he had spent enough time in both buildings to know that people mattered far more than pipes.

Of course, that was his perspective as someone who already lived at the New Israel; it would be different if he, like Andrew Ross, was trying to convince people to move in or make a donation.

"How much?"

Andrew Ross smiled. Then he wrote a number on a Post-it note and passed it across the desk.

That the numbers all fit on the one small rectangle was reassuring. The sum was significant, but it might have been worse.

He slipped the Post-it into his pocket. "One condition. My wife gets our double in Tel Aviv to herself—"

"Your wife? Three fourteen is a single."

"You looked up my finances, but not my marital status?" He stood. "Here's the deal: My wife stays in Tel Aviv and gets whatever help she needs for as long as she needs it. I move to Jaffa, which, courtesy of me, starts looking a heck of a lot better."

He held out his hand. Andrew Ross walked out from behind his desk but didn't extend his hand until he'd opened his office door.

They didn't bother with good-byes. At Ross's age, Harold too would have made certain assumptions about an old man leaving his wife. And like the CEO, he wouldn't have understood that even the very old could grow apart, that the husband might innocently develop new hopes, dreams, interests, and abilities, until suddenly he looked back and saw a giant chasm between himself and his wife, and that even if there were a way back to her, he might not be able to convince himself to cross back, afraid he no longer wanted or knew how to live on the other side.

She hadn't asked to see the doctor, but Zeni had insisted that she had an appointment, so here she was. It was one of the young ones from the university again, doctors who appeared for a while on a certain day of the week and then disappeared forever, and of course he was running late.

Through the open exam-room window came bursts of guttural conversation. The morning was uncharacteristically cold and windy for September, but bad weather never stopped the Russians at the New Israel. They went outdoors wrapped in thick coats and scarves no matter the season or temperature. Or so Harold claimed. Most of what she knew about them she'd gathered from his complaints: they kept nonkosher foods like sausage and buttermilk on their windowsills; they distrusted the Residents' Council, even though that body was meant to represent them too and interpreters were provided at all meetings; they rarely smiled when passing others in the hallway, except people they already knew. For the exact same reasons, she admired them tremendously.

The doctor entered the room tucking his long black hair behind his ears like a schoolgirl. Why otherwise perfectly fine looking young men chose women's hairstyles these days, she had no idea. He sat down on a little wheeled stool and slid forward until their knees were just inches apart and she could see his remarkably white, shiny teeth.

"Ralph Nguyen," he said. "I'm one of the interns working with Dr. Blumenfeld. I heard about your husband. How're you doing?"

He'd heard? Already? She'd only just heard herself.

"The nurse." He waved a hand toward the closed door. "You must have told whoever brought you over . . ."

But she hadn't. Apparently, at the New Israel, even husband-wife arguments were part of the public record.

The doctor leaned forward. "It would be totally understandable if, under the circumstances, you felt sad or upset."

She resisted the urge to say *No shit, Sherlock.* Sometimes it was better just to keep quiet.

"Hey," he said gently, ducking his head so they were eye to eye. "I want to help you. But I need you to help me too."

She wondered whether he'd grown up without a father, so feminine were his movements and gestures. But before she could ask, someone knocked at the exam-room door. The doctor swiveled and stood. He didn't push off, simply rose and crossed the room in two quick strides. At the door, he said, "When I'm done here," then he pivoted—really it was more of a pirouette—took one giant step, and lowered himself to a perfect landing on his stool.

She winced. The poor man. He would never find a wife. Besides, what could be explained to someone so young and agile?

"Sorry," he said. "Where were we?"

As she recalled, they had been at the part where he'd commented that her distress at the dissolution of her sixty-two-year marriage might be something other than pathologic.

When she didn't answer, he launched into the usual questions about the pain in her back and shoulders and hips and the shadows she saw whenever she looked at anything head-on. Then he asked her a series of questions, circling yeses or noes as she told him that yes, she'd dropped most of her activities and interests, and yes, her life was empty and boring, and yes, she often felt helpless, hopeless, and worthless, which explained why no, she was not basically satisfied with her life, and no, she did not feel happy most—or even some—of the time, and no, she certainly did not think it was wonderful to be alive now. Finally, he opened the chart that was the sum total of her life at the New Israel and began writing.

Sitting up exhausted her. The pain in her joints and spine had begun to crescendo from its usual hum to a chorus of distinct but colluding voices. She looked at the clock. It was still morning. All the time and effort Zeni and the aides had spent getting her up and dressed and across two buildings for her appointment, and after all that, there remained nothing but worse pain and another long, empty day ahead.

"There's never enough time, is there?" the doctor asked without looking up.

There was, she thought, but only once you had no use for it.

He wheeled her out into the reception area. "You'll take one pill at night before bed," he said. "This medicine isn't a cure for grief, but it might help make things bearable."

More wasted time and money, she thought as he disappeared back into the exam room. Unless this one was a magic pill that would help her recover her eyesight, independence, house, and husband.

When the lunch bell rang, he hurried to meet his friends at what would soon be his regular table. He loved that the dining room in Jaffa was nothing like the one in Tel Aviv 5, with its wheelchairs and feeding tables. Here, residents walked themselves to and from meals and sat four to a table, the tables in two neat rows, each with a crisp white tablecloth and a bright yellow flower in a tiny vase at its center.

Someone called his name, and he scanned the room until he spotted Gisela waving from a table at the back. She was sitting with Stanley Luft, who played fiddle and mandolin for We Three Hebes.

"We thought you forgot us," Stanley said when he was close enough to hear.

"Not a chance." He glanced at Gisela. "I had a business meeting this morning that ran late. Luckily, it went very well."

Gisela smiled slightly, but in accordance with their plan, she didn't otherwise acknowledge his good news.

"We're still waiting on our fourth." Stanley pointed his spoon at the last open seat at their table. "A recent arrival," he said. "And supposedly a very big deal in St. Louis, but the daughter and grandkids are here."

No matter how functional they were, the New Israel residents were assigned seat placards so they could be served whatever diet their physician had ordered. Sitting down, he saw that Gisela had diabetic/weight reduction and Stanley had renal, low salt. He had regular and could only hope the others had noticed.

Gisela spoke with her mouth full. "We met her at breakfast, but big deal or not, if she keeps with the lateness, they'll move her to Eilat like that Tova Fishman last month."

"What's she like?" he asked.

"See for yourself." Gisela, still chewing, jutted her chin toward the path between the tables behind him.

He tried to turn his head but found he couldn't rotate it far enough, so instead he backed up his chair and stood just as the new person approached the table.

"Oh," said a voice on the low end of contralto. "A gentleman."

He pulled out her chair. She wore a white silk blouse over a black and white striped skirt and had tied back her silver hair with a thin velvet ribbon. She was gorgeous and clearly knew it, taking her time as she reached the table. In her right hand was a silver-tipped ebony cane that matched her outfit but that she didn't appear to need.

He waited as she leaned the cane against the wall and greeted the others. Finally, she turned to him and extended her hand as Stanley made the introductions.

She wore a perfume he didn't recognize. He let his wrists brush her shoulders as he pushed in her chair. Returning to his seat, he realized he was still smiling.

Gisela looked from him to the newcomer. "Mary O'Brien," she said. "Not exactly a Jewish name."

Mary nodded at the server who brought her plate. "My fourth husband was Irish."

"Fourth?" Stanley repeated with raised eyebrows.

"Unlucky in love," she said, tucking her napkin over the large bow at the neck of her blouse. She added both salt and pepper to her soup before tasting it, then tore her bread into chunks and dropped it in as well.

It was all he could do not to stare. He took a bite of his sandwich and concentrated on chewing, aware of Gisela's eyes on him and also, for the first time, of how he might inadvertently have raised her expectations of their relationship.

On the far side of the room, an argument erupted at one of the tables of Russians.

"Luck, schmuck," Gisela said to Mary. "Maybe you're like those gold diggers over there, just pretending to be a Yid to get in here."

"Oh come on," Stanley said. "Who would have the last laugh if Russian Christians started posing as Jews in order to find comfort and security in America? Honestly, who would even make that up?"

Once, he might have been as oblivious as Stanley, at least where it came to females. Now he realized he had only seconds to defuse the situation with Gisela. Pointing across the aisle, he said, "So that guy over there with the schnoz, that Vladimyr Moyshe Vaynshteyn—he isn't Jewish?"

Stanley and Mary laughed.

Gisela's nostrils flared. "I didn't say they were all crooks, but you can't always know what people are up to."

"No," he said with a wink. "And they *are* often up to something."

He watched her relax. She knew perfectly well she was the only one he'd consulted about leaving Ruth and moving to Jaffa.

Mary blew on a spoonful of her soup. "What does it matter? Maybe some things are quite simply other people's business."

"Take that approach around here," Stanley warned, "and you'll die of boredom."

"Here, here," seconded Gisela, raising her water glass.

After each sip of her soup, Mary licked the corners of her lips to make sure she had it all. He could not imagine that a woman with an appetite like that wouldn't have other, equally compelling passions.

"And the name Mary?" he asked as the servers cleared their plates.

"Oh, that." Mary laughed. "We lived in Crown Heights, a world of Malkas and Leahs. To my mother, it was both original and wholly American."

He laughed, unable to contain himself. He couldn't wait to get into his new room and start his new life.

The knock on the door came just as a hideously tattooed young chef on TV poured chipotle chocolate sauce over potato-chip-crusted pan-seared elk. "Come in," she said when Zeni was already well into the room.

"You do not drink?" asked the nurse, lifting the full can of liquid food from the bedside table.

She hated the supplements and how Harold and the staff seemed to believe they would transform her, somehow solving all her troubles. Every day, the little cans arrived at ten in the morning, two in the afternoon, and before bed. And without help, she couldn't even pour the sick-sweet liquid down the sink or find a place to hide the unopened containers.

Zeni pulled up the shades and opened a window. "It is good for you."

"Like hell." She pushed the can away and pulled the pillow over her head.

They went through this every day. Early on, Zeni had tried to coax her, offering different flavors, occasionally attempting to bargain or command. Eventually they'd reached their current standoff, neither of them with any illusions about the outcome of the conversation.

Now she waited. Soon she'd hear the door shut, and then she could decide whether to go to the trouble of sitting back up to see which chef had made the best use of the required crazy ingredients in order to win the contest's cash prize.

The bed moved behind her. Surely, today of all days, Zeni wasn't going to force her to drink the so-called food?

A hand touched her back and began gently rubbing. She tried to shrug it off, but then a second hand began massaging the other side. The hands, small and strong, moved up and down her back, then side to side. They kneaded, pressed, and pounded, lingering on the tightest and most tender spots. She could hardly bear it at first, and then she wished it would go on forever. Why had Zeni never done this before? Warmth rose from her neck and along her spine, where for the longest time there'd been only pain.

After a while the hands slowed, then stopped. "Me too," Zeni said quietly. "No more husband."

She rolled over, and they looked at each other.

"What happened?"

"He said I have too many opinions, and I am too fat."

Zeni definitely had her opinions, but she wasn't fat. It made no sense.

The nurse ran her hands along her torso, showing the shape hidden beneath her scrub top. "Now I am not fat, but before, yes. For one year I ate only dinner. No breakfast, no lunch, no McDonald's, no *pancit*. I wanted him to feel sorry about leaving." She stood up. "You can do the same."

Ruth waved away the idea.

Zeni parked the wheelchair alongside the bed. "In the Philippines, we have a dog. This dog, she love another dog down the road. For a long time, you see one dog, you see both dogs. Then that other dog he found a different dog to be his friend. For a while, my dog stayed only at home. She did not run around like before. Then one day I see her go down the road to the house of the other dog and pee. They shoo her, but every day she go back. She pee again."

"Did she get her boyfriend back?"

Zeni shook her head. "You do not understand. Harold goes everywhere. He meets many people. You stay always on Tel Aviv five." She dropped soap and shampoo into the carry bag at the back of the wheelchair. "Maybe some people do not know even that he has a wife."

Clearly, she had underestimated Zeni. Not only did she have chutzpah but she understood perfectly what made Harold tick.

*

He stared in disbelief at his closet. While he was in the music room, Ruth had had one of the aides take his suits to Jaffa 314.

"You said you were moving," she explained. "I figured you'd want out right away."

"The damn room's not ready yet. I can eat in the dining room, but I can't move in until after the High Holidays."

"Poor man. How will you bear it?"

"Look. I didn't have to tell you now, but I did so you'd have time to adjust before I left."

"So considerate. Always a gentleman. Now, that should impress your friends."

He didn't have time for this. Not one jacket remained, and he had to find something nice enough to wear to temple. He'd never make it to Jaffa and back with a suit in time for services.

She rolled up behind him. He couldn't recall the last time he'd seen her propel herself. If his leaving got her up and moving, it would be a bonus beyond his wildest dreams. She too could be happy at the New Israel if she let herself. He was sure of it.

"What I don't understand," she said, "is why you're going to services in the first place. You don't believe in God. You never went before we moved in here."

So she was up, but otherwise unchanged. He moved pants right to left in his closet. There was nothing appropriate for him to wear, certainly nothing nice enough to impress Mary O'Brien. "I believe in community. Everyone's going."

She laughed. "Everyone? The atheist Russians? Those living corpses on Masada who don't even know their own names anymore?"

"Of course not. What's gotten into you?"

Incredibly, she didn't offer another snide retort. She looked as if she were actually thinking about the answer to his question.

"Get out of my way," she commanded. When he did, she rolled up to the closet and scanned his clothes. Suddenly he realized what had changed. They'd finally convinced her to take a shower. There was a special one down the hall with a waterproof support chair and room for an aide. Her hair no longer lay along her head in greasy clumps. She smelled of soap and shampoo.

"The linen trousers," she said. "The blue shirt, the belt with the banjo buckle, and your navy silk tie. It's not a suit, but you'll look pretty sharp."

He held the outfit against his body in front of the mirror. She'd always had a good eye for style.

He sat down on his bed to change. Midway through untying the laces of his sport shoes, he stopped and looked up. "I appreciate the help, I really do. And I'm very grateful. But it doesn't change anything."

"I didn't imagine it would."

He wished she'd turn on her television the way she usually did, blaring the absurd food shows one after the other as if to reprimand him for taking her away from her kitchen and her favorite restaurants. But she just sat in her wheelchair studying him.

He pulled on his trousers, careful not to wrinkle the linen, then buttoned the shirt and secured his belt and tie.

Ruth gave him the once-over. "Handsome," she declared. "You'll stand out in the crowd as usual."

He checked himself in the mirror, pleasantly surprised that she was right. If he hurried, he might still be in time to have his choice of seat and seatmates.

She kept her head down as Zeni rolled her to Jerusalem, not that anyone was likely to recognize her. At the synagogue, they slipped in through a side door; it would be just like Harold to be watching the main entrance. Inside the temple, the fluorescent lights and heavy, stale air surprised her. At the New Israel, it seemed, worship took place in a room that looked and smelled like a high school gym.

She easily spotted Harold's blue shirt in front on the left. He was surrounded by women. She pointed to a spot in the same section, far enough back that Harold wouldn't see her and close enough that she'd be able to wheel herself to the front. Zeni parked her there and pretended to set the wheelchair brakes before touching her shoulder and walking away.

And then Ruth waited, watching as late arrivals crowded into the wide, windowless space and scanned the room for the best of the remaining tan folding seats. Her neighbors, with their round faces and heavy sweaters, appeared to be Russian. She nodded and smiled, and they did the same, so either they weren't Russian or Harold was wrong about San Francisco's most recent Jewish immigrants. But since no one said anything, not even hello, there was no way to know.

A walker squeaked as its owner hurried by. Every few seconds she touched the wig on her head, the huge glasses that actually did help her see, and the corners of her lipsticked lips, but everything had stayed in place.

The lights flashed off and back on. At the front of the room, a stylish Filipina lit the candles and the rabbi signaled to a young man who lifted the huge double-twist shofar to his lips and blew: a piercing, primitive blast that echoed through the room.

One of her neighbors reached up to adjust his hearing aid. Seconds after the sound ended, she continued to feel it in her chest. Maybe that was what life was like at the end: one long cry that wiped out everything else.

The next blasts were shorter, nine staccato sobs that sounded as if they came from deep inside a wounded animal. Harold was right that sometimes instruments were more eloquent than words. How often she had wished she could make such a sound herself.

As the shofar's last note faded, she reached for the cool metal on either side of her chair and pushed. The wheelchair rolled down the side aisle faster than she would have thought possible. They had always been different, she and Harold, and she hadn't put up with him for so long to end up like this.

The rabbi moved to the podium and adjusted the microphone.

As she reached the front of the room, one of the women beside Harold leaned over to whisper in his ear.

The rabbi cleared his throat.

"Wait," she called. "Me first."

Only then did she realize the fault in Zeni's plan. In her wheelchair and with everyone seated, only those close to Harold would see what happened next. That would ruin everything. But if she stood up . . .

Harold saw her then. His mouth opened.

The wig shifted on her head as she rose.

Harold jumped to his feet.

The plain gold band slid easily from her fourth left finger, and she held it out to him even as she felt her legs give way.

He stayed with Ruth all night at the hospital, as much to have time to sort out what had happened as to monitor her condition. Had she hoped the fall would kill her? Or had she gambled that it wouldn't? She would have known that he would never walk away if she were injured, and also that he'd blame himself for not understanding her as fully as she understood him. With the entire community as witness, she had known that her downfall would become his as well.

It was lunchtime when he got back to the New Israel. He entered the Jaffa dining room with his back straight and his face closed like the heavy wooden doors of a boardroom. Crossing the short distance from the doorway to his table, he walked a gauntlet of whispers and stares. Even the Russians looked away when he glanced in their direction.

"Afternoon," he said to Stanley and Gisela. He didn't say *good*.

"That it is," Stanley replied, holding out a hand, though they didn't usually shake except at council meetings.

Gisela took a bite of her sandwich.

"Soup? Sandwich?" asked a server once he'd sat down.

He nodded, then looked over at their table's empty chair. "Late again?"

"Mary moved to table six," Stanley said. "At breakfast this morning. She insisted."

A second server put a bowl and plate before him. His favorites: tomato basil soup and grilled cheese on rye. He tried to feel pleased but failed.

"So," Gisela said, "have they told you much?"

He poured himself some water. "She's got a broken hip, a broken arm, broken ribs, and a concussion. She's in intensive care."

"Conscious?"

He shook his head. "Sedated."

Stanley stroked his mustache, his index finger tracing from the center down one side, then the other. "It's always something in a marriage," he said. "No way to be ready." Stanley's wife, in her thirteenth year with Alzheimer's, had been moved to Masada 4 that summer.

He didn't tell his friends the worst of it, that the doctor had said the fractures wouldn't kill Ruth, only make her more fragile. That she'd need lots of help from him through the months, and possibly years, of her recovery.

In silence, they ate. He chewed and swallowed, tasting nothing, and then began again, moving his spoon from bowl to mouth and back, repeating the motions of eating as he would be repeating the motions of his life from here on out.

LUCKY YOU

WEDNESDAY, THE DAY THE boy fell, Perla Weldon walked her afternoon dogs out over the saddle of Bernal Hill. Because it was early December, after the first of the El Niño rains, the mud was orange brown, slippery in some places and as thick as peanut butter in others. It clung to her boots and splashed on her jeans as she threw sticks and rocks for her charges. Perla and her dogs covered most of the hill's twenty-four leash-free acres that day, from the Monterey pines in a lonely cluster on the highest peak to the grassy eastern slopes and short red rock bluffs to the west. She praised the dogs in her usual voice—which was childishly high—and reprimanded them in deep tones that required her to lower her chin to her chest. Heading back to the K9 Safari truck, they walked along the cliff path that would be closed off three hours later and planted with indigenous grasses the following week.

I watched as a group of neighborhood volunteers planted the grasses. Perla had told me her version of the story by then, and my wife had read the brief account in the *Chronicle* aloud one breakfast as a warning to our boys, but I wanted to get a sense of the place for myself. Leaving work early, I drove to the gate at the top of Bernal Heights Boulevard and retraced Perla's route. I wondered how many afternoons she had passed the boy, walking home from school with his friends. The paper said the friends always walked together, Maya Cohen and Jessica Fernandez, both age ten, and Dylan Hunter, age eleven, who had been admitted to San Francisco General Hospital in critical condition. Perla had said she couldn't remember seeing them, but she didn't pay much attention to kids unless they were harassing her dogs. Children, she believed, were cute one minute, unspeakably cruel the next, the demands of their bodies and imaginations endless and unpredictable. She much preferred animals.

In the parking area, I imagined Perla's K9 Safari camper truck with its trademark paint job: frolicking canines and squat, flat-topped trees on a background that was savanna tan on the bottom and the brilliant blue of African skies on top. Then I pictured Perla coming down off the hill toward the truck. She glanced at her watch and, instead of opening the tailgate, whistled that unique series of notes all her dogs knew. Standing alone on that flat stretch of rocky rubble a week later, I could almost hear the sound—the pitch rising, then retreating, then rising some more, like a complicated question.

The dogs looked at Perla sideways, the whites of their eyes showing and their tails poised in midair, equally prepared to drop or wag, depending on her command. Having made good time that afternoon, she owed her pack and their owners another thirteen minutes, long enough for a jog down the pedestrian-only portion of the boulevard that runs through the park below the cliffs. Feigning indecision, she made the dogs wait an unnecessary second, their bodies tense and trembling.

Moments like that one, she had said while telling me the story, reminded her why she loved dogs, their complete engagement and unrestrained joy in the face of life's simple pleasures.

Perla pointed past the gate at the pavement curving north down the hill. The chocolate labs, Silo and Seamus, barked, and a black-and-white collie named Bailey turned circles. The others sprinted forward with raised tails and lowered shoulders, and Perla ran with them, enjoying the stretch of her legs and the catch of cold air in her chest. She ducked under the gate. Beside her, Taco's nails clicked on the blacktop. They passed the patch of giant cacti and the graffiti-tagged view bench that looked west toward Twin Peaks. At the curve, Perla heard her own panting, the swish and rustle of the wind in the eucalyptus, and just beyond the Esmeralda Street steps, an abrupt, high wail that stopped her mid-stride.

She registered only color and motion at first, something bright red tumbling past the yellow grass and orange rock. Then, twenty yards down the road, the figure rolled off the cliff, and a second after it landed, she heard the thud of skull on asphalt.

Some people would have run to the boy right then. They would have forgotten themselves and their usual responsibilities and just reacted. Perla noticed a plane buzzing overhead and the wind blowing strands of hair into her face. She said that even at a distance she could see that the body was small, with a red sweater and long blond hair.

The dogs stopped running when she did. Now they sensed Perla's tension and hovered close. She ran a hand along Taco's trembling back and let the beagle crawl into the space between her feet. Just then, several people—an older man, two women pushing strollers, a teenager—hurried by, headed toward the body.

Rasta stiffened.

"No!" Perla snapped. "Come." She tapped her left thigh twice with her hand. In slow motion, ears low and flat, the shepherd slouched forward and sat on her left side. She gave him a hunk of the cheese she kept in her zipped upper coat pocket for emergencies. The other dogs stared at her without blinking, licking their lips. She led them into the small clearing off the road beside the steps, made them sit, and gave each of them one of the small training treats from her lower pocket. A trickle of sweat rolled down her neck and into her shirt. Unless the kid needed CPR, she reasoned, little could be done until rescue arrived.

Though she didn't say so, it seems entirely plausible that Perla hoped an observer—and surely some of the people going by recognized her bush jacket with its dog-and-baobab-tree logo—might believe she was doing her part by keeping her pack out of the way. But then she came to her senses. She checked her watch; the human brain can survive only six minutes without oxygen.

Perla told the dogs to stay and moved, faster than walking but slower than a jog, toward the crowd. People stood in two clusters, one around the boy, another a little farther away. She pushed through them without looking up. A heaviness slid into her shoulders and neck.

The boy lay completely still but for the rise and fall of his chest. When she saw that he was breathing, she realized she was not and took a big gulp of air. Blood, already clotting, pooled around his left ear. A man Perla recognized knelt at the boy's side, his eyes wide and mouth slightly open. She knew his yellow Happy Tails truck, that he walked large and small dogs separately, drank too much coffee, and didn't do weekends, but she'd never bothered to learn his name. As she dropped to a crouch opposite him, he leaned forward toward the boy's small ear.

"It's okay," he said. "You're okay. We're getting help."

Perla reached for the child's wrist. He'd landed perpendicular to the road, with one leg caught beneath him and his arms flung to the sides. At his feet, a woman wearing a tapered navy skirt suit and bright purple five-toed running shoes pointed at the silver earpiece and microphone that curved over her cheek in front of her mouth. "Nine one one," she said. Then she cocked her chin at the child. "How old do you think she is?"

"He," said a man carrying infant twins, one on his chest, one on his back.

The boy's pulse fluttered under Perla's fingertips, rapid but regular. A tiny tuft of saliva hung from the corner of his mouth. She stared at the pretty face and delicate hands, at the low-riding jeans, red V-neck sweater, and unlaced high-tops.

Sirens sounded from somewhere down the hill in the Mission. People exchanged quick, relieved smiles.

The Happy Tails man said, "She's a girl, definitely."

Perla moistened her lips with her tongue. "A boy," she said. "A ten- or eleven-year-old boy." His chest rose and fell. His heart raced. The scalp wound had slowed to an ooze, and there was no other visible bleeding.

"A nine-year-old girl," the cell phone woman said into her machine with authority.

The man with twins looked at Perla and shook his head. She shrugged her shoulders. Up the hill, a dog barked a guttural warning. Without letting go of the boy, Perla leaned to one side until she could see that all her dogs were still on the shoulder where she'd left them.

"There were two others," the cell phone woman said into her mouthpiece. She tilted her head back and squinted up at the cliff path. "But I don't see them now."

The boy moaned. He didn't open his eyes or move.

"Please," whispered the Happy Tails man. "Hang in there." He rested a hand on an edge of red sweater and slowly moved it up and down. Perla tracked the boy's pulse. She watched the lift and descent of his torso, faster than before. She held his wrist two inches above the ground, then let go. His arm dropped like a doll's.

The sound of sirens came from several directions now, louder and closer.

Perla squeezed the tip of the boy's second finger; he didn't retract his hand, but within seconds his blanched nail bed regained its pink tint. The engines were close. Close enough, she felt sure, that soon the paramedics would arrive in time to help the boy.

Something shoved her shoulder from behind, and a man's voice said, "Hey, what are you doing? Are you a nurse?"

Perla shook her head. She let go of the boy's wrist. At that exact moment, his eyes twitched and the tendons on his neck strained with inspiration. When he exhaled, the noise sounded like bubbles blown through a straw.

"Oh my God," said the Happy Tails man. He looked at Perla. "What's happening?"

Perla thought the boy was going into pulmonary edema. Or that his lungs were filling with blood. She didn't construct a more elaborate differential diagnosis than that two-item list. Instead, she imagined that she had thrown balls to her dogs on the rocky flat beside the parking area rather than running with them down the road. Or that she'd driven to the beach at Fort Funston that afternoon, or to the Presidio, or to any one of the other two dozen dog parks spread throughout the city.

"They're here," she heard the cell phone woman say. Everyone looked down the hill.

Red flashing lights lit the asphalt from the fire engine and rescue truck arriving at the park's lower gate. Two paramedics, each with a fluorescent orange tackle box, scooted under the barrier and began jogging uphill carrying a stretcher between them. It would take them at least a minute, maybe two, to reach the boy.

Now the boy breathed in again, making a gurgling sound. His skin looked ashen. Perla reached for his wrist and couldn't find a pulse, but he took another gasping breath.

"Hurry, hurry, hurry," intoned the Happy Tails man, looking back and forth between the boy and the paramedics.

Perla felt for a pulse in the boy's neck. She thought she sensed a flutter beneath her fingertip, but she couldn't be certain. She willed him to breathe again.

"Jesus!" shouted the cell phone woman. "Goddamn dogs."

Halfway down the hill, terriers, Chihuahuas, and a shih tzu, some trailing leashes, yapped and lunged for the paramedics.

"Oh God," said the Happy Tails man. "I forgot." But he neither stood nor called his dogs.

Perla watched as a pale pink bubble formed between the boy's lips. He looked as if he were wearing lavender lipstick. He looked like a girl.

"Can you imagine being the parent who gets this call?" asked the man with twins. "Can you just imagine?"

The paramedics dropped to their knees. One began assessing the boy, and the other threw open his tackle box. Perla stepped out of the way. She couldn't imagine receiving the call about the child, but she could imagine making it. She walked to the edge of the asphalt and retched into the dirt.

No one who knew Perla as I did would call her thoughtless or irresponsible, though she was one of those people who had been slow to find her place in the world. K9 Safari, a year and a half old when the boy fell, was only the latest of her independent ventures. In the decade since she and I had worked together, she had also run a catering business, done a two-year stint in real estate, and worked as a personal trainer. But Perla said K9 Safari was her best job yet, her favorite by far, and the most successful. She had a twenty-dog wait list and bookings for holidays more than six months away. And it was true that she excelled at her work. In the aftermath of the boy's fall, when she wouldn't have minded if her dogs acted up, making it necessary for her to escort them back to the truck, they remained in an orderly pack on the shoulder of the road, sniffing the air and throwing sidelong glances downhill toward the growing group of worried humans.

You can see San Francisco General Hospital—where I work and where Dylan Hunter was taken by the paramedics—from the cliff where the three young friends were walking the afternoon of the fall, and you can see Bernal Hill from certain parts of the hospital. Not from the pediatric ICU, where Dylan spent ten days, or from the wards, where he spent another three weeks before being transferred to a long-term rehabilitation facility. But you can see much of the hill from my office, its eastern slopes jutting like an island of primordial wilderness above the neighborhood's expanse of intersecting freeways and tightly packed houses. If I stand to the far left of my windows and look up and to the right, I can even see the stretch of asphalt where Perla waited with Dylan after the fall. I look at the hill often these days, noting the greening of the grass with the winter rains and the different hues of the rocks as the light changes throughout the day. I would like to tell Perla that I now see those colors and changes and the opportunities they represent when I look at Bernal Hill, but she and I are no longer in touch.

* * *

Fourteen years and five months before the boy's fall, in the third week of June, Perla and I both arrived in San Francisco (me from Baltimore, she from Chicago) to begin the family medicine residency at SF General. Looking at Perla then, you couldn't have guessed that she'd already had second thoughts about being a doctor.

That first morning, a low, wet fog hung over the city from San Bruno Mountain to the Golden Gate. As we gathered on the steps outside the hospital's main entrance, water dripped from rusted pipes along the cement façade, and people passed wearing the sort of clothing I hadn't expected to need in California—knit watch caps and leather gloves, long coats and colorful woolen scarves. The residency director, Dr. Ernest Westphall, told us to line up for the official class photograph, and then the ten of us—five women and five men, all bright-eyed and vaguely self-conscious—jockeyed for the front-and-center positions while pretending not to care where we stood, until at last we'd assembled in two uneven rows. We had stethoscopes draped casually, almost elegantly, around our necks and pagers clipped to our belts. Each of us wore a pressed white coat with his or her surname embroidered in red script across the left side of the chest, after which were written the same two letters, *M* and *D*, as if being a doctor is a singular experience. When Westphall said "code blue" instead of "cheese," one short second before the shutter clicked and the flash exploded, most of us tried to smile.

We all got a copy of that photograph. Mine hangs above my office desk so our new recruits—I replaced Westphall five years ago as residency director—can see that I began just like them. (Of course, that isn't what they see; they notice only the dated clothes and our pockets stuffed with books, the contents of which they now carry in slim chrome or black handheld devices weighing less than the most benign pocket manual of yore.) Still, it's a great pre-digital-age photo, the sort of flawed, overly revealing glimpse of life that would be deleted these days, inadvertently constructing an artificially polished historical record. Four of us married within the group, and with the exception of Perla—I was the only one who remained close to her—we've all stayed in touch; you don't go through what we went through without forming intense bonds. We helped mold and define one another, both as doctors and as people. So it matters that the photograph exists. It's a reality check that we can hold up against our memories, a glimpse of what we were like untainted by all that followed.

In the snapshot, I'm standing in the center of the front row, wearing a red bow tie I still own and resting my arm on Josette Rivera's shoulder. She's pressing her hip comfortably into my thigh, both of us elated to have a familiar presence in our new city, three thousand miles from the medical school where we weren't particularly close despite being the only two Pinoy in the class. Josette looks like a child playing dress-up, clogs poking out from below a pantsuit that doesn't quite fit. Beside her, Nam Tran pulls a face. At thirty-one, he's the oldest in the group, but he has no intention of growing up. He's had to do that already in his life, first at a detention center in Hong Kong, then in a housing project in Lowell, Massachusetts. Behind him, Darius Shah, homeschooled through age thirteen, then Harvard cubed—B.S. '91, Ph.D. '95, M.D. '98—just twenty-two years old, stares at the camera as if daring it to challenge his right to be there. Diminutive Tea Tores, next on the upper step, has a wide, beautiful smile and plans to start a free clinic in the Central Valley for the children of farm laborers like her immigrant parents. Lamar Johnson, to her right, has an M.P.H. as well as an M.D. and muscles straining the sleeves of his shirt. Beside him, Sumita Banerjee has close-cropped hair, piercings the length of both ears, and a key ring hanging out of her pants. She's looking down at Althea Bukowski, who appears flushed, excitement and anxiety radiating from her moist blue eyes and bright orange lips. Only Marcus Rosenberg, standing beside Althea's half-turned back, isn't smiling. Finally, there is Perla, completing the front row. She's wearing a pale yellow blouse tucked into a black pencil skirt and a necklace made of tiny Lego blocks in primary colors. Unlike the rest of us, she looks intelligent and calm, mature and prepared. In other words, unlike the rest of us, she looks like a doctor.

The four patient-care wings at the General were distinguished only by signs labeled A, B, C, and D, as if the administration couldn't be bothered to provide more specific or interesting designations. I had trouble finding the lab, the stairs, my patients. The hallways all looked the same, especially at night: speckled off-white linoleum, fluorescent track lighting, stained, dingy walls that might once have been colored in a drab, subdued palette. In addition to my deficits in navigational skills, my new job also seemed to have exposed interpersonal inadequacies. My resident—a pediatrician, as I had started on the pediatrics service—hated me. Ditto, apparently, my patients and their parents, or so it seemed on those rare occasions when I managed to locate them. (I had no idea then that this generalized antipathy had little to do with me. My patients had spent enough time in the hospital to know that nurses provided comfort while doctors caused pain. My resident—one week remaining in his three-year training stint—was what I soon learned to call *toxic*, a phenomenon for which we now have jargon in the form of the words *burn out*, words evoked with increasing frequency by my exhausted, angry, dysphoric residents, who brandish them in order to secure time off for yoga and navel-gazing instead of just sucking it up as we did.) During that long first day of my internship, I worried that I wouldn't make it through my shift, much less the year.

Eighteen hours after our class photo was taken, I sat pen in hand over an open chart at a nurses' station thinking about the word *green*. Up until that night, if I thought of *green* at all in reference to myself, it was the noun I considered: the communal central greens of the East Coast towns and universities I'd unknowingly given up by moving to drought-plagued California; green, the slang term for money, which I hoped to have more of now that I'd finally be receiving a paycheck; and the green paint in the bathroom of my new apartment, made by combining my leftover yellow (bedroom) and blue (kitchen). By contrast, as an adjective, *green* had always seemed to refer to others, such as the patients at the refugee clinic where I'd volunteered during high school: the newly arrived Hmong elder we found squatting atop the handicapped toilet, his first pair of tennis shoes leaving footprints on the seat, or the Sudanese woman who burned herself and her two daughters after starting a fire in the living room of her new American home in order to cook dinner. And then suddenly, at the start of my internship, a practicing doctor for less than twenty-four hours, there I was, trying to access data from a computer in a hallway on the toddler-to-teen ward of a San Francisco hospital, living the adjective: "not in condition for a particular use; deficient in training, knowledge, or experience; not fully qualified for a particular function."

I needed to locate one Rayshawn Marley Harris, age two, whose IV had fallen out and required replacing. I had admitted four patients already—twin sisters with failure to thrive/rule out abuse, a three-year-old boy with illegal parents and new diabetes, and an FLK, or funny-looking kid, all the nurses knew and loved, who had an inherited metabolic disorder I'd never heard of and hoped to look up later. Six hours left on call, a full day ahead, there were seven other patients I barely knew with my name listed under Physician on their charts. Already I smelled different—of nervous sweat and institutional soap, of the fluids and filth of my patients, and of the breakdown products of the oversize muffins I had discovered and would consume every third or fourth night at midnight meal for the next three years.

Someone knocked on the side of the desk, and I startled. The nurse had strawberry-blonde hair and long silver baubles in each singly pierced ear.

"Need some Tylenol for a patient with a fever," she said.

I smiled and introduced myself without using the word *doctor*, motivated by the absurd and very green belief that the physician was just one member of the health care team and that the gorgeous nurse standing before me had chosen to ask me for the Tylenol because she found me as attractive as I found her.

The nurse blinked twice and glanced down at my ID badge.

"Just Tylenol," she said. "That's all I need."

The patient's name didn't sound familiar. I flipped through the index cards I'd inherited from an outgoing intern.

"He's not yours," she said.

"Who's taking care of him?"

"Does it matter?"

I thought, Is this her way of flirting? What if the patient had liver disease? Weak kidneys? What if his fever was the first sign of serious infection? I said, "I'll need to examine him."

The nurse shook her head, air huffing through her nostrils, and walked away.

Knowing I had failed some sort of test, but certain I was in the right, I decided to go after her, to protest and also to defend myself in case our encounter had been some bizarre San Francisco–style foreplay. I grabbed my cards and stethoscope off the table and pushed back from the desk.

I didn't see the second nurse until my rolling stool slammed into his legs. A medication tray fell, its hard plastic making a single sharp clap against the linoleum. Liquid medication spilled out of the little plastic cups and mixed together, a strangely beautiful blend of bright purple and lime green, of dark yellow and red and blue.

"I'm sorry—" I started.

"Oh, yes," the nurse said. "You are."

He was exactly my height and twice my age, with graying brown hair pulled back into a ponytail and cartoon-character tattoos down both forearms. I started laughing. Maybe it was the late hour or the sugar high or simply the release of all the tensions accrued during that long and stressful first day, but I laughed and laughed. At first the nurse just watched me, his mouth slightly open. Then he smiled. Not a friendly, *poor you* type smile, but a sadistic grin that darkened his eyes and revealed no teeth.

"Great," he said, projecting his voice as if he had an audience in that dim abandoned hallway at two A.M. "A blind *and* crazy new doctor. Just what we need around here."

I wish I'd thanked him. I rode the furious adrenaline he'd inspired in me through the next hour while Rayshawn cried, "Why, Mommy, why?" and I stuck him, over and over, until on my fourteenth try I finally hit a vein and restarted the antibiotics that kept him alive.

Our first intern outpatient clinic began during my thirtieth consecutive hour awake and in the hospital and ended four hours later when Dr. Westphall gathered the ten of us together for our inaugural monthly check-in. These were hour-long, after-clinic pizza-and-bitch sessions he claimed to have instituted by popular demand, as if our predecessors had begged him to let them spend more time in the hospital. In the small, windowless conference room, we interns sat upright in curved plastic chairs on three sides of the rectangular table, and Dr. Westphall lounged solo on the fourth side, a greasy paper plate in his lap, his black dress socks and Birkenstocks resting comfortably on the tabletop.

His topic was stress, anticipating it and coping with it.

"Anyone can start," he said. "This is meant to be informal."

No one spoke. We took huge bites of pizza, filling our mouths and then arranging our faces to suggest that we knew good manners precluded speech.

I ached to go home. The room was too hot, the chairs too hard, and what fool would discuss his secret fears with a group of strangers destined to become rivals for the chief residency and jobs? Dr. Westphall lifted a stray mushroom off his plate and dropped it into his mouth. Sprawled serenely at his end of the table, he didn't seem to mind waiting for a response to his question. Josette nudged me with her elbow. In medical school, I'd often announced events: the children's health advocacy group, the poverty 911 project, the family medicine interest group, and the homelessness outreach coalition. She knew I wasn't shy.

"Sleep," I said, ending the unpleasant silence. "I love to sleep."

Josette smiled and nodded. I winked at her. Dr. Westphall took a deep breath, then another bite of pizza.

"Like-wise," Lamar said. His New Orleans drawl made two words out of one. Like me, he had been on call the previous night, but in the morning he'd changed back into his dress shirt and slacks while I was still in rumpled scrubs.

Nam said, "I like to dive into a job headfirst, no worries."

"What about seeing your wife?" Dr. Westphall asked.

That got our attention. Nam didn't wear a ring, and it was the first we'd heard about him being married.

"Same deal," he answered with a grin. "Dive in, head-first . . ."

"Yo," said Sumita with an exaggerated swagger of her shoulders. "That's my line."

Dr. Westphall blushed. Of the interns, only Marc didn't laugh. "Does anybody ever do such a bad job you have to kick them out?" he asked.

Dr. Westphall wiped his mouth with a torn paper napkin and straightened his legs, visibly relieved to be back on safe conversational territory. "Never. And it's not that we wouldn't make other arrangements if a resident really couldn't do the work."

"Do we talk about medicine at all at this conference?" Darius asked.

"Not much," Dr. Westphall conceded before turning back to Marc. "Residency is tough but totally doable. People who get into med school generally have what it takes to be doctors. In my day, we lost about a quarter of the class. Still, if a man made it to the clinical years, as you all have, he knew he'd go the distance. What it comes down to is how much you want it."

I glanced at Josette, sure we were thinking the same thing: an old-timer's war story, a bullshit waste of time.

"*If a man . . .* ," Tea echoed, gazing at Dr. Westphall with her huge, unblinking eyes. "Wasn't there even one woman in your class?" She was so beautiful that three weeks of residency passed before any of us could have a normal conversation with her. I nudged Josette's arm with my elbow.

"Four, actually," said Dr. Westphall. "One of whom was my wife until she was killed by a drunk driver."

"Ouch," Josette whispered. "Also, touché."

Althea's brows lifted and her eyes widened as she gave the rest of us what we'd already come to call her "more later" look. Having gone to medical school in San Francisco, Althea could provide biographical sketches complete with bed partners for all the attending physicians we'd be working with.

Dr. Westphall moved his pizza plate onto the table and sat up. "Okay. If there's another topic you guys would like to discuss—"

Lamar held up a hand. "Sorry, Ernie. We're acting like children. We can do better with this topic. C'mon guys."

Ernie? I put down my slice.

"Down boy," Josette whispered.

"Seriously," Nam said. "We all knew what we were signing up for. Right? Now we just need to do the job."

"Or not," said Marc. "People do quit."

Sumita shook her head. "Yeah. Like one in a hundred thousand."

Perla leaned out over the table so she could see all of us and we could all see her. "I'm worried I don't know enough," she said. "Not that I'm stupid or careless, but that I won't even realize the mistake while I'm making it."

"Good," Dr. Westphall said. "Now we're talking."

But of course, *we* weren't. Darius doodled in the pepperoni grease on his plate. The rest of us studied the table.

Nam said, "You ask your resident."

Tea nodded. "Or your attending."

"You stuh-dy," Lamar drawled, looking only at his best pal *Ernie*. "And you question yourself and your actions at every branch in the decision-making tree."

I still hadn't thought of anything worth saying aloud, but it didn't matter: problem solved, case closed. Most of us relaxed a little.

"And what if you make a mistake anyway?" Perla asked.

Someone groaned. I couldn't tell who.

"Luckily," I said, "you'd only be killing a fellow human being."

Only Josette laughed.

Dr. Westphall turned to me. "Possibly, Dr. Bautista. And let's say that's exactly what happened. Then what?"

Lamar and I answered simultaneously. "You keep going."

For the remainder of the session, Dr. Westphall lectured us on the moral and legal benefits of admitting to one's missteps. Later, as we walked to our cars, Josette wondered whether Marc was depressed or just uptight. The idea of quitting was insane. We'd already devoted so many years to get to this point. Not just the four of medical school but all the years leading up to that, years when some people partied every weekend and traveled around the world with backpacks, years we couldn't get back.

For the next twelve months, turnover defined our lives. Daily, we sent patients home only to admit new ones, and every four weeks, we changed services, taking care of patients from newborns to the elderly and moving from wards to ER to intensive care. But it was only Perla for whom the theme extended to personal life and possessions as well; her boyfriends, stethoscopes, and even apartments also came and went with astonishing rapidity.

Her first apartment, a newly remodeled Victorian in the Castro, sold within two weeks of her arrival, subjecting her to that now-ubiquitous con, the fake-owner eviction. Though the new owner claimed he'd be living in what had been Perla's apartment, when she drove by a few months later, she took note of the red BMW convertible with Florida plates parked in the drive, and she knew the owner—a local—had found himself a more lucrative tenant. Her second place, the top floor of a single-family home in Cole Valley, was flooded after the homeowner fell asleep while smoking. (Josette, rotating at the university hospital, saw the blaze from the fifteenth-floor labor and delivery unit.) Next Perla moved to Golden Gate Heights, where she lived for nearly four months in a converted garage she entered and exited with the push of a button, her life-size Amelia Earhart and Marion Carstairs posters temporarily coming to rest on the ceiling. She settled in, let down her guard, and then the shortage of street parking pitted neighbor against neighbor, and snitching to the housing department led to a crackdown on illegal units. After seven months in San Francisco, she found herself homeless for the third time, camping out on Josette's living room floor in the Inner Richmond.

At first I thought the stress and drama of her housing and other upheavals explained what Perla did a few weeks later. She and Nam were the two interns in the ER on the night in question. In Nam's version of the events, it was a challenging shift but in no way exceptional.

Their evening began with the death of an eighty-year-old on home hospice whose children panicked at the last minute and brought him in. The next patient was a teenage girl who'd been raped at school but hadn't told anyone until—waiting with her family in their car in the Burger King drive-through line—she burst into tears. Then came the usual: shortness of breath and chest pain, sickle-cell exacerbations, fevers and overdoses and asthma attacks. Five hours later, the ER took the fallout from the latest Mission District gang showdown. In Trauma 1, Nam and the third-year worked on a corpse. Perla went into Trauma 2, where a sixteen-year-old with just the beginnings of a mustache lay curled up, clutching a blood-soaked pressure dressing to his side. There was one cop in the room and another at the door. The boy's left wrist was hand-cuffed to the side rail, and he cursed and thrashed as the nurse tried to take his pulse and blood pressure. Perla introduced herself, then began a head-to-toe survey to see if there was more than one wound.

"*Puta*," the kid said. "Don't fuck with me."

Before she could say that it might not be the best idea to call the doctor trying to help you a whore, the building shook. At first, Nam said, they all thought it was an earthquake. But the shaking continued at regular intervals, and soon they heard sirens and a voice shouting over a bullhorn. Later they learned that the dead guy's crew had pushed a Dumpster into the steel doors of the delivery bay over and over, trying to force their way through the back after being turned away at the ER's main entrance.

Perla stayed focused. She put a hand on the boy's cuffed wrist. "You're hurt," she said in Spanish, "and I want to help you."

"*Pinche cabrona*," he answered with a lewd wag of his tongue.

Nam said he thought that was the key moment, though a nurse later told me she wasn't sure. And Perla? She said she asked for the cops' help and, without uttering another word, did what needed doing. Then she wrote some orders and a quick note, and although the ER was overflowing, she turned off her pager, dropped it into Dr. Westphall's mailbox along with her ID badge, handed a two-word message for the ER attending to one of the nurses ("Quitting. Sorry."), got in her car, and drove away, leaving medicine for good.

Thirty-five minutes after Perla's departure, Josette's pager went off. She was in the outpatient clinic that month, which made her the jeopardy intern called in to take Perla's place. Since Perla was supposedly working that night, I'd slept over at Josette's. At the time, we still thought our relationship was secret, though it turned out that everyone in the program knew we'd hooked up, including Dr. Westphall.

As Josette dressed, I announced that Perla would head south toward sunshine but come to her senses by San Luis Obispo and turn around. In fact, Perla drove to a downtown hotel and went to bed. "Like a regular person does in the middle of the night," she told me when she finally resurfaced. "Just exactly like a regular person." The next day, she drove north, crossing the borders of California, Oregon, and Washington, and, fifteen hours after she left San Francisco, onto the ferry in Seattle that took her home to Whidbey Island.

I learned all this a few days later, when she called Josette about the things she'd left in the apartment and got me instead.

"I guess it was a really bad night," I offered.

"You don't get it, Rey," she said. "It wasn't about the kid or the shift or any of that."

"Explain it to me, then. Because you're right, I don't get it."

Perla sighed. "I don't know that it was any one thing exactly. Not the job, or the train wreck that was my living situation, or the fact that no way could I seem to keep a guy around for more than a couple of weeks. It was more like there was one person I thought I ought to be, and then there was the real me and what I really want from my life. I know that sounds trite and selfish, but I think that's it."

"I don't know," I said. "Sounds like you did what you felt you had to do."

I'd been lying on Josette's bed studying for part two of the medical board exams when Perla called. Now I sat up and closed the book. Although there were three good texts with slightly different formats, I'd made my selection based on the painting on the cover. It was by Joan Miró, one of my idols way back in college.

"It's okay," Perla said. "You don't have to be nice. I don't expect anyone to understand."

The painting showed a stick figure with huge eyes, one red and one blue, looking surprised and anxious. Surrealist or not, it was a portrait of every sick patient I'd ever taken care of. Maybe the painting got to me, because I didn't mean to say what I said next.

"Back in med school, I almost quit too. Twice." My room-mates at the time had known, but I hadn't told most of my friends or my parents, not then or since. And I'd never mentioned that phase of my life to Josette.

"No way," Perla said. "You're like Mr. Doctor."

"Not then. It was first year. I wasn't flunking out or anything, but I hated it. Felt like I was being squeezed into a tiny little box. What I really wanted to be was an art historian or a painter or some shit like that."

"What happened?"

"Are you kidding? No way did my parents immigrate to this country, then work their asses off so I could make art. I got over it. These days I might buy an art book or go to a museum now and then, but mostly I don't even think about that stuff anymore."

"Reymundo Bautista, I totally underestimated you."

"Yeah." I laughed. "I get that a lot."

We spent the next hour and a half talking—our first real conversation. I didn't hang up until Josette got home.

Josette still can't believe Perla left, not so much because of what she did to her career, but because of what she did to us, her supposed friends and co-interns. The program couldn't find a midyear replacement worth taking, so for the last five months of internship, when we all would have become toxic anyway, the remaining nine of us took on Perla's call nights and ER shifts in addition to our own. Since residency is equally about machismo and teamwork, Josette never complained, but she never forgave Perla either. Their friendship basically ended with Perla's departure, which was ironic, as it was only after she left that Perla and I really got to know each other. We talked often, generating huge long-distance bills during the months she was gone, and we began going to art shows and museums together when she moved back to San Francisco the next summer. Josette joined us sometimes, but she usually made some snide comment about Perla not really being the sort of person she wanted to hang out with in her scant spare time. I thought Josette was just being petty and maybe a little jealous, until seven years later, when our first child was born and I suggested Perla as godmother. Josette asked if I'd lost my mind. Surprised but still not understanding, I explained that Perla, unlike our other mostly medical friends, had time for parenting. Josette said there was no way a woman with so little integrity would ever be any kind of mother to her children. She called Perla unreliable and selfish and accused her of living in a perpetual state of adolescence, choosing jobs that allowed her to bypass the rites and obligations of normal adulthood. After that, I tended to see Perla when I knew Josette wouldn't be around.

Until the boy's fall, I had never considered that Josette might be at least partially right about my friend. Listening to Perla tell the story of that Wednesday on Bernal Hill, I was sure the rest of our group—Althea and Sumita are still around (and still together), Lamar was recruited to Stanford as the youngest department chair in that institution's history, and the others, though spread across the country, keep in touch—would be as shocked as I was by Perla's choices. They would wonder what physician, former or otherwise, wouldn't immediately step forward to help an injured child. They would argue that the basics of resuscitation—airway, breathing, circulation—are like riding a bike, and even if Perla couldn't remember how many compressions or how many breaths to give the kid, she at least should have started some kind of

CPR. In other words, just like me, they would have missed the point.

*　　*　　*

It's funny how random things can impact your life. Sometimes I wonder whether Perla would have told me about Dylan Hunter's accident, much less gone into such detail, if we hadn't had long-standing plans to hang out at my house that Saturday evening. Josette and our boys were spending the weekend with cousins in Fresno, a road trip that I, attending on the wards, had to miss.

Perla sat across from me at my kitchen table as she told the story, a bottle of Napa Valley cabernet and a plate of artisanal cheeses between us. I tried to picture the characters and events she described so vividly: the dogs and the scream, the injured boy on the road, the cell phone woman and the man with twins, and, of course, Perla herself. When she finished, I felt certain she wanted me to find out whether the boy had survived, and if so, how he was doing. Because she had hesitated initially and then done little to help, I assumed that she didn't feel comfortable calling the hospital.

"I'll check the ER log for you tomorrow," I offered. "Or, better yet, I'll swing by the peds ICU."

"Tomorrow's Sunday," she said.

"I'm on inpatient this month, so no days off."

"Lucky you," she said, laughing as she did each time I mentioned some of the less glamorous aspects of my work. "Anyway, there's no need. I saw him this morning."

I put down my wineglass. "You're kidding."

"The dad posted a 'Did you save my son?' sign on the hill's

219

upper gate. I called the number, and he asked me to stop by. The kid looks like hell, but they say he'll pull through." She smiled.

"You called?"

"Well, yeah. They wanted to be called. That's why Tom put up the sign."

"Tom?"

"Dylan's dad."

So now she was on a first-name basis with the family. I couldn't think of anything to say that wouldn't sound accusatory. How could Perla not see how badly she'd behaved? Didn't she know that dogs can never be put before humans? That once again she'd failed to follow through?

She poured herself more wine. With her trim, toned body and sun-bronzed hair, she looked as if she belonged in an advertisement for our new black leather barstools and the marble table Josette had said she couldn't live without.

"Actually, I think I've seen them around. They have a sheltie mix."

"You did recognize the boy!"

Perla laughed. "It's the dog I recognized, of course. And probably also Tom. He's seriously cute." She grinned. "But get this. Turns out the parents separated about two months ago, and Dylan was supposed to be going to his father's new apartment. He forgot what day it was. He shouldn't even have been on Bernal Hill!"

"Wait. You've met the father?"

She grinned again and tossed her hair. It caught the light from the colorful glass diffusers on the Italian light fixture I'd bought in exchange for agreeing that Josette could buy the table. Looking up at me through her bangs, she seemed relaxed and very happy. "In certain circles—mostly those where it's normal to walk around carrying one or more plastic bags of dog shit—I have quite the rep."

She just didn't get it.

"You have a medical degree," I said as calmly as I could, "and you knew what to do, but instead of starting the resuscitation, you checked on dogs and waited for the paramedics. It's entirely possible that you cost that boy part of his brain and some of his function." She could make up some bullshit story for herself if she wanted, but those were the facts.

Her face fell. She looked suddenly smaller and nothing like her usual brash self. She traced the rim of her wineglass with one finger, and I could almost feel her mind turning over what I'd said.

A moment earlier, I had felt angry at Perla and scared for her. Now I saw that if I could get her to face what she had done and not done on Bernal Hill, she could face everything else in her life too and things would finally come together for her. I put my hand on her forearm. "I'll help you with this. I'll be there with you every step of the way."

She removed my hand. "There's nothing I need help with," she said, her voice hard and so quiet I almost couldn't hear her. "All is good in my world of dogs and regular, predictable work schedules and people who understand that sometimes in life bad things just happen." She took a deep breath. "You, on the other hand . . . did you really never ask yourself why you stayed friends with me when no one else did?"

I decided to handle her as I would a difficult patient. I walked around to her side of the table and used my most empathetic facial expression and tone of voice. "You don't have to pretend with me. We could talk through it together, review the protocol, and then next time—"

"Rey!" she interrupted. "Stop. I'm done talking about the boy. I didn't tell you the story so you could diagnose and treat me. I told you because it was a horrible experience and you're supposed to be my friend. So, since me getting sympathy obviously isn't happening, let's move on to something more interesting and not ruin our Saturday night." She topped up our glasses and squinted slightly as she handed me mine. "Remind me. What sort of painting was it that you wanted to do after college?"

As my faithful companion at art shows for more than a decade, she knew the answer to that question as well as I did. "That's not what we're talking about."

"Isn't it? C'mon, Rey, you want to talk motive, means, and opportunity. Well all right, mister big shot doctor. But don't pretend you don't know what's really going on here."

I took her glass, placed it carefully on the table, and grabbed her arms. Then I pulled her toward me until her face was just inches from mine.

"Rey!" she screamed. "What the fuck?!"

Her lips and tongue were purple from the wine, and her breath smelled sharp from cheese and alcohol. I couldn't tell what I wanted more: to punish her or to devour her.

We stared at each other, breathing hard. She tried to wriggle free, but I wrapped her arms behind her back and held on tight. I could feel her, hot and rigid and foreign, along the length of my thighs and torso.

"Rey," she said. "Get off me."

My younger son often used the same words when the older one had him pinned. I imagined my boys bursting through the front door, home a day early and eager to see Daddy, with Josette following close behind.

I let go. Perla grabbed her purse off the floor. I sat down in what had been her chair. "Oh shit," I said. "Oh my God."

Seconds later, the front door banged shut.

*   *   *

Over the next few weeks, I caught sight of Perla several times at the general—in the cafeteria she'd always griped about, on the pediatrics unit I loved and she dreaded, and in the stairwell we'd both always preferred to the elevators. If she saw me, she didn't let on. But apparently Althea also ran into Perla at SFGH, and the two of them rekindled their friendship. Althea said that Perla visited the boy most days around lunchtime—between her morning and afternoon dog groups, I figured—even though Dylan was too impaired to recognize his parents, much less appreciate a stranger's attentions. Eventually Perla admitted to Althea that her presence at the hospital had more to do with the father than the son; she and Tom Hunter were dating.

For a while I worried that Perla would say something about what happened that night in my kitchen, but I don't think she will. Knowing Perla, she probably just put the whole thing behind her and moved on.

Not me. After she left, I cleaned up, finishing off the bottle of cabernet. Then I went into the den and looked up at my art books. I keep them on the top shelf of our huge built-in bookcase, just under the ceiling's polished, naked beams and well out of the children's reach. They all have moved with me, my painters and sculptors, from East Coast to West, from apartment to starter house to the three-bedroom Potrero Hill home Josette and I recently bought, with its views of downtown and the East Bay. It's a beautiful house, and I am very pleased to provide such a home for my family.

Over the winter holidays, Josette noticed that I was spending more time with my art books, and she bought me a drawing pad, charcoals, and watercolors. Now I occasionally steal away from work, drive up to Bernal Hill, and plant myself on a patch of grass or red rock. Then, for thirty or forty minutes, I capture some piece of my world, upping the ante on the challenge to my fledgling skill set and offering a slight nod to modernism by using charcoal when watercolor might be best, and vice versa. So far I have rendered a giant ant colony against a tiny downtown San Francisco skyline; the famous Bernal coyote slouching in the high winter grass, her eyes as sentient as any human's and the backlit sky framing Mount Diablo in the distance; and a pack of dogs running down the pedestrian-only portion of Bernal Heights Boulevard alongside a trim, athletic woman, the wind blowing fur and hair, and their bodies loose and carefree, as if they might keep running forever.

Returning to work after such jaunts, I often pause before that internship photograph hanging behind my office desk. I notice not just the clothing and facial expressions but our positions and postures on the steps as well: Josette, shy and awkward, laying claim to me with her hip; Lamar flexing his muscles; Nam pretending he isn't taking seriously the business of being a doctor; and Sumita and Althea positioned both close enough to each other and far enough apart to heighten the charge between them. I stand front and center, a place I fought for, while Perla stands off to one side, at the edge of the frame. It's funny, but I've only just recently realized that if we have changed over the years, it's only in the most superficial of ways, and also that most of us have ended up right where we wanted to be that very first day.

THE PROMISE

HATTIE ROBINSON WAS A jazz singer in the 1930s, the only female black labor leader in Northern California in the '50s, and a regular in the Letters to the Editor section of the *San Francisco Chronicle* for decades. At ninety-six, she began nude painting—not portraiture of disrobed others, but art made by her in a totally naked state and in the absence of most other social conventions. I met her the following summer, called to her home by a social worker for Adult Protective Services.

I'd recently given up my clinic and academic responsibilities as the family medicine program director at San Francisco General, but unwilling to fully succumb to retirement, I had begun spending my mornings making house calls to patients in homes and apartments across the city. My wife, Carly, a former advertising executive, suggested that I call my new venture From Projects to Penthouses. Throughout the twenty years of what had been for both of us a midlife second marriage, Carly had expressed both pride and fascinated repulsion at how I sometimes spent my days. She felt that a catchy, accurate, but possibly misleading title might be my only hope of building a viable practice.

As it turned out, no marketing was necessary. More so than most urban centers, San Francisco's world-famous hills have produced a city replete with ancient and otherwise disabled people rendered invisible by their inability to go out. Referrals poured in by word of mouth alone, and within months of starting the practice, I had to increase my work hours to keep pace with demand; I couldn't abide the very real possibility that the time a potential client spent on my waiting list might exceed his or her life expectancy. Carly noted that most retirements looked significantly different from mine, but I could see no better way to spend my time than to offer patients good care and a dignified death at home.

The social worker told me that Hattie had been seen in the emergency department several times in the space of a month, each time for something silly: an ingrown nail, a bruise not black and fresh but with a halo of lighter brown, a cut so small no sutures were needed. Each time, her daughter brought her in, dropped her off, and disappeared. Each time, the daughter was slow to return when the hospital called to say there was no reason to keep her mother.

They lived in a worn but still handsome Victorian in the Lower Haight, a neighborhood of drug addicts, pierced and tattooed young professionals, and people like Hattie, who predated not only the current counterculture fashionistas but also their flower child predecessors. In the broad, high-ceilinged foyer, I was greeted by a huge Benin plaque and African masks elaborately decorated with feathers and what looked like real human hair. Framed reprints of book covers lined the long, wood-paneled hallway in pairs: *Cane* and *Their Eyes Were Watching God*, *Another Country* and *Native Son*,

Black Fire and *Letter from Birmingham City Jail*, *Beloved* and *The Color Purple*. Just before we turned into the bedroom, a collage of the numbers 1, 9, and 3 provided the single false note in an otherwise impressive decor. Nineteen thirty-one, explained Hattie's daughter, Patricia, was the year of her parents' marriage. They lived in Harlem then, but came to San Francisco after the war.

Hattie stood in one corner of her room, naked and painting as promised. She sang an aria of sorts and turned circles on a tired patch of carpet. When at last I got her attention, she couldn't tell me who she was or where, though she remembered how to scream and scratch and kick, all of which she did when I examined her, careful to steer clear of the urine-soaked rug and elaborate swirls of stool on the walls and bed. (Later, Carly cringed at these graphic details when I told her about my new patient. "Oh God," she said. "I had no idea it could get that bad.")

When I finished my evaluation, Patricia brought two chairs in from the kitchen and said, "Momma always did tell me she planned to live forever, but no way did either of us ever imagine something like this."

"What did you imagine?" I asked.

Patricia glanced up at me, surprised. "I suppose we thought she'd be like my daddy. He took sixteen pills a day and needed a wheelchair his last two years, but he was still himself, right up to the end." She pointed at her mother's vanity, where a halo of photographs encircled the mirror: Hattie and a bald man about my age waving from a car beside Willie Brown; Hattie speaking through a bullhorn outside a factory while the same man—younger and with a full head of hair—stood to one side holding a picket sign; Hattie posing in front of the Victorian at a time when the paint looked fresh and new, while the man—middle-aged but sporty-looking despite the cane in his left hand—grinned up at her.

"So now you're wondering how best to take care of your mother?" I asked.

Patricia nodded and looked across the room. Hattie sat on the sofa rapidly turning the curled pages of an old magazine.

Seeing Patricia's profile, I realized she too was quite old, early seventies at least. ("*Quite old*," Carly said that evening with a laugh. "Should I remind you of your own birth date?")

"Sometimes," I said to Patricia, "we can make an educated guess about what a person would have wanted based on their choices when they could make their own decisions. How did your mother handle her health? Did she go for regular check-ups or just see a doctor when she got sick?"

Patricia threw back her head and hooted. "Mother never did care for doctors, said they were always thinking they knew best and how could some stranger who saw you once or twice a year know what was best?" She smiled. "No offense, Dr. West-phall."

The tone of her apology concerned me. It was the overly accommodating tone of a caregiver pretending that she wasn't exhausted and angry and utterly convinced that there wasn't anything that could be done to improve her situation.

"But your mother did see someone occasionally?"

"Not unless I dragged her. And that never did any good anyhow, because she'd just refuse the mammogram or Pap smear or whatever else they wanted to give her."

That morning, I spent more time with daughter than with mother. We talked of Hattie's weight loss and her incontinence and how hard she fought when Patricia tried to clean her up. And then we discussed what could be done and what couldn't, what should be done and what shouldn't. When I proposed a fairly conservative approach to Hattie's care, Patricia said, "Whatever you think, doctor. You're the expert, not me."

"But you're the one who's with her twenty-four seven."

"Ain't that the truth." She went to the window. She had a hitch in her step I hadn't noticed earlier, and I wondered what sort of medical problems she had of her own. Just as I was about to break the silence, she turned with her hand outstretched. "Thank you for coming, Dr. Westphall. You've been a big help already. Mother and I will look forward to seeing you again."

As I was leaving, Hattie stood, paintbrush in hand, and said, "Let's tulip the lampshade while climbing the cradle." I made the hospice referral from my car before pulling away from the house. "No rush," I told the intake nurse. "This could take months."

Three days later, I received a message from Patricia that Hattie was being admitted to the hospital. She had a fever and didn't seem able to move her left side. When they'd put a catheter into her bladder, pus drooled into the bag.

"Comfort care," I told the residents. *Comfort care*, I wrote in my note.

That night Hattie got three IVs, five medications, a spinal tap, a CAT scan, and a Posey vest restraint. Together, teams of neurologists and radiologists localized the lesion in her brain. She'd had a massive stroke, the result of a clot in the artery that controlled her right side as well as her ability to speak and swallow. When I inquired why my orders had been ignored, the intern said there was no advance directive and her attending didn't want to withhold care just because the patient was old.

When I called the attending, he said the daughter had told him to do what he thought best.

"But this isn't what Hattie wants," I argued.

"There's no advance directive," he said. "You can't know what she wants." It was a point I had to concede.

I phoned the old Victorian five times that morning and continued calling over the following several days but never reached Patricia. I assumed she was at the hospital or that she'd taken advantage of her mother's absence to run some errands or go out with her friends. (Carly, the cynic, suggested that maybe Patricia had caller ID and no interest in speaking to me.)

On her fifth day in the hospital, Hattie developed black heels and a chasm around her tailbone. A white cotton cuff looped around her left wrist, which was fixed to the metal bed frame by two long straps tied with bulky knots. Her right arm lay flaccid on the sheet, the hand already beginning to curl in on itself. She couldn't speak, but she looked my way when I spoke to her in the singsong voice I generally reserve for pets and my youngest grandchildren. Her left arm bucked against its tether, and a feeding tube hung from her right nostril, its other end disappearing down the back of her throat. Every few seconds, the machine beside her bed clicked, and a drop of liquid food, pale and pasty, fell into the clear plastic tubing and made its slow way to her stomach. (I had a similar tube once myself, in medical school; they made us insert them into one another in hopes of teaching both proper technique and appropriate restraint. I gagged repeatedly, the plastic rod an assault on the natural order of what does and does not belong in the human body. I tried to be strong but lasted only seconds. Worse, although I'd skipped breakfast as instructed, after my lab partner pulled out the tube, I heaved into a trash can. And I wasn't the only one. That night, I told Carly that I'd have to be tied down or drugged to let anyone do that to me again.)

At the end of the week, the intern caring for Hattie left a message on my voice mail. "Ms. Robinson's rallying," she said. "Her numbers look good." Code words for *I want her off my service*.

We've all spoken similar words.

I called back, and the intern said they'd filled out the paperwork for a local nursing home. I told her I only did house calls, but I'd be happy to continue caring for Hattie if her daughter wanted to try taking care of her at home.

I didn't hear from the intern again and so went on with my life and work, as one must. ("How can you?" Carly sometimes asks lately. To which I answer, "How can I not?" I want to help, and often I do, but my role comes with inherent limitations. What's more, I see only a sliver of each family's story, so it's impossible to judge decisions that might equally be considered selfish or the single available route to legitimate salvation.)

"It's disgusting," Carly declared when I told her what had happened to Hattie. We'd driven out to the Mission District to try the latest Nuevo Latino sensation, a Peruvian restaurant that blended traditional flavors and California cuisine.

"I think you mean shameful."

Carly speared a hunk of halibut from the bowl of ceviche between us and waved it in the air as she spoke. "No, I mean disgusting. What's shameful is your behavior. Can't you do something for the poor woman? Isn't that your duty, if not as a doctor, then at least as a decent human being?"

I spotted a small curl of green chili in the ceviche and avoided it. Spicy foods had begun giving me indigestion.

"I couldn't reach the daughter. I don't go to nursing homes any more than I go to San Jose or Afghanistan. What exactly do you think I should be doing?"

Carly raised her eyebrows and lowered her voice. The restaurant had received a bomb in the noise-rating category, so I had to read her lips to understand her.

"*Help* her. And stop being obnoxious; you know perfectly well what I mean. According to her daughter, her wishes were clear enough."

I put down my fork. Carly, her hair pulled sleekly back into a perfect bun to show off the dangling diamond earrings I'd bought for her birthday, cut into a small fish laid upon a bed of wilted greens and enormous white corn kernels. I put my hand over hers.

"What if I came home one night and said I'd strangled Hattie? Put a pillow over her head? Injected—"

Carly shook off my hand. "Stop it! I didn't mean that. You know I didn't mean that."

"Is there a difference?"

"There has to be."

She abandoned the serving spoon and fork. Beside us, a young foursome argued the pros and cons of public and private education.

Carly folded and refolded her napkin. I lifted fish and accoutrements first onto her plate, then onto my own. The restaurant deserved its three stars; the fish melted in my mouth.

"What if it were me?" Carly asked. "If I were like Hattie is? Would you help me?"

For the past couple of years, Carly had had trouble coming up with names of acquaintances and movies we'd seen, little slips that might have been part of normal aging. At first, like many of our friends, we'd made jokes about senior moments. Then my daughter had told me that Carly called our grandson twice the same morning to sing "Happy Birthday," and a short while later she'd turned the wrong way up a one-way street and didn't notice until a car came toward her head-on.

I reached for her hand again and held it tight enough that she couldn't pull away. "Whatever happens, I'll take care of you."

Our next course arrived, though Carly hadn't even begun her fish.

"Poor service," she said. "I hate that."

One of the men in the young foursome beside us said, "Then you'll have to move to Marin or Palo Alto. I mean, if you really believe that's what's good for a child."

"Listen," I said. "If things get bad—and I'm saying *if*—I won't let it get to where Hattie is now. I promise."

But Carly had been my wife long enough to know this was a promise I might not be able to keep. Prior to the stroke, Hattie hadn't had so much as a cold in the long years of her dementia.

We looked at each other across the table. Despite the room's thunderous mix of music and conversation, I had the sensation that I could quite clearly hear my own pulse.

"Eat your dinner," Carly said finally. "It's getting cold."

Seven months after Hattie's hospitalization, I made an exception to my usual practice and went to the large skilled-nursing facility in the Western Addition, where a patient of mine had been taken temporarily upon the hospitalization of his wife. Since it was my first visit to the institution about which I'd heard both horror stories and great praise, when the administrator offered me a tour, I accepted.

Hattie sat in a recliner in a large room labeled ACTIVITIES, though the only apparent activity of the many patients parked in two neat rows of wheelchairs and recliners was sleeping.

"The recreational therapist must be on break," said my guide.

Walking past, I almost didn't recognize Hattie. She'd gained weight and lost hair, but her left hand gave her away. It wove through the air, fluid and purposeful, as if she were painting a large, invisible canvas. I went over to pay my respects. Standing by her bed, I could smell the sweet liquid now entering her body through a tube that disappeared under her bedcovers and also its inevitable aftermath, pungent and foul in what must have been a full diaper. Greasy hair splattered her forehead, and she wore a faded patient gown imprinted on the chest with the words CALIFORNIA PACIFIC MEDICAL CENTER. Looking around, I saw that they all wore them, though the colors and hospital names varied: ST. LUKE'S HOSPITAL; UCSF; ST. MARY'S MEDICAL CENTER; SAN FRANCISCO GENERAL. A parallel image flashed through my mind: my grandson's birthday party, where each small boy wore the jersey of his favorite major-league team.

Across the room, my guide looked at his watch. I walked back between the twin rows of patients to rejoin him and resume my tour.

I tried reaching Patricia that evening and discovered that the phone number had been disconnected. The next day, I drove by the old Victorian and saw that it had recently been sold. The following week, though I could more efficiently have phoned or faxed, I made a second trip to the nursing facility to discharge my patient home to his wife. On that visit I didn't check in with the administrator, just walked around, peering into rooms until I found Hattie's. (It's an unspoken truth that a man of my age and race with a stethoscope slung over his shoulder and an authoritative expression has free rein in most medical settings.)

When I said hello to Hattie, she farted. Her left hand swooped, dived, fluttered, and her feeding machine clicked and purred. Unlike the magnificent Victorian house with its art and photographs, the walls and surfaces of Hattie's current personal space offered no clues about her life. On her bedside table lay a box of blue latex gloves, size small, and a cheap black barbershop comb. I used the comb to move the hair off her face and neck. She blinked once—a reflex—then kept painting the air. After just three passes of the comb through her hair, flakes of skin covered the black plastic like pox. I looked around but found myself the only fully sentient and still-functional person in the room. Hattie's roommate's eyes were open but staring into some space to which I didn't have access.

I pulled the curtain around Hattie's bed, opened my work-bag, and from the forest of syringe- and tourniquet- and swab-filled plastic bags, selected the one I'd packed that morning with Hattie in mind. Donning gloves, I poured the liquid into one palm and then rubbed the waterless shampoo into Hattie's scalp. She leaned into my hands like a kitten. With her hair returned to a thin but lustrous white, I washed her face, applied Carly's moisture cream to her cheeks and forehead, and put Vaseline on her lips. I hadn't asked to borrow Carly's cream but felt sure she wouldn't mind.

Before leaving, I placed the toiletries on Hattie's bedside table, took a business card out of my pocket, and circled my phone number. Then I wrote "call anytime" beside my name and propped the card against the box of latex gloves. At the hallway door I turned and, with a glance at Hattie, fingered the loaded syringe in my jacket pocket. It was a flu shot for my other patient, but it might have been anything.

A MEDICAL STORY

S O MUCH OF MEDICINE is stories. Or potential stories. For example: the year before I began doing palliative care, I visited an elderly couple in an apartment complex named for Martin Luther King. Rogelio said that was the only good thing about the place. Beer bottles and cigarette butts ornamented the sidewalk; urine and streaks of barely clotted blood garnished the walls. A woman reeking of dust and sweat reached for my jacket and stumbled, smearing saliva on my sleeve. The guard checked me over, then buzzed me in, showed me where to sign, told me to take the elevator, not the stairs. The elevator wobbled and creaked. On its walls were faded admonitions about garbage disposal and the use of fire escapes printed in English, Spanish, Chinese, Russian, and Tagalog. Rogelio and Carina lived on the fifth floor, in the last apartment along a narrow, windowless corridor. Someone had obliterated the hallway lights. I turned on my otoscope and held it in front of me to light my way. It helped just enough.

By the time I finished my eight years of medical training—the year I met Rogelio and Carina—I had abandoned the midwestern friends of my childhood, the mountain biking I'd taken up with such enthusiasm upon moving to San Francisco, the ability to sustain a romantic relationship, and any reading that artfully conjured the pain of others or took longer than half an hour to complete. By way of trade, I had acquired expertise in internal medicine, a twenty-pound diabetic cat with a fondness for sushi, and a spacious apartment on Russian Hill from which I could walk to Chinatown, North Beach, and Fort Mason. Still unsure of what I wanted from my career, I signed up for a year of locum tenens, filling in for doctors on vacation or family leave, moving from one clinic or hospital to another every few weeks or months, and sometimes juggling more than one job at a time in hopes of paying off my student loans before I turned forty.

Very quickly, stories of lives damaged, unnoticed, and discounted accumulated in my imagination. I could neither forget nor make sense of them, so I began taking notes and then signed up for a writing class online in hopes of capturing and better understanding my work and my patients' lives. The class reminded me of the person I'd been before my medical training—a happy, caring person I liked and hoped to become again—but the time I devoted to writing was time not spent reading medicine or making money. I began to wonder what counted as meaningful work and, by extension, as a meaningful life. I didn't see that those questions linked my writing to medicine as surely as did my subject, each story the tale of a patient or doctor I knew or had heard about.

So many medical stories are about death, or potential death. From the fifth floor of the Martin Luther King apartments, where I occasionally visited them as part of an outreach team for an understaffed neighborhood health center, Rogelio watched helplessly as his wife disappeared. He was a tiny man, so frail that once, when I passed him with only a foot of space between us, he wobbled, clutching his walker as if it were the safety bar on a roller coaster. His wife, Carina, sat smiling and mute in a wheelchair, fat and healthy except for her brain, a not so vital organ if you have the right husband.

Each visit was the same. Rogelio wouldn't discuss any of his many worrisome diagnoses, just his guess about how much longer their luck would last. And he wouldn't consider a nursing home. With a nod at the caregiver, he'd say, "I must watch them with her." And, "I am so lonely."

The aide sat beside her charge, engrossed in a soap opera. Carina smiled. When I left, Rogelio squeezed my arm and whispered, "She must die first. Promise me."

Young and hung up on mistaken if well-intentioned notions of professional integrity, I made no promises.

Medical training had done something to my attention span. In high school and college, I had kept journals and turned out five- to fifteen-page essays on a biweekly basis. During residency, I had worked eighty-hour weeks and thought nothing of it. Having finished my training, I wanted nine hours of sleep a night, weekends off, and another human being with whom to share those large swaths of unstructured time. Though I aspired to write articles that told a moving story, then explained how the world needed to change so that, for example, people like Rogelio and Carina would be better cared for and safer, I couldn't seem to generate more than a paragraph at a time. Worse, more often than not, I produced writing best described as minimalist, sardonic, and self-referential.

One of the earliest pieces I wrote was called "Guilt," and it was a one-liner:

If she spent half as much time working as she did feeling guilty about not working enough, she wouldn't have to feel so guilty.

The night I finished that piece, I invited over a man who'd had a crush on me for years. He was a friend of a friend who'd landed in San Francisco shortly after I did and bicycle commuted sixty miles a day to and from the Redwood City children's video game start-up, where he worked as creative director. When he arrived, I went into the kitchen to pour us some wine, and when I returned to the living room, he was holding my story.

"What's this?" he asked.

"An essay."

"It's a good start."

"It's done."

He sat on the couch, downed half his wine, and read the piece again.

"I get it," he said finally. "It's like one of those witty, paradigmatic, semiautobiographical thirty-page essays reduced to a single sentence?"

I kissed him. That night, we began dating.

Doctors, you see, aren't so different from patients. Every day we hope someone will see past our elaborate and very impressive window display to the jumble of expired products weighing down the shelves and choking the aisles of our psyches.

This is a classic medical story: It was three in the morning. I was covering the night shift at a small Catholic hospital when I was called to see a patient seven hours dead and zipped into a white plastic pouch brought back up from the morgue. He had been dying for so long—first at home and, more recently, in the hospital—that no one had bothered to call a doctor when his heart stopped. Legally, he was still alive.

The nurses and aides—two Filipinas and a plus-size Barbadian with a strong, charming accent—wouldn't go into the room. They clustered, nervous and giggling, just outside the door, speaking of spirits and ghosts. The room was all dim lights and long shadows, the body bag glowing as I pulled at the long central zipper, then parted the plastic edges. I placed my stethoscope on the patient's cold chest, and it teetered on his ribs. I thought, As if nurses don't know death. As if the diagnosis couldn't have been made by the tech in the morgue.

A little while later, since they were the only other people awake at that hour of the morning, I told the story to the doctors and nurses in the emergency department downstairs. I knew it was disrespectful of the patient, but I couldn't help myself. He was so dead. We had a good laugh, then went back to work.

Of course, what most doctors call stories aren't really stories at all. They're anecdotes, which my Webster's dictionary tells me are "usu. short narrative(s) of an interesting, amusing, or biographical incident."

Here's an example of one I'd forgotten until I was sent to Chinese Hospital for a two-week stint and it turned out that what they needed was a surgeon, not an internist:

As a medical student, I cut off a woman's foot. I was doing my required surgery rotation, and one night, around midnight, I was told to go down to the emergency department to see a woman whose foot hurt. All these years later, I can't remember her exact age, though I remember that she looked decades younger than what it said on the chart. Her foot was gangrenous; it must have been hurting for weeks. Her brother had brought her in and said she'd probably hurt herself gardening. Or maybe that was just how she liked to spend her time. She was unmarried, lived alone in the family home where she'd been born the better part of a century earlier, and had never seen a doctor. No childhood vaccinations, no broken bones. "She never even catches colds," said her brother.

She was overweight, so probably she'd been diabetic for years.

I could easily picture her in one of the many similar small houses in Ingleside near the 280 freeway. A well-kept but worn house, everything faded, its contents exactly as they had been when her parents were alive and slowly filled their home with furniture, commemorative plates, and children. Everything left just as it had been when the parents died. A dark, quiet place with a pervasive odor of age and dust, of mildew and microwave dinners and the fresh flowers she sometimes brought in from the garden.

This was toward the end of my two months on surgery, so I did the admission without much help. There was no question of what needed to be done.

The next morning, the surgery resident offered me the foot.

His exact words were, "If you want it, it's all yours."

I thought, Why not? When will I ever get another chance to cut off a foot?

Many doctors would call that a story, though it's not: no conflict, no crisis, no resolution. It is, as we like to say in medicine, necessary but not sufficient that the description is vivid and detailed and true. Nor does learning more about me, a key character and potential protagonist, guarantee the transformation of anecdote to story. Case in point: my first day on surgery, as the attending and residents worked for more than six hours to remove and reattach parts of a man's intestine, I marveled that anyone could survive an operation, their innards exposed to the air for all those hours, cut and rearranged, sewn and stapled like cloth or paper or aluminum siding, and then wake up, groggy to be sure and in some discomfort, but basically fine—better, in fact, than prior to the operation. But the second day of the rotation, standing through a few quickie surgeries (one appendix, one gallbladder, and one hernia) and then another six-hour intestinal procedure, I felt like Ronald Reagan on his visit to the Redwoods: seen one, seen 'em all. I realized then that I wanted to take care of patients, not parts, wanted conversation and connection, not instrumentation, resection, and redecoration. Though I couldn't have articulated it correctly at the time, what inspired me most in medicine was the opportunity to go beyond everyday exposition to life's trigger problems and rising action, its culminations, turning points, and denouements.

In contrast to anecdote, story—at least in the literary sense—offers so much more: narrative arc, movement, unification of action, irrevocable change. Meaning.

It seemed that in the process of becoming a doctor, I'd also become quite literal, unable to bend fact for the sake of drama or significance. Or perhaps I'd always been that way, and that was why I'd become a doctor in the first place. In any case, having come up short in my attempts at advocacy journalism, I decided to try to exercise my creative muscles by writing fiction, in the hope that it would help me move beyond my own myopic and overly anecdotal point of view to some larger truth with a capital *T.*

To my surprise, most of my earliest stories contained a protagonist who could invariably be described as a young female doctor who was always having to adjust to new hospitals and patients and couldn't quite figure out what she wanted to do with her life. Nevertheless, I avoided the first person unless the "I" was so certifiably crazy that no one could possibly mistake her for me. Most of the time I chose a classical, all-knowing, and thus appropriately doctorly narrator. Physicians, we learned in medical school, should function as objective interpreters of other people's behaviors, confidently providing reflections, judgments, compassion, and truths at key moments as the action unfolds. In theory, as in great eighteenth-century novels, that stance made good sense; in real life, unlike in fiction, I sometimes found it hard to manage.

This is an old story; most doctors have one that's more or less the same.

I'd been sent to a large group practice near the old Mount Zion Hospital. Two hours into an overbooked clinic of patients I didn't know, Rose Fong walked in off the street with a funny feeling in her chest. The nurse said she didn't look good and put her into a room right away. Rose said she'd never had the squeezing feeling in her heart before and also that she wanted a sandwich. "Please," she said to me in precisely articulated, very slightly accented English. "I am so hungry." The T waves on her EKG, normally tiny upside-down U's, looked like tombstones, tall and broad and evil. *Tombstones* is the actual medical term, not a word I slipped into my story for dramatic effect.

As we waited for the ambulance, Rose said, "I don't care what kind—ham, tuna, cheese, even peanut butter." Her EKG went up down, up down, slithering like a snake—a pattern even more distressing than tombstones.

"Just a glass of milk," she begged as the paramedics arrived. Then she mentioned nausea, and her EKG became a line, straight as an arrow, and it stayed that way for the next forty-five minutes as we tried unsuccessfully to save her.

Among us locums docs, the joke went: the good patients died and the bad ones stuck around to torment you. A lie. Both died, at least now and then. What was true was that deaths were easier than primary care. Fewer phone calls. No prescriptions.

If you were a nice locums, a team player, you'd fill out all the appropriate forms before finishing your placement so all the doc you were covering for had to do on his or her return was send a note to the family.

In other words: no epic account of an impoverished provincial childhood, young love, migration halfway around the world, pursuit of the American dream, invisible illness, sudden death, and small, orphaned children—just a condolence card.

The night of her death, I told my boyfriend that all I'd been able to think about for the rest of the day was how I wished I'd given Rose a sandwich.

Some medical stories never get told in quite the right way. Such stories almost always involve a doctor behaving badly according to certain widely accepted though rarely articulated codes of physician conduct. This is the sort of story you tell one way if you're its protagonist, unconsciously but quite understandably suppressing and internalizing, then forgetting certain details while exaggerating and elaborating others. If, on the other hand, you were a secondary player, such as— hypothetically speaking, of course—a senior doctor who owned a large group practice and did nothing more than peer over shoulders during a prolonged and unsuccessful resuscitation, you are free to tell the story in a completely different way, making modifications for the sake of humor and misplaced sympathy and, most important by far, to discourage future lawsuits against the practice by relatives of the deceased, and you are free to do so whether or not such alterations occur at the expense of the facts, such as the poor prognosis associated with tombstones on an EKG, the patient's accented but actually entirely intelligible pronunciation of the names of certain types of sandwiches, and a somewhat inexperienced junior colleague's well-meaning but perhaps ill-advised—possibly even lethal—decision to get an EKG before calling 911.

Some people believe this means the story has been told. Those same people, while fluent in the languages of shame and humiliation, of ass kicking and ass covering, lack even the most rudimentary understanding of point of view.

Once upon a time, Rogelio and Carina had four children. The oldest died in Nicaragua of what sounded like cancer but might have been the sort of infectious disease we don't see much in the United States. The third and fourth died in a school bus accident in El Paso; they were nine and ten at the time. Their only surviving child, a daughter, married a man who moved a lot for work. She lived in Chicago when I met her parents, but soon thereafter she moved to Raleigh-Durham, then Orlando. I gathered that there were grandchildren but also that there wasn't money or time for visits.

Sometimes in medicine, entering a story in medias res can be problematic. In those instances, you wonder what you're missing and assume the worst: that frail Rogelio used to cheat on Carina, and his current kindness stemmed from guilt and retribution; that, frustrated by failures at work, the inability to save enough for a down payment on a house, or the death of his sons, he ignored, abused, or disparaged his daughter, who consequently wanted little or nothing to do with him; that the son-in-law's frequent moves stemmed not from a quest for more lucrative work, but from a need to escape the law; that the daughter wanted her mother dead so she could inherit the earrings, necklace, and bracelet bought in better times and worn even now, day and night, over cornflower-blue flannel pajamas and floral housedresses.

The possible backstories, limitless and nefarious, can make you question a patient's or family member's every plea or explanation and search the subtext of even the most straightforward comments. Such as when Rogelio and Carina's daughter said, "You're too kind," in reference to my having gone out of my way to make sure her mother got the right antibiotic for the pneumonia that might otherwise have killed her, when what she might have meant was *I wish you hadn't.*

It's rare but not unheard of for a medical story to start as an anecdote but—because it appears to be about one thing when really it's about something else entirely—end up one step closer to being an actual and successful story, one with what might almost qualify as an Aristotelian reversal. In that sort of story, you get to the end and it changes everything. Such as the story I told my increasingly serious boyfriend about Svetlana Kamenetsky, a patient I cared for in the large clinic near Mount Zion, where I ended up working for more than six months, covering first the regular doctor's preterm labor and then her three-month maternity leave.

Respecting Russian tradition and the family's well-documented requests in the chart, I didn't mention bone marrow failure to Svetlana. She went for transfusions and never asked why. Words like *Chernobyl* and *mortuary* were spoken only furtively, in the tiny hallway outside my exam room, whispered over the screeches and whoops of the children running in and out of the waiting area shared with the pediatrics clinic next door. One afternoon, when I put Svetlana last on my schedule and asked that the entire family be present so we could discuss the few remaining options for treatment, she said never in the Soviet Union did they have a doctor so nice. She said, "We are very thank you," and the entire family— Svetlana, sunken and swollen, gray and dying; her ancient parents; her husband and brother; even the teenage children— were all smiles.

Hearing the story to that point, my beloved boyfriend was also all smiles. But then I told him how sometimes at work I felt like a fraud, pulling options and assertions with the bright colors and plasticity of Play-Doh from the empty pockets of my long white coat. Right away, my boyfriend stopped smiling, which was good, because boyfriends, like patients, sometimes get confused. Too often they think a nice doctor is a good doctor. Too often, they notice the affection but not the brutality, the gratitude but not the obvious, unspoken question. For example: Cultural tradition aside, what kind of doctor lies to a dying woman?

Not infrequently, medical stories tend toward sentimentality or humor, as if outrage at the injustice of illness and the necessary violence of medical care are downers better left to novelists and bloggers.

"That's interesting," said my new fiancé on the Saturday morning after the cloudless Friday night atop Twin Peaks, the lights of the city and bridges sparkling below, when he dropped to one knee and asked me to marry him. A few hours later, naked, his curly hair wild from the wind on the hilltop and the burrowing of my fingers, he was reading the titles of the books on my writing desk.

"What is?"

"Your books. They're all about war."

It was true. As models for writing about medicine, the war books came closest to achieving what I was after. They had stories of good deeds and bad, but no heroes or villains. They had descriptions of horror and obscenity and crazy things that should never have happened but did, again and again, and so struck me as profoundly and irrevocably true. In other words, they were honest. I wanted to be honest, too.

To ensure objectivity and accuracy, doctors' notes avoid the first person pronoun. Instead, they are written in the style of textbooks, using the dispassionate third person with lots of jargon and a relative paucity of the sort of telling detail that might allow a patient to transcend the page and emerge a fully formed and unique human being in the imagination of the reader. Mostly made up of something called history (which shouldn't be confused with story), the best such notes contain quotations (dialogue, if you will) in the actual voice of the patient. These conventions, particularly the avoidance of the subjective and responsible "I," may partly explain why, when describing certain emotional events in my writing, I do so by using the second person. But rest assured that whenever I use the word *you*, I am not referring to you, the reader, but to myself. This is a common literary usage of the second person but also, I've found, a common usage in real life as well. So often, when a person says *you*, they mean *me*.

"You're too easily upset," I said to my fiancé one night when he appeared on the verge of tears at the end of one of my patient anecdotes. Then I reminded myself that he worked in a world in which young, healthy college-educated men and women spent their days debating pressing issues such as whether the villain should be a lion or a bear in their latest animated children's video game, and I softened my tone. "It's my work, you know. Somehow, you're going to have to get used to it."

When Rogelio talked about his life, games were a recurrent theme. He'd been a player of bridge and dominoes and *loba*, seeking out games on the weathered green or gray picnic benches in the concrete parks that punctuated the Mission District. This was back when Carina managed every aspect of their household, before his world shrank to the confines of their most basic needs and the two rooms of their government-subsidized apartment. The games had brought him friends and fun and, on occasion, a little extra spending money. But he'd given all that up the day Carina put an entire bag of unopened tortillas on the stove's open flame and walked away. His life ended that day in so many ways, yet it also went on and on, the years that followed an excruciating expanse of structured, hollow time, the only game around the game of life, a game at which he considered himself hopelessly and unequivocally a loser.

His death was abrupt. I'd visited them just two weeks before. At that time he'd had some vague symptoms that he said weren't important, telling me instead about the aide he'd fired because she would change Carina's diaper only twice a day. I suggested doing some tests, but Rogelio said he felt good enough—"*Regular*," he said in Spanish with a shrug and his usual wan smile. He said he'd call if the symptoms continued. His exam was normal, and he looked the same as always, so I didn't insist.

That was the worst: when you didn't know whether you'd killed them, when you wondered whether, if a certain hand had been played a slightly different way, maybe the whole thing would have gone in another direction and there would still be dominoes standing in their usual neat lines at the end of the long hall on the fifth floor of the Martin Luther King apartments. Maybe Rogelio would still be in the game, making sure his wife lived and died in her home with the best of care to the very end, her hair neatly brushed, and every inch of her skin clean and rich with the scents of baby powder and cooking oil and love. But there was no way to know, so you stayed awake nights wondering, and then sometimes, for the next several patients, you ordered every test imaginable, careful to miss nothing. You tortured them and found that some got better and some didn't, and you were no closer to a definitive answer about what constituted good care and enough treatment and what was too much.

This next medical story, though an official chapter in the history of medicine in America, is considered sacred by some and blasphemy by others. It all depends on people's biases when it comes to plotlines in medicine: Are the only legitimate scenarios the archetypal classics Man v. Disease, Man v. Man, and Man v. Death, or might tales that lack metaphors for battles and quests—scenarios such as Man with Man, Man accepts Fate, or Man with God—have a place in the canon as well?

Way back in the mid-1990s, when mostly no one besides doctors on call carried cell phones and Internet skills weren't essential for keeping up to date with the latest scientific developments, a new species of medical conference emerged and spread across the country like an epidemic. From the enthusiasm of certain doctors and nurses, one might have thought there'd been a major medical breakthrough. The conferences had sessions with such titles as "Giving Bad News," "The Good Death," and "The Spiritual Lives of Patients." During the breaks between lectures, multicultural pain scales with selections ranging from smiley faces to frowns and plastic pocket cards listing useful phrases to use when breaking bad news were snatched from display tables as quickly as free wine or cookies.

It was the birth of medical modernism, when a subset of doctors finally acknowledged that not all patients could be cured, and then they went one step further, admitting that in fact not just some or many, but all patients—and also, eventually, their doctors and nurses and everyone else would die. The movement's leaders declared that if patients were to find meaning at the ends of their lives, medicine could no longer countenance the traditional and up to that point supremely dominant narrative in which cure alone constituted therapeutic success. Moreover, they argued that there should be no singular approach to patient care at the end of life. Each person should be viewed as his or her own text—complex, contradictory, playful, ironic, ambiguous, and absurd—and not all stories would have the benefit of happy and tidy endings.

By the time I came along nearly a decade later, death had become a fashionable specialty in medicine. But it wasn't until my locums year that I had what could be called my Chekhovian realization or Joycean epiphany: I wanted to be right there when people died—in the trenches, as we doctors like to say, as if battling disease and death in others is a first person experience.

Good medical stories capitalize on the myriad opportunities for imagery, analogy, and metaphor offered on a daily basis in medical encounters and settings. In the spring of my year doing locums, I was sent to a large nursing home on the southern edge of town where I watched two chatting young women in baby-blue scrubs wheel a body draped in a single white sheet from one building down a long glass corridor to another, then wait in the main lobby among the potted plants and Easter decorations and a crowd of visitors and residents for an elevator down to the morgue. Walking by, I thought of those old brokerage commercials in which mention of the famous broker's name caused immediate silence: all movement and conversation stopped.

I had seen enough by then to know where people went after death. Nowhere. They remained in bed, wearing death like a face-lift, an orgasm, a new persona, the change obvious from the doorway. The afternoon of Rogelio's death, for example, the aide and I watched as the paramedics rolled him down the darkened hallway in a black rubber sleeve, like a giant garment bag for his ultimate journey.

Sometimes, when it was over, when the coroner and the funeral home had been notified, you didn't know what to do. The more you wanted to leave, the longer you stayed. In those moments, setting became all important: a shiny black rotary phone that wasn't ringing, though you'd left a message for the daughter; the acrid smell of urine from a diaper in need of changing; the faded green recliner you didn't sit in, because you'd never seen anyone sit there but Rogelio; the painting of the Cerro Negro volcano erupting over the city of León, painted by Carina from a photograph long after they'd moved away.

One warm Sunday evening in mid-May, as the grass on the city's unmanicured hilltop parks faded from green to the golden brown hues that signal summer in San Francisco and shortly after my new husband and I had driven ourselves up to Reno and tied the knot, I scrolled down the document I'd been working on for the better part of that year. It consisted of a series of anecdotes, each describing a patient I'd seen or a "story" I'd heard from another doctor. Each anecdote had a beginning, middle, and end but felt incomplete on its own. They shared themes and locations in San Francisco and occasionally a character who appeared in more than one anecdote. I knew they belonged together but hadn't figured out how.

Looking up from his Sunday *Times*, our obese feline fluff ball comfortably ensconced in his lap, my husband asked, "Have you considered that progress is slow less because of what you're trying to say and more because how you're saying it needs to be completely different?"

"Meaning I need to choose between personal essay and fiction?"

"No. Meaning none of that matters. Meaning you keep trying to seduce your reader with setting and synonyms, humor and allusion and allegory, and maybe all you need to do is just be straight up about how much your patients mean to you and how difficult these situations are and how lost you feel when you don't know what to do. Meaning forget the fancy footwork and ironic remove, and just tell the damn story!"

At the county hospital where the neighborhood health center admitted its patients, the residents called admissions *hits*, unless they called them *hurts*. Hits were just work, while hurts were admissions made especially painful by either the amount of work required or the certain knowledge that one's efforts were ultimately useless. Carina was a hurt. Obese and demented, she kept getting sick. At each admission, she seemed weaker and more disturbed by the hospital sounds and smells and people, the IVs and breathing treatments and everything else. I offered to try managing the crises at home and explained about alternatives to 911, up to and including hospice. But Carina's daughter, who had moved her entire family across the country and into the Martin Luther King apartments in the week after her father's death, insisted on hospitalization. "But I thought—" I began, recalling that she had seemed disappointed when I'd cured her mother's pneumonia a few months earlier, and then I let it go.

Carina's daughter had become her official caretaker, work that came with a small but reliable paycheck from the state. Between hospitalizations, she hand-fed her mother small bites and spoonfuls of her favorite foods. From what I could tell, Carina's diet consisted of tortillas and bananas and ice cream, only some of which made it to her stomach. The rest went down her trachea, and a few days or weeks after her most recent admission, I'd receive a call saying she was back in the hospital. With each hospitalization, the residents would talk to the daughter about Carina's obvious suffering and apparent distress, but the daughter said that Carina was happy at home, and it was true that on my visits she sat smiling in her wheelchair between bites of strawberry ice cream or lay in her bed smiling, her grandchildren lying beside her doing their homework and watching TV. But it was also true that Carina's ongoing existence and care needs secured for her family a low-rent apartment and a regular paycheck. When my locums year ended, this was Carina's life: *tortilla hospital home tortilla hospital home tortilla hospital*.

As is the case for all medical stories, with the exception of things I've altered in obeisance of the Health Insurance Patient

Protection Act and, at my husband's insistence, for reasons of esthetics and art, everything I've written here is true. For their sakes, I had to change patients' names and biographical details. For my sake, I had to downplay some aspects of my professional and personal lives. The heartbreak and incredible sex, for example, but also the joy. In real life, there was more of it. In real life, if you're as lucky as I have been—with work that is long on characters, drama, and significance—there's always more joy. But that doesn't make for much of a story.

ACKNOWLEDGMENTS

In medicine, the "history of the present illness," or HPI, is the critical first portion of the medical note that describes the onset, duration, character, context, and severity of the illness. Basically, it's the story, and without it, you can't understand what's going on with your patient. Similarly, to really understand this book, you need to know that its onset occurred decades ago, that the symptoms have waxed and waned over time but have been increasingly prominent in recent years, that it's been a wonderfully messy business full of emotional highs and lows and legions of supportive, generous characters, and that I am hugely grateful to each and every one of them.

In retrospect, the symptoms started shortly after my birth at one of the hospitals described in this book. The context was the parents to whom I was born: I am a writer because my mother talked to me from before I could answer her, taught me the rules and beauty of language, and provided me with endless recommendations of good books; and I am a doctor because my father modeled the excitement of science, the importance of evidence and logic, and the thrill of making a difference in the world. My parents have supported my every venture and interest, and a person doesn't get much luckier than that.

Within weeks of completing my medical training, I began taking writing classes from talented and dedicated writer-teachers. I thank Shelly Singer, Paul Cohen, Tom Jenks, and Carol Edgarian for their wise instruction and forbearance in the face of my early efforts, and Judith Grossman, Peter

Turchi, Debra Spark, David Shields, Adria Bernardi, and the rest of the faculty at the Warren Wilson Program for Writers for teaching me all I needed to know to continue developing as a writer long after I'd earned my M.F.A.

For some people in medicine, fiction writing is a foreign and questionable activity. I have been fortunate to work for people whose open minds and flexibility allowed me to take on a second career not only without compromising my medical career but in a way that enriched both. Jay Luxenberg was the first to invest in me, and I will be forever grateful for his unwavering support even as months bled into years and there was no outward sign that I was actually doing what I claimed to be doing. Like the best of bosses, Seth Landefeld let me follow my unique and unconventional trajectory, offering sage advice and financial support at key moments when many others would have offered neither. Molly Cooke, David Irby, Nancy Ascher, Paul Volberding, Brian Dolan, David Elkin, Patricia O'Sullivan, Talmadge King, and many others at UCSF expressed interest and confidence in my efforts and helped me blend my passions for medicine and writing into UCSF Medical Humanities and a better book.

My job is sufficiently demanding that stretches of months often passed during which I did no writing. What saved me, and the book, during those years were opportunities to go to beautiful places where I was provided with the space, time, fellow artists, and good food required to make otherwise impossible leaps of progress. I thank Ucross, Ragdale, and Hedgebrook for giving me just what I needed to move forward.

Critical to the development of these stories has been the feedback and community I have had from my writing groups: Lindsey Crittenden, Rachel Howard, Ken Samuels, Adrienne Bee, and Frances Stroh in the early years, and more recently the Grotto group extraordinaire: Natalie Baszile, Bora Reed, Suzanne Wilsey, Katherine Ma, Susi Jensen, and Catherine Alden. Thank you all for putting up with this long, slow process and for having the courage to give honest, constructive feedback.

The fact that this book is appearing in print at all is a testament to the generosity of three writers who responded quickly and enthusiastically to an acquaintance who had the audacity to ask if they'd send the manuscript to their agents. Thank you to Peter Orner, Chris Adrian, and Bill Hayes.

So much of success is luck, and my next lucky break came in the form of Emma Patterson, a young agent who started reading my manuscript and told her boss, Wendy Weil, to read the book immediately. I knew from the start that I was in good hands with Wendy and Emma at the Wendy Weil Agency, and it became even clearer when they led me to my editor, Nancy Miller, at Bloomsbury. Nancy's keen eye and gentle questions have done much to improve the book, and it has been a total pleasure working with a team that understood what I was trying to do and believed that others might enjoy it too.

I am particularly grateful to the friends who read, reread, and re-reread these stories. Each offered insights I lacked and needed, and their faith in me and the work kept me going and inspired me to further improve the book. I cannot thank them enough: Kathleen Lee, Annette Huddle, Gina Solomon, and Shawn Behlen.

Finally, there is one person without whom this book would not exist. Jane Langridge makes anything possible and everything better. This book is for her.

READING GROUP GUIDE

These discussion questions are designed to enhance your group's conversation about *A History of the Present Illness*, a collection of original linked stories based on the author's personal experience in medicine. Narratives of doctors at various parts of their careers are woven with stories of patients of varying ages and backgrounds to create a portrait of health and illness in America today.

ABOUT THIS BOOK

A History of the Present Illness explores the truths of medical care in the U.S. today through an examination of what it means to be a doctor and, alternately, a patient, as well as the relationship that exists between the two. Aronson lends her personal experiences to these expressive short stories, correcting any prettied-up or embellished views of what it is to be a doctor by offering a realistic, if sometimes saddening, sense of how this world operates.

Aronson offers a glimpse into the complicated lives of doctors: why they have chosen to become doctors—and why for all of those who love the profession, there exist others who question the decision for varied reasons and at different stages of their careers; the personal turmoil a doctor's career path can wreak on both the individual and loved ones; how a hierarchy of specialties exists; what it feels like to burn out from caring too much; how easy it is to make mistakes, especially fatal ones; how a seemingly-simple moment can become a profound turning point; and how the doctors themselves inevitably become patients.

These stories also provide a genuine portrait of what it means to be on the other side of the stethoscope, as a patient or caregiver. Aronson captures the spectrum of emotions that patients and families feel, be it in rapid succession or gradually and cumulatively over the course of treatment: from Bopha's embarrassment and shame, to Rodney's sense of despair laced with brief bouts of hope, to Maurice's determined cheerfulness. In a number of the stories, the doctors themselves become the patients, yet are unable to acknowledge this truth.

The collection's title, culled from the medical term "history of the present illness" or HPI, which, as Aronson writes in the Acknowledgments, is "the critical first portion of the medical note that describes the onset, duration, character, context, and severity of the illness. Basically, it's the story, and without it, you can't understand what's going on with your patient." These short stories serve as the HPI for the current state of health and illness in America today, and they imbue the world of medicine with the truths of humanity.

FOR DISCUSSION

1. In "Snapshots from an Institution," what purpose do Charles' antics (the story-within-the-story) serve?

2. In "An American Problem," why is this the phrase the Khmer assistant uses to describe Bopha's bedwetting?

3. Do you get the sense that Robert really enjoyed being a doctor in "Giving Good Death"? What about the narrator in "Becoming a Doctor"? Or Ray in "Lucky You"?

4. In "Heart Failure," why does Aronson choose to set Marta's difficulties with her daughter Sophie against the backdrop of Marta's father's last days and death?

5. What do you think the narrator's mother-in-law means by "form is not always content's container" in the story "Twenty-five Things I Know About My Husband's Mother"?

6. What effect does the structure of short stanzas in multiple alternating points of view have in "Fires and Flat Lines"?

7. What tips you off to the irony of "Blurred Boundary Disorder"? Why would Aronson include this seemingly ludicrous story in the collection?

8. Why is "Vital Signs Stable" told in everyone but Edith's point of view?

9. Is Ruth's behavior at the end of "Days of Awe" selfish? Justified?

10. In "Lucky You," why doesn't Perla help the boy who falls?

11. Why does the narrator (or the author) continue to emphasize the themes of objectivity and truth in "A Medical Story"?

12. Many of the doctors in *A History of the Present Illness* face ethical dilemmas with their patients, including Chitra in "Soup or Sex?" and the narrator in "The Promise." There are strict guidelines and laws governing doctors' behavior; do you think it's ok for a doctor to interpret the rules somewhat flexibly, even just a little bit, if he or she believes it will bring comfort to a patient?

13. The phrase "good death" appears in a number of the collection's stories. What does this phrase mean? Why the repetition?

14. What is the role of the narrative of medicine in the medical world? Why is it important?

SUGGESTED READING

Richard Selzer, *Letters to a Young Doctor* and *The Doctor Stories*; Atul Gawande, *Complications*; Abraham Verghese, *My Own Country: A Doctor's Story*; Jerome Groopman, *The Measure of Our Days*; Samuel Shem, *The House of God*; Oliver Sacks, *The Man Who Mistook His Wife for a Hat*; Ellen Rothman, *White Coat*;

Emily Transue, *On Call*; Michael Collins, *Hot Lights, Cold Steel*; Pauline Chen, *Final Exam*; Rita Charon, *Narrative Medicine*

Louise Aronson has an M.F.A. from Warren Wilson College and an M.D. from Harvard. She has won the *Sonora Review* prize, the *New Millennium Writings* short-short fiction award, and has received three Pushcart Prize nominations. Her fiction has appeared in *Bellevue Literary Review* and the *Literary Review*, among other publications. She is an associate professor of medicine at the University of California, San Francisco, where she cares for older patients and directs the Northern California Geriatrics Education Center and UCSF Medical Humanities. She lives in San Francisco.